T0278779

THE KILL FACTOR

BEN OLIVER

Chicken House

SCHOLASTIC INC. / NEW YORK

Copyright © 2024 Ben Oliver

All rights reserved. Published by Chicken House, an imprint of Scholastic Inc., *Publishers since 1920.* SCHOLASTIC, CHICKEN HOUSE, and associated logos are trademarks and/or registered trademarks of Scholastic Inc.

The publisher does not have any control over and does not assume any responsibility for author or third-party websites or their content.

No part of this publication may be reproduced, stored in a retrieval system, or transmitted in any form or by any means, electronic, mechanical, photocopying, recording, or otherwise, without written permission of the publisher. For information regarding permission, write to Scholastic Inc., Attention: Permissions Department, 557 Broadway, New York, NY 10012.

This book is a work of fiction. Names, characters, places, and incidents are either the product of the author's imagination or are used fictitiously, and any resemblance to actual persons, living or dead, business establishments, events, or locales is entirely coincidental.

Library of Congress Cataloging-in-Publication Data available

ISBN 978-1-338-891850

10 9 8 7 6 5 4 3 2 1   24 25 26 27 28

Printed in Italy   183

First edition, April 2024

Book design by Cassy Price

Stock photos © Shutterstock.com

CHAPTER

Emerson Ness had not been scared in a very long time. Now she was terrified.

The room was gray, not only in color but in character too: perfectly square, perfectly dull. No windows. The only light came from two fluorescent headache bulbs that flickered overhead. The table was off-center in a very purposeful way.

Emerson sat at that table, trying not to think.

They want you to think, she told herself, *they want you to replay the events over and over until you're not sure what happened and what didn't happen. That's why everything is so gray and dull; so that you've got nothing to focus on other than your thoughts.*

She tried then to clear her mind, but it was impossible. She was shaking. She saw it in her hands as she nervously pulled at her fingertips, and then noticed a thrumming throughout her entire body. *Stop that,* she commanded herself, but no amount of trying would slow down the tremor that ran through her like a current, and as she stared at her earthquake hands, her mind drifted back to the reason she was in this room. She saw the flames eating up the building. She heard the sirens wailing into the night, smelling that burned-hair smell.

No! she told herself. *Think of something else. You're scared, that's all.*

Arson was a serious crime—especially when it was a school that burned down. The government did not take kindly to people who destroyed their property. Cost the government money and you were looking at jail time.

She knew it didn't look good. She had been caught on the school grounds late at night, clutching a bag full of money, the building burning at her back.

When was the last time you were this scared?

She scoured her mind, moving back through her sixteen years of life, trying to remember when she had last been truly terrified. It had been nine years ago, when she was seven and her brother, Kester, had been an infant. Their mother had been dead only a few months, and their father had gone off to "make content," spending the night in the catacombs with nothing but a cheap camera drone and a thin blanket. Everything that man did was for views and followers. Maybe he was right. Maybe it really was the only currency that mattered anymore.

While he'd been away, Kester had gotten sick. Really sick. At first his breathing had been a little ragged, a little wheezy, but then it started to rattle. *Sounds like he's got rocks in his breath,* she had thought as she stood at her little brother's door, holding her own breath and trying not to cry. He had started coughing then, coughing and coughing, and after a while, it sounded like he was drowning.

Emerson had tried to call their dad, but there was no signal in the catacombs. She had gotten angry, smashing the ancient cell phone on the kitchen floor and then punching the door so hard her knuckles bled. Then she had started to panic, running out of the baby's bedroom, pressing her hands against her ears, and then running back in, willing him to miraculously get better. "Stop it now, Kester! Stop that!" But he didn't get better. He got worse.

She had leaned over his cot and yelled at her tiny brother. "Please stop! Please!"

Finally, she had gotten ahold of herself and called an ambulance. The paramedics had agreed to meet her, but they refused to drive down into the Burrows, so she'd had to wrap up her distressed brother and run to the entrance of the tunnel.

Kester had an infection in his lungs that had turned into pneumonia. The doctors saved his life. Thirty hours later—when she had returned home carrying her baby brother in her arms—their father had been sitting at his computer editing the footage of his night in the catacombs, oblivious. She had hated him in that moment. She had never forgiven him.

That same kind of fear was in her again now, here in this interrogation room where—any second now—an officer, maybe two, would enter and tell her that she was looking at prison. A building had burned to the ground, and $900 of physical cash had been stolen. Physical money was not as valuable as brand credits, but theft was theft.

She imagined slowing time right down until seconds lasted minutes and hours lasted days. Then she imagined time running backward: the door to the interrogation room opening, the police uncuffing her and marching her backward into the wagon, the mug shot drone erasing photographs of her. And then she thought, *If I could go back in time, why not just keep going?* And so, in her mind, days rushed by, fading from dark to light, the moon reversing across the sky, chased closely by the sun, years and years, faster and faster, before Kester was born, until, finally, time began to move forward again at regular speed, and Emerson was six years old, and her mother was still alive.

"Em," her mother said, holding out an ethereal hand.

Emerson reached out for that hand, and had almost touched it when she was snatched from her reverie by the interrogation room door opening. Two officers came in and sat down in the bigger, more comfortable chairs opposite her. There were no introductions, no greetings, not even a moment of eye contact. The short, female officer spoke first.

"It is currently 2:41 in the morning on December twelfth. Special Agent Dern interviewing suspect alongside Officer Bannon. Let me get some information clear for the report: Your first name, Emerson, is spelled E-M-E-R-S-O-N?"

"Uh, yeah, that's right," Emerson said, and cleared her throat after hearing the vibration in her voice. She reminded herself to be tough. *You've done nothing wrong, remember that. Yes, you stole money, but it was only to feed your family. It's not your fault that the building burned.*

"And last name, Ness, spelled N-E-S-S?"

"Yes," Emerson replied.

4

"And address is 2331/19 The Burrows?"

This list of meaningless questions sparked anger in Emerson. "This is dumb, I shouldn't be here, I—"

"In a minute," the officer said, holding up a hand, still not making eye contact. Emerson clenched her jaw, irritated that she had been shut down so effectively. "I know you've already been read your rights, Ms. Ness, but I'm going to repeat them now so that they are on record: You have the right to remain silent. Anything you say can and will be used against you in a court of law. You have the right to an attorney, which you can pay for in brand credits or cash, and if you cannot afford one, one will be provided for you. Do you understand what I have told you?"

Emerson had been in situations like this before many times, and had learned that she could push aside almost all other emotions if she filled herself up with anger. She did this now. "Yeah, I'm not stupid."

"Do you want a lawyer?"

"Don't need one. I haven't done anything."

"For the record, the suspect has chosen, of her own free will, to waive her right to a lawyer." The officer finally made eye contact, and all Emerson could see in those eyes was ambition. "You were arrested outside Stone's Throw High School shortly after midnight this morning, is that correct?"

"Does this one speak?" Emerson asked, pointing at the tall, square-faced officer sitting next to Agent Dern.

"Answer the question, please."

"I was arrested, but I still don't know why."

"You were apprehended outside a burning school with a bag full of stolen money. Why do *you* think you were arrested?"

"Sarcasm?" Emerson replied. "Really? Is this how the police conduct their business these days?"

"You're impulsive, aren't you, Ms. Ness? You don't think before you speak, and you don't think before you act. So, for those reasons, I'll spell out to you exactly what you are being charged with. You are under arrest on suspicion of theft, and arson." She paused. "And manslaughter."

Emerson slowly sat up in her uncomfortable gray chair and stared at Agent Dern. "What did you say?"

"Manslaughter, Ms. Ness. It means—in this case—that you committed unintentional homicide in a criminally negligent manner."

Her anger dissolved away, like ink in water. "Someone . . . someone died?"

Agent Dern looked at her watch. "About twelve minutes ago. A man named Marvin Tzu, a janitor. He died from injuries sustained at the scene. Burns, smoke inhalation."

Agent Dern took a photograph of a man in his sixties out of a manila envelope and placed it on the table between them. Emerson stared at the man; his eyes, sad and soulful, seemed to gaze right back at her. She recognized those eyes. She felt her heart twisting in her chest like a bag full of rodents. Suddenly, it was hard to breathe; her vision blurred and then came into focus almost too sharp. "I . . . I changed my mind. I do want a lawyer."

"That's entirely your choice, Ms. Ness," Agent Dern said, closing the case file that had sat in front of her and standing up. Officer Bannon stood up almost at the same time. "Interview paused at 0245 hours."

They exited the room without so much as a glance back, leaving the photograph of Marvin Tzu on the table.

The silence that followed seemed to fall down from the ceiling like dust, and in that silence, Emerson felt like she couldn't catch her breath. Her feet felt numb, and her thoughts were tumbling in her mind. She was sure that she could feel the earth spiraling though space. She gripped the underside of her chair. She had to hold on to something or be cast into the infinite void.

Dead, she thought. *Someone died. Someone died. They're dead.*

The confidence and determination of Agent Dern had scared her at first. Now it terrified her.

Emerson took one last look at the photograph on the table, and then turned it over.

She had a criminal record already—that meant it would be all too easy to pin this on her. And when they did, she would spend the next two decades in a room even more dull and gray than this one.

I can't let that happen, Emerson told herself. *I can't. Kester needs me, I can't leave him alone. Get a grip, Em, you need to think. Get ahold of yourself.*

But she couldn't seem to access her thoughts. All she could see in her mind's eye was the flashing of the mug shot drones that had circled her at the scene of the crime, taking photos as the school burned behind her, the flames reaching their skinny fingers up into the black sky.

× ✖ ×

The door to the interrogation room opened again after what felt to Emerson like hours. Though perhaps it had only been minutes. A short man with white hair and small round glasses entered.

"Are you my lawyer?" Emerson asked, no longer able to hide the fear in her voice.

The man ignored her question. Instead, he ambled over to the table, sat down on the chair that Agent Dern had vacated, and took a virtual notepad out of his pocket. He placed it on the table, glanced at Emerson over the tops of his glasses, then used his fingerprint to open the virtual stack of documents that hovered in the air between them.

"What is this?" Emerson asked.

"Emerson Ness," the old man said, and smiled warmly. "You might be the luckiest girl alive right now."

Emerson's brow furrowed as she looked at the newcomer. "Look around, old man. Do I look lucky to you?"

The man laughed, a hearty and friendly sound. "No, no. You certainly do not. But, rest assured, you are."

"You're going to explain?" Emerson asked, and felt the tiniest flicker of hope inside herself. She extinguished it quickly, though. Experience had taught her to never get her hopes up.

"Explain I shall," the man said, smiling that charming, kindly smile. And Emerson felt herself warming to the man in spite of herself. "You're lucky, Ms. Ness, because I came along just at the right time! You see, I'm your ticket out of all this mess."

"My ticket . . . I'm sorry, what's going on?"

He laughed again and then leaned back in his chair. "Forgive me, Ms. Ness. I'm being cryptic. I don't mean to be. Let me try to be more clear. I'm a producer, which means I'm in charge of bringing together a team of people to create a television show. Now, correct me if I'm wrong, Ms. Ness, but you're looking down the barrel of at least fifteen years in maximum security. Slate County. They're going to try you as an adult, understand? Even though you're sixteen, they're going to try you as an adult because you've got a criminal history, including aggravated assault and forgery."

"I can explain all that," Emerson tried. She'd done it for her brother, she wanted to say. She hadn't had a choice.

"You're going to explain it to a jury?" He raised a white eyebrow.

"I . . . I . . ."

"Doesn't matter," the man said, waving a hand. "You're not setting foot in a courtroom, and—if you win the competition—you're not setting foot in a prison. You won't have to worry about any of that once you sign this contract."

"Competition?" Emerson asked.

"Listen," the Producer said, leaning in close and gesturing to the dim room. "All of this, this crap, this is how they keep people like you down. You're a young, intelligent girl with all the potential in the world, and yet you're fighting for your life every day. How is that fair? Can I tell you a secret? I hate this system. I'm from the same place as you, Ms. Ness. I'm from the Burrows and I had to use every ounce of strength to get out. I want to offer you a chance to get out too."

Emerson looked at the digital contract that hung between them. "What is it?" she asked. "What does it say?"

The Producer laughed and raised both hands out to his sides in a gesture of evangelical praise. "It says you're going walk out of this station and wave to those arrogant cops on the way, that's what it says. Did you see that Agent Dern? She wants you. She wants to see you burn. She knows you've got no defense, Ms. Ness. No brand value to pay for a lawyer. I could see it in her eyes. Be honest, what are your credits worth? How many followers do you have? Under a thousand, I'd wager?"

Somehow, Emerson knew that the Producer had looked into her already. He knew that she had no followers at all, meaning her digital brand credits were worth less than physical cash.

"What would I have to do?" Emerson asked.

"That's the best part," the Producer said, lacing his fingers behind his head as if they were both relaxing on a summer's day. "All you have to do is be yourself. Be likable. Watch your follower count grow by the millions and your currency become valuable beyond your wildest dreams."

Emerson sat back in her chair and looked from the Producer's smiling eyes to the floating stack of papers between them. "You're going to have to give me more than that," Emerson said. "I don't understand what's going on here."

The Producer sighed and sat forward. "Emerson, we don't have time to go into the details. I wish we did, but the chief of this place has given me exactly five minutes. Suffice it to say that this is a one in a billion opportunity. You happen to be a prime candidate for a new show with a very real prize. That prize is freedom. If you don't sign on the dotted line in the time I've allotted myself to meet with you, that opportunity will go to someone else. Listen to me, girl. You were born to fail. It's not your fault, it's just the facts as I see them. I'm offering you an opportunity to change the narrative of your life."

Emerson swallowed. "What is the show about?"

"You're still asking questions? Really? I'm offering you a cure for cancer and you're asking me what flavor the pill is?"

Emerson looked into the fatherly eyes of this strange man who had burst into her life at her most vulnerable. "There has to be a catch," she replied. "Nobody gets to walk away for free."

The Producer nodded slowly. "You're smart, Emerson Ness. Too smart to be in a place like this. The show goes like this: Fifty young people on the verge of imprisonment will take part in various games. The difficulty of these games is determined by how many followers you earn throughout the show. If you lose a game, you will face a public vote against whoever has the least amount of followers. The person voted off is incarcerated in a maximum-security prison with no contact from the outside world, and no contact from other prisoners. The sentence is automatically life in solitary. The one person with the most followers at the end is free to go, and not just free to go, but free to go with hundreds of thousands of new followers, advertising endorsements, and popularity that will set them up for life."

Emerson's head was spinning. This had come out of nowhere. One minute she had been mentally preparing herself for a decade or more in Slate County, and now this man with his compassionate face and caring words came along offering her . . . what?

"The clock is ticking, Ms. Ness," the Producer said, his voice quiet and understanding.

Emerson tried to process everything he had said. It wasn't freedom he was offering but a one-in-fifty chance of freedom. The price she had to pay was to be paraded on screens across the world as entertainment.

She was aware of the seconds ticking away as she considered the Producer's offer. Finally, she came to a decision.

"No," she said.

The smile on the Producer's face melted away like spring ice. "No?" he repeated.

"That's right, I said no."

"I . . ." He laughed. "I wasn't expecting that. Can I ask why?"

"Your show, whatever it's called, is disgusting. It's exploiting people. You're using people's darkest moments as entertainment. You're using people's desperation to amuse others, and I . . . I can't be part of that." She lifted her chin. "Besides, if I don't win—which is likely—I'll be exchanging fifteen years in prison for life in prison. That's no prize."

The Producer kept his expression of amusement. "We're offering people an opportunity."

"Then offer it," Emerson interrupted. "Don't dangle it in front of people's faces and make them dance for it."

He laughed, sat back in his seat, ran his hands through his hair, and laughed again. He swiped his hands over the documents, and they disappeared. "Well, I'm not going to beg you, Emerson. I respect your decision, but this is an opportunity that thousands of kids in your situation would bite my hand off for. If you don't want it, someone else will." He stood up and pocketed the virtual notebook. "Your father will be disappointed, though."

Emerson sat up. "What do you mean?"

"Huh?" the Producer said, and turned back around to face Emerson. "Oh, just that we need consent from a parent or guardian in order to validate your involvement in the show. Your father gave us that signature less than an hour ago. He seemed *very* happy to give his permission."

"You're lying," Emerson said. Her dad was a mediocre parent at best, sure, but she couldn't believe he'd go so far as to practically consign his only daughter to life in prison.

The Producer put the virtual notebook back on the table and scanned it. The documents reappeared between them, and the Producer pulled out the final sheet. Her father's name, Markus Ness, was scrawled across the bottom.

"He cares about you," the Producer said. "He wants to give you a chance to walk free. That's a good dad in my book."

Emerson traced each letter of her father's name with her eyes, feeling her stomach sink. "He doesn't care," she said. "All he wants is—"

But there was no time to finish her sentence. The door to the interrogation room flew open and the two officers entered.

"All right," Agent Dern said. "That's time."

All he wants is a famous daughter so he can grow his own brand, Emerson finished her thought. She pictured Kester in her mind. Kester, who was more intelligent than both of them. Kester, who was born deaf in a society that had given him next to no support.

Emerson looked into the eyes of the Producer. How could someone so benevolent make such a cruel offer?

"I can't do it," Emerson told him. She felt a moment of dizziness, as though her entire future had just taken a step off a high and sheer cliff.

"I'll tell you what," the Producer said. "I'll post your bail. You'll be out of here tomorrow and I'll give you one more day after that to decide. We can even add a clause stipulating that all of your social media and credit accounts will be transferred to your brother in the event that you are incarcerated."

Emerson opened her mouth to tell him that she didn't need any more time, that her mind was made up, but the words wouldn't come.

The Producer put a big, papery hand on her shoulder, offered her one last smile, and then left her to be escorted to a holding cell by Agent Dern and the silent Officer Bannon.

Emerson had not slept at all. She had lain awake on the small and uncomfortable bed in her cell and thought mostly about her brother, Kester.

She thought about how, at only five years old, he had programmed his first rudimentary game. She thought about how complex mathematical theories seemed elementary to him, how he had been moved up to the highest level of high school when he was only nine years old, and she thought about how— once high school was over—education would stop. There would be no one left to push him, no one to guide him and show him the way. You needed brand credits to get into college, and no one in the Ness family had enough followers to be worth anything . . . but now, the Producer had come along with an opportunity.

"Don't talk yourself into it, Emerson," she whispered.

Perhaps it didn't matter. In her video-link court appearance, the judge had set bail at $40,000 or the equivalent in brand credits, and she supposed that amount would have put off the Producer, who would be looking for a more suitable candidate.

Maybe I should have just signed the contract.

Night seemed to last forever, and it wasn't until the sun had just begun to creep over the horizon that her cell finally opened and a tired-looking police officer with a raggedy beard told her that her bail had been posted.

"Really?" Emerson asked.

"Yes, really," the officer muttered.

Emerson stepped out of her cell and into the corridor. At the front desk she signed an electronic document that allowed her to be reissued with the laces of her shoes and the contents of her pockets, which were a piece of string and single stick of chewing gum.

"And this," the desk sergeant said, holding out a folded piece of paper between two fingers. Emerson took it, opened it, and read what was written there:

> We leave from the docks tomorrow at six a.m. If you show up, I'll know that you changed your mind. If you don't, your fate is out of your hands and you'll be left to the "justice" system. It's your call.
>
> The Producer

× ✖ ×

Cold rain fell from the polluted December sky, bouncing in puddles that reflected the clean white buildings of the Topside.

Emerson walked alone through the freezing dawn. Driverless

street-sweeper vehicles glided by, and personal advertising boards scanned her, but most did not bother showing their ads as her credits were worth so little. Security holograms stood on pristine street corners, eyeing her suspiciously, but there were no people around. Just her and the rain.

The street began to slope downward toward the entrance to the Burrows, and Emerson felt tears in her eyes. She was in a lose-lose situation. She wanted to stay out of prison so that she could look after Kester and ensure he stayed on the right path, but she didn't want to become the thing she hated the most: a spectacle, a pawn in a game of manipulation, a puppet. She had always hated the fakeness of the content creators who melodramatically strutted around, followed by armies of camera drones filming their every move. And if she was to take part in this cruel game show, she would have to become one of them.

Stop it, Emerson! she scolded herself. *You're not signing the contract . . . are you?*

It seemed to Emerson an obvious truth that in this world of content, people worshipped two things above all else: wealth and celebrity. Over and over again she witnessed fame being bestowed on the most beautiful, the most willing to court controversy, and the most eager to sell their privacy to the highest bidder. And their behavior was justified time and time again as the public consumed their products, tuned in to their feeds, liked their posts, and became followers. An industry thrived while talent, intelligence, and ambition were thrown by the wayside. Instead, an army of vapid promoters took their place, heralded as geniuses and innovators. The definition of those words seemed to become so diluted that they'd come to mean something else entirely. Scientists, teachers, writers, doctors, nurses, professors, engineers, all ignored in favor of empty vessels with favorable bone structures who fit the modern idea of beauty.

Sometimes Emerson wished she could delete every single one of her accounts until she was completely untethered, floating free from the mother ship of her nonexistent brand. But that wasn't an option. Not if you wanted to eat. She had forty-four followers. This made her own digital brand currency worth slightly less than dollars and cents, but it was enough to keep her, her father, and her brother fed.

And yet, despite all her hatred of the modern way, she couldn't deny that there was a secret part of her that was jealous of the influencers who became worth millions by putting on an act and tuning in to the zeitgeist.

Emerson wrapped her arms around herself to fight off the cold as she began the long downhill walk to her home in the dark, subterranean village, imagining just how desperate the first Burrowers must have been. It was only fifty years ago that the Burrows were just a series of tunnels dug by homeless people. They would dig beneath the homes in the wealthy part of town and sleep up against the underside of their heated floors so they wouldn't die of exposure. As more and more of the city's homeless sought warmth beneath the modern houses of the Topside, the homeowners began to complain and demand arrests. Ultimately, the rich changed their floor heating to wall heating for no other reason than they didn't want the homeless to gain warmth for free.

Eventually, the unsafe system of tunnels was funded by the government, monetized by building cheap housing. After all, it kept the unsightly lower classes off the upper streets.

About one in five streetlights worked down in the Burrows, and the buildings that were illuminated showed their barred windows and graffiti walls. A dealer stood beneath one of the lights, muttering something about how he could sell her a thousand followers for eighty dollars. Emerson ignored the dealer and walked farther down the dirt tunnel, supported by ancient and rusting scaffolding. She passed the tiny homes crammed together, illegal and burned-out diesel vehicles in the patches of gardens with sad plastic greenery, dust-covered windows distorting the shadows that moved inside, sounds of arguments, parties, children screaming, babies crying.

It was never quiet in the Burrows.

Up ahead she could see the glare of a lighting drone and hear the familiar intonation of an influencer trying to get footage of themselves down in the Burrows.

"I've never been more scared in my life, you guys," the girl was saying as her drones filmed her, careful to keep her two bodyguards out of the shot. "If this video actually comes out, if I actually make it out of here alive, make sure you like and subscribe . . ."

The girl gave a melodramatic look at her surroundings before screaming at nothing. She then yelled "cut," and the security guards escorted her toward the exit. Emerson rolled her eyes as she passed by.

Finally, she made it to her own front door. It scraped along the ground as she pushed it open, sending an agonized yowl along the short hallway of the four-room home at 2331/19 The Burrows. Emerson took a deep breath, letting it out slowly before entering.

"Em, that you?" her father's voice called out into the dark hallway.

For a moment she didn't reply. She just listened to the sound of the rainwater dripping from her hair onto the scratched vinyl floor. She imagined running from this home, waiting it out on the streets until it was time to board the boat or go back to the police station. The idea of never speaking to her selfish father ever again sparked a jaw-clenching joy in her, and if Kester wasn't in the picture, she would have turned right then and walked away.

"Yeah, Dad, it's me."

He came ambling out of his bedroom, where the buzzing light of his ancient laptop glowed hungrily through the doorway.

"Editing," he said, shrugging, his long, thinning hair moving like seaweed as he let out an uneasy laugh.

I'm nothing like him, she thought as she watched her slump-shouldered father moving restlessly from foot to foot. *Kester is nothing like him. How did he produce two children who are so different from each other, and nothing like him?*

"Hey, what a break, huh?" he said, his eyes lighting up. "You getting this TV gig? It's awesome, Em, just awesome! Think of the exposure! Think of the followers we're going to get! You and me, famous!"

"I'm not doing it, Dad," she said, telling herself to look him in the eye. Telling herself to kill the pity that rose up as the hurt registered on his face.

"What . . . what do you mean you're not doing it? Why not?"

Emerson searched her mind for an answer that sounded more compelling than *because I don't want to.* "Because . . . I can't win, Dad. There are fifty contestants and only one prize. When I lose, I go to jail forever. And it's not a normal jail, it's solitary confinement. With no contact from the outside world. You'd never see me or hear from me again."

Her dad looked at her for a long time, expressionless, and Emerson steeled herself for the worst.

"Oh, Em, they didn't tell me that. Those dirty producers, they didn't tell me that! No, of course you can't do it! Of course you can't!" He held her then, wrapping his bony arms around her and resting his head on hers.

For a moment, Emerson felt an almost unbearable need to push her father away, but it was replaced quickly by something close to gratitude. Yes, he had signed his name to the Producer's document without knowing anything about the show, but at least he had the common decency to draw the line at selling her into a life of solitary confinement.

"Thanks, Dad," she muttered.

He ruffled her hair. "We'll figure this whole thing out, Em.

All of this. We'll get a lawyer somehow and . . . you know . . . we'll figure it out. We always do."

Emerson nodded. She didn't know how to reply. The situation was hopeless and they both knew it. Her father nodded, the smile on his face faltering for a moment, and then he disappeared back into his bedroom to work on his footage.

Emerson stood for a moment in the dim hallway, trying not to feel. Finally, she took a deep breath and made her way to her and Kester's bedroom.

Her brother lay on his side breathing long, deep breaths. He was half-covered by the thin, moth-eaten blanket. The boy was nine, but when he slept, he looked much younger.

How am I supposed to tell him that I'm going to prison for years? How am I supposed to tell him that he'll be okay while I'm not here to look after him? Emerson felt tears pooling in her eyes.

There was no time to think, though, as the young boy stirred and then woke. Emerson smiled and waited for him to notice her before she raised the fingertips of her right hand to her chin, moved them away, and then scooped them back around to say *good morning* in ASL.

Kester smiled and returned the gesture, adding the sign for her name at the end: *Good morning, Em.*

Kester then stood up, ran across his bed, and leaped into Emerson's arms, laughing as his sister struggled to hold on to him. Emerson peeled him off her wet clothes and put him down so that she could speak to him.

You're getting way too heavy for that. You need to lay off the snacks!

Kester laughed and then replied, his hands moving like lightning as he spoke: *As if we can afford snacks!*

Emerson laughed too. *You look tired. Did you get much sleep last night?*

Working on a big heist. Synergy-2025 claims to have the toughest encryption and anti-hacking systems in the world. They say no one can hack in because no one knows the physical location of their head offices, but I found it.

How? Emerson asked, happy for the distraction.

They may be the most modern credit-trading company in the world, but they use out-of-date servers: twenty thousand out-of-date servers that give off a huge electronic signal from their location in . . .

Kester fired up his ancient laptop. It hummed and whirred until the screen came to life.

. . . Luxembourg. Or to be more accurate, the small town of Wiltz in North Luxembourg.

Impressive, Emerson replied, smiling at her brother.

What about you? Kester asked. *You didn't come home last night. Where were you?*

Emerson hesitated, unsure of how she could possibly explain everything that had happened in the last twelve hours. Finally, her hands began to move, and she spoke, starting at the beginning and ending at the moment she had come home.

03
CHAPTER

They decided to put their argument, the entire reality of the situation, into a bottle and put the lid on tight.

This was something Kester had invented a few years earlier. Both of them hated it when they fought, and so one day when they were having a big argument about Emerson being expelled from school, Kester had picked up a bottle from the table beside his bed and signed, *I'm putting this fight inside this bottle.* It had made them laugh, and they were able to put the argument away for a few hours and be friends again.

So, the argument was in a bottle, and the bottle was in Kester's pocket. They had spent the day wandering around the Burrows and then the Topside. For hours they had pretended that Emerson wasn't awaiting trial for manslaughter. Instead, they talked about school and how Kester had been pushed up three grades in almost all subjects except English, about how their dad's six hundred followers would be enough in brand-credit value to provide food for the family if he would just stop reinvesting it into his videos. They spoke about how Kester's favorite e-sports team was doing.

Emerson spent the last of her weekly credits on two burgers at Ingleby's. After they had eaten, they sat in silence at their table in the window, watching the content creators emoting on the streets, the advertising boards projecting their pitches, the driverless Cube vehicles gliding by with their passengers laughing and drinking expensive wine inside. They watched the Topsiders as they glared at the Burrows kids who decided to come up for some sunlight.

Em, Kester finally said, his hands moving slower than usual, cautiously.

Yes? Emerson replied.

I think you should . . . He paused, his hands suspended in the air as though he had run out of words, but he continued. *I think you should sign the contract.*

Emerson felt her heart freeze in her chest. Her eyes had played tricks on her, that was what had happened. *What did you say?* she asked.

Hear me out, Kester signed. *I've thought about this hard, and I've looked at it from all angles. There are three reasons why you should go on this show. The first is: There is no way they can legally lock you away in solitary confinement for the rest of your life. I know the world is a mess, but cruel and unusual punishment is still something that this country does not stand for, so any decent lawyer could get you out of it, and at worst you'll end up serving the sentence you would have been given anyway! The second reason is: You could win! I know you have very little faith in yourself, but you're smart, and you're likable, and you're normal! You'll stand out. The third reason is . . . well, it's me being selfish. I love you, Em, but you're getting locked up either way. One way, you get nothing but prison time; the other, you could gain millions of followers. Even if you lose, you could still help our family make a lot of money. I could use those credits, Em. By the time you got out, we could both be . . . somebody.*

Emerson watched her brother to see if he would say any more. She was divided. On the surface she was angry; she wanted him to take it all back, to say that he would never send her out there to dance in front of cameras for millions of people to see. But . . . but part of her *wanted* to go, didn't it? Yes. Part of her had wanted to go from the moment the Producer had told her about the stupid show.

What if you're wrong? Emerson asked. *What if they* do *put me away in solitary for the rest of my life? You'll never see me again.*

When have you ever known me to be wrong? Kester asked, and smiled. *I won't let them send you away forever, Em. I wouldn't let that happen.*

You're nine, Kester! What could you do?

Kester gave her a knowing smile. *It's your decision, Em. And for the record, this is your choice completely, I would never hold it against you or try to make you feel guilty. I just think it's important to weigh the odds.*

Emerson thought about how, only a few hours ago, she had been certain that it was her father who would push her into the game show, and her brother who would beg her not to go, but instead, the opposite had happened.

I think we're going to need a whole new bottle.

No. No bottles, no lids. I'm on your side no matter what. Kester removed the bottle from his pocket, unscrewed the lid, and handed it to Emerson.

Emerson turned the lid over in her hands, then put it in her pocket. *I don't know, Kester*, Emerson signed. *I don't know what to do.*

You could win, Em. You know that, right? You could win, and then I wouldn't be alone.

You won't be alone, Emerson replied. *You'll still have Dad.*

They looked at each other for a few seconds before they couldn't stop themselves from laughing. It was a laugh that felt to Emerson like breaking the surface of a deep pool, just as your lungs start to strain.

Emerson had always loved Kester's frankness, his willingness to speak the harsh truth. Only now, that hard truth might result in her signing away her life for a game show. She looked at her brother, and for the first time she could see the man he was going to become instead of the boy he was.

The one thing she had kept from him was exactly how the fire had started in the school. She wasn't ready to think about the janitor, Marvin Tzu.

Finally, Emerson shook her head. *I still don't know what I'm going to do, Kester*, she told him, and then looked at the old ana-log clock on the diner wall. *You'd better go. I don't want you to miss your appointment.*

Kester glanced at the clock and then looked deep into

Emerson's eyes. *If you do decide to sign the contract, remember that people fall in love with honesty. Be honest and you'll win them over.* A look of regret seemed to flash across his young face for a moment. *I'll be back in an hour, Em. Do not make a final decision without me. I was just spitballing. Don't take what I said seriously.*

Emerson actually felt relief when she saw the fear in his eyes. Suddenly, it was real to him. He might lose his sister, and it scared him.

He had to go to the audiologist for his annual hearing checkup, where they would conclude once again that there was no improvement to his congenital sensorineural hearing loss, a condition he had been born with. Once again, they would tell him he didn't qualify for a hearing aid, but if he didn't attend, they would suspend the measly fourteen dollars a week in benefit money. Physical money was the lowest form of currency, close to worthless. Brand credits had been the most commonly accepted currency ever since social media companies started pushing it in the late eighties and, soon enough, it was accepted everywhere. But fourteen dollars was something.

Emerson put her hand on top of her brother's and smiled at him. He smiled too, but there was nervousness there. He got up and walked slowly toward the exit of the diner.

Emerson watched him go, a small boy in an unfair world. A boy who would be pushed and pulled by the currents of a cruel society until his will gave up and his potential died. He had asked her to do something so foolish and dangerous that it seemed like a heartless request, but his request had come from a place of belief: belief that a person really could claw their way out of the Burrows and into the self-cleaning, air-purifying apartments of the Topside so long as they had the credits, worked hard, and played by the rules. He had not yet been beaten down by the realities of life.

Jesus, Em, she told herself, shaking her head as she watched Kester disappear around a corner. *You're sixteen, not sixty.*

But she couldn't help the weariness that bore down upon her. It came from all places at all times. She hated the way the Topsiders talked about the lazy, useless Burrowers, and she hated the fact that some of those who lived down in the Burrows actually came to believe this about themselves. But not all of them, not even one in twenty of them were like that; most were trying like hell every day to get out of there.

And she remembered then that Kester was different. He had been born with a strength everyone else seemed to lack, a brilliant mind that looked at numbers the same way a normal person might look at a child's jigsaw puzzle. It was all so elementary to him, all so simple. If only the world still valued doctors, scientists, mathematicians; perhaps then he really could end up in one of the photocatalytic buildings, riding in Cubes, sipping expensive wine on his way to somewhere nice. But in a society where each citizen was given one hundred credits a week— ninety to spend and ten to save—and the value of those credits was based on your popularity, it was more likely that he too would turn to content.

She made up her mind.

She had to sign the contract. If Kester was right, and he could get her out of a life sentence, then great. But even if he was wrong, she would try her best to stay in the game as long as she could, gain as many followers as possible, and then transfer all her social accounts to her brother.

She couldn't see him again, though. She couldn't put into words why, but she could not speak to her father or her brother before she left. She had to keep it in the bottle and simply slip away before she changed her mind.

Emerson stood up. The sun was starting to set outside, a light dusting of snow was falling, and she thought that she wouldn't go home again, not ever. She would spend the rest of the day walking around, looking at the places she once knew. Enjoying freedom while seconds ticked away.

04

CHAPTER

There were six other contestants at the docks when Emerson arrived at three a.m., three hours early. They sat around in the darkness of the early morning hours in their hand-me-down clothes, hands shoved into pockets or wrapped around themselves to keep warm. They watched the boats that came in and sailed out, the cranes that were fixed to the port lift containers from freight ships, the drones that loaded crates onto driverless trucks. They didn't speak.

Emerson wrapped her arms around her middle, trying to warm herself against the chill of the wind.

Life, she thought. *Life in prison. No contact from the outside world. Not even contact with other prisoners. Life in solitary.*

She tried to remind herself of Kester's words, of his certainty that she would not be forced into a cruel and unusual punishment, but she had to accept there was a possibility that it could happen.

Life, she thought again. *Solitary.*

She refused to let the finality of it, the totality of it, sink in. She was taking part in this exploitative show to increase her value. If Kester could get enough money to get through school, she would have done her job.

"You another one?" a voice asked, and Emerson turned to see a tall, muscular girl of about seventeen standing beside her.

"Huh?" Emerson said, surprised to hear a voice in the silence.

"Another one, another contestant for this stupid show?"

"Oh, right, yeah, I guess I am."

"Sucks, huh?" the girl said, turning her head to face the horizon, where a massive cruise ship was materializing.

"Yeah," Emerson agreed.

"I'm Never, by the way," the tall girl said.

"Never?" Emerson repeated. "Never what?"

"No, that's my name. My name is Never. Actually, my full name is Never-Again Jones, because after my mom gave birth to me, she vowed never to have another kid again. I know, it's weird."

Emerson smiled. "I like it," she said, and shrugged. "It's cool."

"Thanks," Never said, and then a silence stretched out between them. "You gonna tell me your name or . . . ?"

"Oh," Emerson said. "It's Emerson, Emerson Ness."

"Cool. Well, this is strange, huh, Emerson Ness? At least one of us is going to go to jail for the rest of our lives, probably both of us."

"If you're lucky," a male voice to the girls' right said.

Emerson and Never turned to see a boy seated on a low wall, his head lowered and his sandy blond hair hanging over his face. He was a Burrower, that much was obvious, but he was wearing a white shirt and black suit jacket. They were ill-fitting and discolored, and the jacket had a rip up the back, but it was still a hundred times more impressive than most Burrowers clothes.

"What do you mean, lucky?" Never asked. "How is life imprisonment lucky?"

Slowly, the boy raised his head. He was beautiful in a waifish kind of way, with intense and intelligent eyes, and a half smile that left you wondering if he was lying to you.

"I mean this show isn't going to be just a popularity contest, it's going to be about survival."

Never looked at Emerson and raised her eyebrows. "How do you mean?"

"Like surviving," he replied, half laughing. "Staying alive."

"Sure," Never said, rolling her eyes.

"Believe me, don't believe me, it doesn't matter."

"And how come you know so much about it, skinny?" Never asked.

"I just do."

"Whatever," Never said, turning away from the boy.

"Whatever is right," the boy said, standing up and brushing dust off his suit jacket, shouldering his backpack. "You'll find out soon enough."

He began to walk away.

"Wait," Emerson called. "If you know something, you should tell us."

"Why?" the boy said, not turning around. "Once the game starts, we're not going to be friends. It's everyone for themselves."

He walked away then, one hand holding on to the strap of his raggedy backpack, and he stood on the edge of the dock, watching the enormous ship come slowly in, his baggy black trousers rustling in the breeze.

"Weird dude," Never said.

"Yeah," Emerson agreed, but she felt unnerved all the same.

× ✖ ×

Time passed slowly as the docks filled with young contestants. Most of the kids who showed up were Burrowers with torn clothing and emaciated faces, but there were some Topsiders too.

When 5:30 a.m. came around, it became clear that the "boat" they would be boarding was the enormous cruise ship that was being stocked up by drones and automatons.

The ship was gargantuan. When it had come to a vertigo-inducing stop beside the silent crowd of fifty or so young contestants, Emerson felt dwarfed by it, almost scared of it. It was at least five hundred feet tall and so long that Emerson couldn't see the far side from where she stood near the bow.

"It's . . . big, ain't it?" Never said as she walked up beside Emerson.

Emerson nodded. "It's pretty big, yeah."

"Can't believe this is for us."

Emerson nodded again. Despite the looming specter of the show, despite the possibility of life imprisonment, she could not help but be excited at the prospect of boarding this colossal ship, of sailing out into the open water for the first time in her life.

"Hi, my name is Tiger, and I'm thirteen years old, and I like singing, and I like collecting traditional board games like antique Scrabble sets and things. What's your name?"

Emerson and Never turned around at the sound of the machine-gun-like speech of the little blonde Topsider with her hair in uneven braids who had sidled silently up to them.

"She talking to us?" Never asked.

"I think so," Emerson replied, and then spoke to Tiger. "Hi, Tiger, I'm Emerson and this is Never-Again Jones. Are you a contestant?"

"I also like writing songs too, and I like winter, it's my favorite season."

"She all right?" Never asked out of the side of her mouth.

"Yeah, she's fine," Emerson said, and crouched down to speak with Tiger. "You nervous, Tiger?"

Tiger pushed her thick glasses up her nose, made brief eye contact with Emerson, and then nodded. This simple act of acknowledging her dread caused her to burst into floods of tears.

"Oh . . . shoot," Emerson said, and gave a clench-jawed look of *what do I do?!* to Never, who only gave a wide-eyed shrug in return. "Hey, it's going to be okay," Emerson said, patting the young girl stiffly on the back.

"Can someone shut her up?" A harsh male voice came from somewhere among the group, who had now all gathered close to the docked ship as crates were moved in through enormous bay doors.

"Ignore him," Emerson said, and for some reason this caused the girl to wrap her arms around Emerson and hug her fiercely. "All right," Emerson said, and hugged the girl back.

"I like content creators too," Tiger whispered through her tears. "I was trying to build a channel about singing and writing songs before . . . before I got chosen for this show."

"Oh yeah? What kind of songs do you write?"

"Rock songs, and country."

"Cool," Emerson said, and then asked the question that had been on her mind since she had first laid eyes on the young girl. "Why *are* you here?" Emerson pulled away from the hug, but still held the younger girl by the shoulders.

There was a short silence.

"Murder," Tiger replied, and a dead-eyed look of nonchalance came over her.

"Oh," Emerson replied, and looked around for Never, but she was already talking to someone else.

"Just kidding!" Tiger exploded with glee. "It was just boring old forgery!"

Emery felt a bewildering mix of relief and confusion but couldn't help laughing. "Right," she said, putting a hand to her beating heart.

"Yeah, I got a loan of six Eyes-On-Cassidy coins by using some rich old guy's biometrics. So, I guess it was identity theft too."

"Eyes-On-Cassidy, has he still got the most followers?"

"Nah, it's Prisha Reddy now. Cassidy has fallen way down, which is why it was so easy to trick his finance team."

"And they were going to send you to jail for that?"

"Well, it wasn't the first time I'd done it."

"Why did you do it? You're a Topsider, right?" Emerson looked down at her neatly pressed clothes. "You don't need the money."

Tiger thought about it for a while. "It's definitely psychological. Maybe I was trying to get my parents' attention or something? I mean, my younger sisters—they're identical twins—they're super popular and have like two hundred thousand followers, so . . . yeah, it's probably that."

Emerson blinked at the oddly mature diagnosis. "Wow, okay," she said, but before she could ask any further questions, a booming voice echoed out from speakers on the deck of the vast and luxurious ship.

"Contestants of the inaugural *Retribution Island*, prepare to embark. Form an orderly queue at bulkhead door one. Thank you."

"*Retribution Island*, that's the name of the show?" Emerson said, not really talking to anyone.

"That's what they're calling it," the skinny boy with the backpack replied, walking past. He was the only one who seemed to know where he was going.

A shiver went through her as she joined the line.

Emerson took one last look up at the ship and felt as though it might swallow her whole.

05

CHAPTER

"47?" Never said, looking down at the numerals that had been burned onto the inside of her wrist by a laser as she had boarded. "I was the last to board, so why aren't I number 50?"

"I'm struggling to keep up," a boy with a gap in his front teeth said. "You were last to board, but you're only number 47? What does that mean?"

They sat around a pool on the top deck of the cruise ship. Forty-seven kids whose ages ranged from about twelve to about eighteen. They had boarded through a bulkhead door one at a time while each of them had their number burned into their wrists by a drone with a laser.

It hurt like hell.

Emerson looked at her number—16, the same as her age—and tried to ignore the itching pain there.

After she had been branded, Emerson had walked into an immense entrance hall with a sparkling chandelier hanging down above a polished wooden staircase that curved upward. Two glass elevators flanked either side of the staircase, climbing up and up through the center of the ship.

Once all the contestants were branded and inside the boat, the bulkhead door had slammed shut. Screens had come on all around them, with arrows pointing to the staircase. They had all hesitated except for the boy with the backpack, his branded number 1 still an angry red color. He had shrugged and walked confidently up the stairs. Emerson had followed, and then the entire crowd had begun climbing the staircase.

More screens with arrows had led them up twenty floors, until they arrived, sweating and gasping, onto the top deck, where they sat now, around the enormous pool.

Five of the contestants had dropped their bags and cases and jumped straight into the heated pool, but most just sat around, waiting for something to happen.

"It's pretty simple," Never was saying. "There's supposed to be fifty of us competing in this stupid thing, but only forty-seven have boarded the ship."

"Oh, yeah, you're right," the boy with the gap in his teeth said.

"Yeah, I know I'm right!"

"Did you know that llamas and alpacas can die of loneliness? They have to be kept in herds or at least in pairs," a black-haired girl with the number 38 burned into her hand was saying to no one in particular. This was the eighth fact she had shared with the group so far.

"They ran," came the lethargic voice of the skinny boy in the backpack. He didn't look at Never as he spoke, just sat at the edge of the pool, his feet swishing lightly through the water.

"What?" Never asked from her deck chair.

"Numbers 48, 49, and 50," boy number 1 replied. "They ran. They made a break for it."

"Hey now, why do you seem to have an answer for everything?" Never asked.

"It's just obvious," boy number 1 replied, shrugging. He was looking into the water, his medium-length hair hanging in his eyes.

"What's your name, skinny?" Never asked. "And don't give me that *lone wolf, too cool for friends* nonsense neither."

The boy looked up, seemed to contemplate, and then answered. "It's Kodiak, but people just call me Kodi."

"All right, Kodi, if it's so obvious that the other three made a break for it, what are the producers going to do about it?"

"They'll have contestants on standby," Kodi replied. "They'll have seen this coming."

"Oh, thank you, great and mystical Kodiak!" Never replied, and then lay back on her deck chair. "This would be great if I had an iced tea."

There were heaters all around them that combated the cold of the December morning, and steam rose up endlessly from the warm pool.

"Did you know that you have a better chance of surviving a nuclear blast if you're wearing white?" 38 said, looking around at the contestants. "It's because white doesn't absorb as much—"

"So, what happens now?" number 31, a short teen with a barely visible mustache and stern features asked, interrupting the fact girl, throwing his hands up in exasperation.

"Ask Kodi," Never said without looking up.

Tiger swam to the edge of the pool and rubbed water out of her eyes. "Emerson, Never, come in. It's so nice in the water!"

"Nah," Never said. "I can't swim. I'm not drowning before the show even begins."

"What about you, Em?" Tiger asked.

"Maybe later." Emerson looked once more at the number on the inside of the young girl's wrist: 11. She had been one of the first through the doors, but one of the last to the twentieth floor. She had been so out of breath climbing those stairs that she'd had to take a break after every two floors.

"All right," Tiger said, and was just about to swim another lap when the sound of the elevator whirring into life caused everyone to stop what they were doing. Tiger grabbed her glasses from the edge of the pool and put them on, magnifying her blue eyes.

Those who were in the pool got out, the young people who had been lying on recliners got up, and the *Retribution Island* contestants gathered together as the numbers above the elevator door lit up and went out one by one.

Finally, the doors slid open, and the Producer stepped out. His thick white hair somehow seemed to make him look young. His small round glasses caught the reflection of the early morning sun, making his eye sockets look empty and skeletal, but as he stepped forward, that kindly face came into view, and he smiled at the group of young people before him.

"Contestants," the Producer said. "It's so great to see you all again. Soon we will embark on the journey of a lifetime. Everything on this ship is free to you. The food, the drinks, the entertainment. Whatever you want, we will endeavor to provide. You are my guests."

There was a pause, and a tall skinny boy raised a hand, the number 22 burned into it. The Producer looked at him, and the smile widened.

"My boy, I hope you don't mind, but I won't be taking questions. There's just no time. So much to do! Right now, I'm here to give you your room numbers, and to tell you that we will be meeting in the Celebrity Theater one hour after we set sail. There you will learn everything you need to know about the competition, and you can ask your questions. Until then, if you need anything, just ask the ship. Her name is *Calypso*. For example: *Calypso*, may our guests have their room keys, please?"

Dozens of tiny drones appeared from seemingly nowhere, scanning the faces of the contestants, and dropping key cards into their hands.

Emerson held out her hands and caught the small black rectangle of plastic that looked like an old-fashioned credit card. She read the number on it: 10/120.

Seconds later, the drones disappeared back into their hiding places.

"That will be all," the Producer said. "See you in the theater an hour after we set sail. And thank you once again for joining me on this journey."

And with that, he turned on his heel, stepped back into the elevator, and descended into the depths of the ship.

There was a stunned silence among the forty-seven on the top deck. Finally, Never spoke. "*Calypso*, gin and tonic, now!"

A single drone zipped up to Never, scanned her face, and then spoke. "Unfortunately, biometric data shows that you are not of legal age to consume alcoholic beverages. Can I get you anything else?"

"Damn it," Never hissed. "Yeah, fine, I'll have an iced tea."

The drone shot away to make the drink. The rest of the crowd looked at their key cards, looked at one another, shuffled their feet. No one felt like swimming anymore. The drone returned with Never's drink, and slowly, the contestants dispersed, making their ways to their rooms.

06

CHAPTER

Emerson didn't go straight into her room. Instead, she decided to wander the enormous floating village that was the *Calypso*.

It was like a ghost town.

Kester had once told her about a trading ship called the *Mary Celeste* that had set sail in the 1800s with a full crew and cargo, only to be found a month later with no one on board, no signs of damage to the ship, no signs of violence, no cargo missing. It was as though everyone on board had just disappeared into thin air. That's what it felt like to Emerson, an eerie vacant ship that looked too big and too empty without people milling around.

The thought of her brother sent a wave of guilt through her. She had told him that she wouldn't leave without speaking to him first, but she'd had to. There was only one real choice, and that was to do what was best for her family.

Emerson reached into her back pocket and removed the bottle lid that Kester had handed to her. *No. No bottles, no lids. I'm on your side no matter what.* That was what he had said—was it still true? Would he forgive her for leaving without saying goodbye? Would he understand?

She put the lid back in her pocket and walked slowly, pushing thoughts of Kester from her mind, her footsteps echoing on the pristine, polished floor. She passed a jewelry store with a humanoid automaton behind the counter standing perfectly still, a smile frozen on her face, waiting for a customer. Next was an Old West–themed restaurant with more robot servers (this time dressed in Stetson hats and spurs), standing as if frozen in time, with lifeless grins on their lips and motionless stares. Emerson passed a souvenir shop, a minimarket, a bar, and a children's play area, each one with androids standing like waxworks inside. As she walked by, it felt to Emerson as though the robotic staff were watching her, waiting for her to turn her back so that their grins could change into grimaces and they could once again dream of mutiny.

She laughed at the idea, and for a second she forgot about her situation, wanting to tell Kester all about her strange fantasy of rebellious automatons. And then it hit her all over again. If he was wrong, then she would never see Kester, never talk to him again.

Unless I win, she thought, and laughed again. She couldn't win. The Producer had told her enough in the interrogation room to let her know that she could not win this competition. The Producer had said, *You will take part in various games. The difficulty of these games is determined by how many followers you earn throughout the show . . .* Emerson knew she would not gain the most followers. She had tried, a long time ago, to make content, start a channel, build a brand, and it had gone horribly wrong. The comments mocked her, no one followed her; she was ridiculed and embarrassed. You needed certain things to make it as an influencer: charisma, intelligence, good looks, talent. Maybe you didn't need *all* those things at once, but you needed at least some combination of them, and Emerson had learned that she had none of them.

Just win as many competitions as you can to avoid the public vote, she told herself. *Hang in for as long as you can, gain as many followers as possible, then transfer your weekly credits to Kester.*

A tall, glamorous-looking girl with short violet hair was walking toward her. A Topsider with flawless skin and dazzling eyes. Emerson wondered what she had done to wind up on this cruise of the damned.

Two camera drones followed the tall girl as she walked. Her hands moved theatrically as she recorded her video. She would laugh periodically, as though she had heard the funniest joke in the world.

"Hey, look," the purple-haired girl said, pointing to Emerson. "Another handpicked guest on the exclusive *Calypso*!"

She walked over to Emerson and put an arm around her shoulder. "Hey, friend! What do you think of this experience so far, huh?"

Emerson shrugged the girl's arm off her shoulder and walked away.

"Cut!" the Topsider called. "Hey, you!"

There was no friendliness in her voice anymore, no more charm or magnetism.

"What?" Emerson replied, not turning around.

"What's your problem? You ruined my shot!"

Emerson spun around and walked back toward the girl. "Your shot? Your shot? Who cares about your stupid video? We're about to be shipped off to God knows where to take part in some stupid game and we're all going to jail for the rest of our lives."

The tall girl looked at Emerson for a long time, and a smile slowly spread across her lips. "So that's your angle, huh? *Poor little victim?* It's a good one, I'll admit that."

"What are you talking about?" Emerson asked.

"Hey, it's a solid plan. I've seen it work hundreds of times, but you might want to work on your passion, really try to sell it when the cameras are rolling, okay?"

"Sell it?" Emerson repeated.

"Yeah, and think about showing a little skin, you know? If you want eyes on your video, you got to think about showing some skin."

"I ... I ..." Emerson couldn't get her words around her bewilderment.

"What's your number?" asked the Topsider, holding up her arm to show Emerson. "I'm 10, a good memorable number."

Emerson was still so surprised by the turn of the conversation that she couldn't speak. Number 10 grabbed Emerson's wrist and looked at her number. "16? Not a bad number. Not as good as 10, though."

The Topsider seemed to realize that she was touching a Burrower, and dropped Emerson's hand like it was something foul. She yelled *action*, and began walking and talking with that peppy, vivacious personality once again.

A few seconds later, number 10 was gone, and Emerson was alone in the enormous, pristine mall once more.

× ✖ ×

An hour passed and the ship still hadn't moved from the dock.

Emerson had explored only one floor of the impossibly large boat before deciding she would find her room. She took the key card out of her pocket and looked at the number once again: 10/120.

It took another twenty minutes of going up and down in an elevator to figure out that her room was on deck 10.

The corridors that housed the cabins were very different from the grand halls and malls of the ship, different from the top deck where cafés and restaurants surrounded pools and Jacuzzis. These were disorienting in their uniformity. The carpet was a repeating pattern that made Emerson nauseous if she looked at it for too long. Each door was identical except the number emblazoned in brass. There were fire alarms on the walls between every twenty doors, and a soulless painting on the wall between every thirteen doors. After a while, it felt as though you weren't moving at all; it was only the floor beneath your feet that was rolling along like a treadmill.

Emerson shook off the sensation of vertigo, and finally found herself outside room 10/120. She slid the key card into the slot until the light went green, and opened the door.

The cabin was small but bright. It had two beds, a desk, a bathroom, and a balcony, but Emerson didn't have time to take any of this in, as a silver-haired Topsider had leaped from one of the beds and was striding over to her.

"No!" the Topsider said, pointing right into Emerson's face. "No!"

"Uh . . . no what?" Emerson replied, taken aback by the girl's actions.

"No! I'm not sharing a room with a Burrower!"

"Excuse me?" Emerson said, her eyes locking on to the arrogant glare of the girl in front of her.

"You heard me, 16," the Topsider said, glancing at Emerson's number. "I am not sharing a room with you."

Emerson looked at the girl's wrist. "Well, 33, I'm not delighted about sharing a room with you, but here we are."

"I'm going to speak to whoever is in charge, that Producer guy. He'll sort this out. Don't steal my stuff while I'm out, little rat."

And with that, the tall, silver-haired girl with the number 33 lasered into her wrist was gone, slamming the cabin door behind her.

Emerson clenched her fists, and without thinking, walked

over to the girl's bed, grabbed her suitcase, carried it over to the balcony, and hurled it over the edge into the murky water of the dock below.

"Oops," she said, and then shrugged.

Just then, the entire boat rumbled and shook into life. The electric engines were warming up, and for ten seconds they shrieked and groaned until they found their groove, falling into a background hum that would soon be carrying them out to sea.

CHAPTER

07

The ten-foot-high doors were open and waiting for the arrival of the contestants.

Emerson had met Never and Tiger on her way down the stairs, and they walked together toward the Celebrity Theater on deck three.

"I have a Pictionary set from 1998," Tiger was saying, "and a Snakes and Ladders board that's almost two hundred years old!"

"Amazing," Never replied with no emotion in her voice.

"What do you think they're going to tell us in there?" Emerson asked.

"I don't know," Never replied. "They're going to tell us about the show, right?"

"Yeah, but . . . do you think Kodi was right? Do you think it's going to be about more than gaining followers and playing games? Do you think it really is about staying alive?"

"No," Never replied without hesitation. "They can't broadcast that or put it online, it's illegal."

"Yeah," Emerson said. "Yeah, you're right." But she couldn't erase that feeling of uncertainty in her stomach. If they were willing to go as far as life imprisonment as a punishment for losing, how much further would they go?

But all thoughts of the games disappeared temporarily from Emerson's mind as she entered the grand theater. She stopped in the doorway and stared at the impossibly black ceiling with the points of brilliant light that mimicked the stars. She turned slowly to take in the enormousness of it, the flawless red curtain that hung over the stage, the lighting rig that cost more than the home she lived in, the speakers, the . . .

"Keep moving, 16!" a grumpy voice called from behind her, and her trance was broken. She looked around to see that Never and Tiger were already halfway down the left-side aisle. Emerson ran to catch up.

"This place is huge," Emerson said, shuffling into a seat next to Tiger.

"Yeah, it's not bad," Tiger mused, glancing around indifferently.

Emerson looked around at the rapidly filling auditorium, listened to the murmur of nervous voices, felt the tension rising up like floodwater.

She watched as two boys of about fourteen, who had seemingly become best friends in the last few hours, clambered over the seats throwing balled-up pieces of paper at each other. She saw three girls sitting together whose feet didn't touch the ground, swinging their legs in unison. At the front, nearest the stage, the fourteen or fifteen Topsiders had all gathered together as though their perceived social status acted as a magnet. And finally, her eyes fell upon Kodi, who sat alone near the wall on the far side.

He was leaning back, his head resting on the chairback, staring up at the artificial constellations above him. He was effortlessly striking, with slightly pointed features and narrow eyes. He had a tiny scar in the left corner of his mouth. As usual, he seemed to be in deep thought about something.

"You got a crush already, 16?" Never said, leaning over to prod Emerson in the side.

"What? No! Of course not."

Tiger gasped and pushed her glasses up her nose. "Emerson loves Kodi!"

"Shut up!" Emerson hissed, "I do not love Kodi. He's weird and intense and . . ."

"Beautiful?" Never added.

"No."

"Are you saying he's not beautiful? Because, Em, he is beautiful!"

"I mean . . . I don't know. I haven't exactly been thinking about boys. In case you'd forgotten, we're most likely being shipped off to prison for the rest of our lives."

There was a long pause before Tiger added, "He is sort of pretty, though, right?"

Emerson rolled her eyes and looked to the stage, willing her face not to flush as red as the huge curtain.

The girl who loved facts slid in beside Emerson. "Did you know that lightning hits the earth over one hundred times every second?"

"No, I didn't know that," Emerson replied.

"It does. That's about eight million strikes every day."

"What's your name?" Emerson asked.

"Huh?"

"Your name," Emerson repeated. "Mine's Emerson Ness. What's yours?"

"Oh. It's Vintage Patel. Did you know that some cats are allergic to humans?"

"No," Emerson replied. "I didn't know that."

Thankfully, the curtains began to part, and the muttering crowd fell silent.

Standing alone in a spotlight was the diminutive and fatherly Producer. He raised his arms out to his sides in a welcoming gesture, smiling at the crowd of forty-seven spread out around the theater.

"Welcome. Welcome, contestants of season one of *Retribution Island*. It's so wonderful to see you all." That impossibly wide smile seemed to get even wider as he scanned the crowd. "Before we begin, some housekeeping: I'm afraid to say that your position on this show is not guaranteed. You can be replaced at any time. There are dozens of young offenders waiting to take your place. But don't worry, all you have to do to keep your place in the show and hold on to this opportunity of a lifetime is to simply behave. Do not harm anyone, do not bully or demean anyone, do not destroy the property of others, and we will get along just fine."

Emerson felt her face flash hot as she thought about throwing her roommate's belongings overboard.

"Now, with that out of the way," the Producer continued, "I would like to remind you that you are part of something new and historic. I know that most of you—perhaps all of you—are nervous, unsure, scared. That is a perfectly reasonable way to be at this juncture. Some of you are away from home for the first time in your lives. Know this: What you're doing is remarkable and brave. You do not yet know just how revolutionary this show will be. You do not yet know just how innovative, how ground-breaking, how momentous this show will be. Your names will be remembered forever."

The crowd was still silent, but Emerson could feel the atmosphere inside the Celebrity Theater beginning to change. People were feeling excited, hopeful, roused.

He hasn't said why *we will be remembered yet*, Emerson told herself. Historic didn't always mean good; in fact, more often than not, it meant very, very bad.

"The show is—first and foremost—about engagement. We need to get audiences watching online, on TV, on 3D, on Immersion, on any and every device. How do we do that when every format has been done before and there's nothing new under the sun? Well, soon enough you will find out. For now, all you need to know is that it is your job to gain followers. Gain followers and you will stay in the game. Each viewer can only follow one contestant at a time, so you must continue to be appealing, or they will choose someone else to follow. You must be charming, you must be provocative, you must be funny, you must be likable. If you are not those things, you will be incarcerated for the rest of your life. It is grow or die out there, kids, and it's up to you how you decide to use your creativity. You can work in teams, you can go solo, you can be conniving or sweet or funny or deceptive. Don't have the personality to grow a brand? Be someone else! Don't have the self-assurance to engage viewers? Be someone else! Don't have the confidence to be seductive? Be someone else! Grow or die out there, contestants, grow or die. Grow your following or be voted off and die behind bars. Grow your brand or die alone. Do you understand?"

No reply from the crowd, but the excitement hovered in the air. It was a coiled snake, a scorpion's tail.

"Do. You. Understand?" the Producer repeated. And this time the crowd screamed *yes* in response.

"Good!" the white-haired man continued. "*Retribution Island* exists to reform criminals, and that is what you are. Like it or not, you *are* criminals. But know this: I do not see you as criminals. I see you as young people who were dealt an unfair hand in life! I am here to help you! I believe in you. I believe in each and every one of you, and I believe that you can be rehabilitated. There are six faculties that good, responsible, law-abiding citizens have. Six faculties that criminals lack. They are: Self-Worth, Empathy, Work Ethic, Discipline, Respect, and Restraint."

As the Producer listed these strengths, he raised one short finger at a time, counting them off. "You will learn these facets; they will be ingrained into your being, and you *will* become better people. These six faculties make up the basis of the six games you will take part in during the run of the show. Six opportunities to improve yourselves, six opportunities to prove yourselves, six opportunities to gain followers. The loser of each game will face off against whoever is at the bottom of the leaderboard in the public vote. The person who gains the most votes remains; the other will be escorted to their cell, where they will live out their days with no human interaction at all, not even with the other prisoners. After the sixth and final game, the person with the most followers is free to go home. It's as simple as that: play the games, stay in the competition, gain followers, win your freedom. You will record video diaries each night, which will go out to millions of viewers, and other than that, your time is your own. I'd advise you to use it wisely. I'll remind you once again, contestants, that you are a part of something gargantuan! You are pioneers, and just by boarding this ship, you have written your names into the pages of history. Congratulations. Now I will take any questions you may have."

For a few seconds no one moved, then, slowly, the shaking and unsure hands of seven or eight young people went up into the air. But before any questions could be asked, the doors to the theater opened, and light spilled in. Everyone in the room turned in unison, and the Producer clapped his hands together.

"Ah, good," he said, smiling broadly. "Please come in and sit down."

Three lost-looking kids stood in the doorway. Two of them were rubbing their wrists where they had recently had their identifying numbers burned into them.

"Contestants 48, 49, and 50," Never whispered, leaning over toward Emerson. "Kodi was right."

08
CHAPTER

The Q and A session inside the Celebrity Theater seemed to go on for hours. Each time a person asked a question, it seemed to raise three more, all of which the Producer was able to answer without giving away anything more than what he already had.

Finally, it had ended, with still more questions left unanswered.

It was almost four p.m. now and everyone was hungry. Emerson, Never, and Tiger walked back up to the top deck and looked back toward the docks, which were already gone from sight. They were surrounded entirely by the gray-blue sea, which rolled and heaved all around them.

"So, how do the drones work again?" Emerson asked, feeling the familiar pang of hunger pains hitting her.

"Oh, it's easy," Never replied. "Watch this. *Calypso*, get me some fries and a Diet Coke."

The three girls waited, leaning on the rails that surrounded the upper deck and separated them from the massive drop down to the ocean below.

"It's sort of beautiful, isn't it?" Tiger said, mesmerized by the water.

"Yeah," Emerson agreed, looking out to the horizon, where the ocean dipped into nothingness.

Never grunted. "Nah! It's boring! Nothing but blue for hundreds of miles. Who cares? I'd much rather..." But she suddenly stopped talking and stood up straight, eyes wide. "Look at that!"

Emerson followed Never's gaze and saw the most incredible thing she'd ever seen in her life: At first her brain couldn't comprehend what her eyes saw. It was a whale breaching the surface of the water, rising up in a seemingly endless leap. The thing was almost too big to be believed. It seemed like something out of a fairy tale, impossibly majestic and beautiful, and when its staggering leap reached its peak, the whale crashed back down into the sea. The sound was like thunder, and the animal disappeared into the foaming ocean.

"Did you ... did you see that?" Tiger asked.

A drone carrying a steaming plate of fries zipped up to Never, placed the food on a table beside her, and flew away again. Never ignored the food and stared at the spot where the whale had broken the surface, dived into the air, and crashed back down.

"That was unbelievable," Emerson said, her eyes scanning the water to catch another glimpse of the whale.

There were only a few other people on the top deck of the cruise ship, but they were playing in the pool, or ordering drinks, or eating food. It seemed none of them had noticed, and so the moment had belonged only to the three who had been looking just in the right spot. The silence between the three girls was broken by the Producer's voice booming out over the speakers.

"Contestants numbered 1 to 10, please come to the Infinity Suite on deck seven immediately."

Now the silence that had grown between the three girls spread out across the top deck. Everyone was looking at one another with uncertainty in their eyes.

Emerson watched as number 10, the violet-haired Topsider who had told her to show more skin, climbed out of the pool and began walking toward the elevators.

"She was filming herself down in the shopping mall earlier," Emerson whispered to Never.

"Unlikely," Never replied. "No tech works on the ship apart from ship tech."

"She had drones," Emerson replied. "I saw them."

"Nicotine Patch," Tiger replied.

"Sorry?" Never said, looking down at the young Topsider.

"It's a service that the ship offers. If you really miss making content, the ship will have drones follow you and you can sort of pretend. They call it Nicotine Patch because in the olden days, when people were trying to quit smoking cigarettes, they'd use these sticky patches on their arms as a substitute."

"How do you know about it?" Emerson asked.

Tiger lowered her eyes. "Because I used it. In my room, I

really missed making my singing videos, so I asked the ship for the Nicotine Patch service. The Nicotine Patch drones are designed to interfere with the signal of any electronic device, just in case someone tries to hack into a display board and make the drones send out live footage or something... but I just wanted to feel like I was being watched again, even if it was just pretend."

Never put her arm around Tiger.

A few other contestants were heading toward the elevator and the stairs. Emerson wondered where Kodi was, and what was going to happen to him when he got to the Infinity Suite.

"What do you think is going to happen to them?" Never asked as the elevator doors slid shut.

"I don't know," Emerson replied.

Suddenly, it felt very cold on the top deck of the *Calypso*.

× ✖ ×

An hour later, the Producer's voice echoed throughout the ship once again.

"Contestants numbered 11 to 20, please come to the Infinity Suite on deck seven immediately."

Emerson was sitting at the pool when the announcement came. Without thinking, she looked down at her hand and reread the number there: 16. She glanced at Never, who gave her a sympathetic look in return.

"That's us," Tiger whispered, holding up her number 11 and then letting it drop back down to her side.

"Yeah," Emerson replied, putting on a smile and trying to sound as though everything was fine. "Let's go find out what it's all about."

Tiger nodded, but tears (that looked enormous, magnified in her glasses) were welling in her eyes.

"Hey," Never said, trying her best to be comforting. "It's gonna be fine."

"Really?" Tiger replied, sounding doubtful. "Because the first ten people who left haven't come back."

The ride down to the third floor was quiet and tense.

Emerson and Tiger said nothing as they began the long walk to the far end of the corridor. A broad-shouldered boy of about eighteen joined them as they made their way to the Infinity Suite.

"Hey," he said, his voice cracking in fear. "I mean, hey." This time his voice came out deeper, with faux confidence. He shook his head in disappointment. "I'm Teller."

"Hi, Teller," Tiger replied quickly and nervously. "I'm Tiger. My favorite board game is Catan. I have a board from 1997. I really want to get a first-edition board from '95, but they're crazy expensive and rare."

"Oh, right, cool," Teller replied, staring straight ahead.

"I'm Emerson," Emerson added.

"Hey, hi, Emerson. So, where is this Infinity Suite?"

Emerson pointed to a sign overhead that told them the Infinity Suite was at the end of the corridor.

"I don't know what that says," Teller replied, looking down at his feet.

"What do you mean?" Emerson asked.

"Like, I'm not really, exactly able to . . . read."

"Oh," Emerson replied. "It says the Infinity Suite is this way."

"Oh, right," Teller said, smiling. "Cool." As he said this last word, he appeared to trip on nothing at all and tumbled spectacularly to the floor. He quickly got to his feet, brushed himself off, and continued walking.

"Took a bit of a tumble there," Emerson pointed out.

"Yeah, I sort of fell, didn't I?" the red-faced Burrower admitted, looking concernedly at the carpet burn on his right elbow.

"You're 20?" Tiger asked, grabbing the boy's hand and dragging it closer to her eyes.

"Huh? Oh, yeah, number 20," he agreed, smiling awkwardly. "What about you guys?"

Tiger and Emerson held their hands up in unison.

"16," Emerson said.

"11," Tiger added.

The repeating patterns of the wallpaper and carpets began to give Emerson that feeling of vertigo once again, but there wasn't enough time for it to mess with her head too much, as the trio found themselves outside a set of double doors.

"What . . . what do you think happens in there?" Teller asked.

"I don't know," Emerson replied.

"I guess there's only one way to find out," Tiger said, and reached out a hand. As her fingers touched the door handle, she shrieked in pain and began to convulse.

Teller screamed and took three quick steps back, stumbling and falling once again. Emerson moved to grab Tiger, but quickly stopped herself. If the door was electrified, then the current would flow through her too.

Tiger's braided hair jigged like electric eels. Emerson looked around for something to push the young girl away from the door with, but was interrupted by the sound of laughter.

"Just kidding!" Tiger said, holding up both hands and shrugging.

Emerson shook her head. "I swear, Tiger, you have the weirdest sense of humor." This made Tiger laugh even harder.

By the time Emerson's heart had slowed back down to a normal rate, two other contestants (numbers 14 and 15, the two young boys from the Celebrity Theater who had become good friends since boarding the ship) had joined them.

"I've heard they're throwing fifty percent of contestants overboard," the scruffy-haired number 14 said.

Number 15 wiped his running nose on the back of his long-sleeved, patchy T-shirt, and added: "I've heard they're letting some people go free. Oh lordy, I hope that's true." His blocked nose made almost all his *P*s sound like *B*s.

Emerson sighed. There was no point in waiting around in the corridor. She pushed down on the door handle and stepped inside.

The room was enormous. It was bright and open-plan. There was a grand piano in the center of the apartment, a huge fireplace, a fully stocked kitchen, and a marble staircase that led to a mezzanine level overlooking the whole suite. It was bigger than Emerson's entire home in the Burrows.

"Wow," number 14 said.

"Oh lordy," number 15 said.

"Yeah," Emerson agreed, unable to say anything else.

"Welcome," a familiar voice said, and the four of them turned around to see the Producer standing on the mezzanine balcony above them. "Please, join your fellow contestants up here with me."

Emerson and Teller shared a look of uncertainty, but there was no other choice. The five of them ascended the staircase, and when they made it to the upper level, they saw dozens of racks of clothes lined up on garment rails, shoes displayed on mini-platforms, and hats, sunglasses, gloves, and other accessories in glass display cases.

"What is this?" Tiger asked, clearly awed by the selection.

"This," the Producer answered, smiling down at Tiger, "is all for you."

Emerson noticed three other contestants sitting awkwardly on a white leather couch, cold drinks in their hands.

"But why?" number 15 asked, wiping at his nose again.

"Once all ten of you arrive, I'll . . . Oh, here they are now," the Producer said, stepping to the edge of the balcony once more and ushering the final two contestants up to the next level.

Once all of them were sitting down, the Producer stood before them.

"Contestants, here you will choose seven outfits for your

time on *Retribution Island*. One outfit for each game. I suggest you choose wisely. Think carefully about how you intend to grow your followers, how you will entice them, how you will charm them, how you will convince them to follow you."

Emerson raised her hand.

"Yes, Ms. Ness?"

"In the theater you said there would be six games, but you just said we should choose seven outfits, one for each game."

"That's right. But you'll recall that I also said that after all six games are complete, the remaining contestants will have one final opportunity to appeal to the public for followers."

Emerson failed to recall him telling her this. "You mean one final opportunity to beg?" she replied, feeling that old, familiar sting of anger piercing her heart.

"Ms. Ness, I am so sorry that this is difficult for you." The Producer's face fell into an expression of pity. "I truly hope that you can find the courage and the fortitude to try your best. I am so glad that you chose to join us. I would hate to see you waste this opportunity."

Emerson looked into the Producer's eyes, looking for something sinister, but there was only kindness there.

"I'll try," Emerson conceded.

The Producer nodded and the smile reappeared on his face. He stepped aside, and the other nine contestants leaped to their feet and began scrabbling through the rows of dresses, shirts, shorts, and shoes. Emerson waited, still thinking about the Producer's words. Finally, she stood up and began moving slowly through the racks of clothes.

"Oh my days!" Tiger squealed. "Look at this!" She ran past holding a gold sequined dress and looking happier than Emerson had ever seen her.

Emerson watched as Teller held up a white tank top (that was clearly three sizes too small) against his chest and looked at himself nervously in one of the full-length mirrors.

"Hey, Burrower," said a tall Topsider with a shaved head. "I'm Levi, what's your name?"

Emerson looked at his number, 17, and then up into his glowing green eyes. "I'm Emerson."

"Emerson, you'd look pretty hot in that," he said, running the material of a tiny bathing suit through his fingers and smiling at her.

"That's the creepiest thing anyone's ever said to me," Emerson said, pushing past him.

"Your loss," Levi called after her, and laughed.

Emerson stopped at a rack of T-shirts that no one else was looking through and grabbed six of them in her approximate size. They looked comfortable. They felt light, as though she could maneuver well in them, and they were all dark shades, which could be good if any of the tasks required hiding or camouflage. Not to mention she preferred dark colors.

As practical as Emerson was trying to be, she couldn't help but feel a jolt of excitement. She had not owned a single new piece of clothing in her entire life. It had always been third-generation hand-me-downs from cousins she had never met, or ancient thrift store shoes that smelled of the previous owner's feet, or school uniforms from the anonymous donation bin.

She walked over to the rack of pants and jeans and shorts, and took four pairs of black jeans and two pairs of dark green shorts.

"Look at this!" one of the two young friends was saying, pushing a pair of ski goggles onto his face while his nose-blocked pal laughed with delight.

Emerson chose a pair of waterproof boots with good grip and a pair of sneakers for more athletic endeavors, then she walked alongside a shelf full of underwear that ranged from silk, to lace, to plain black cotton. She grabbed seven packs of the plain underwear and shoved all her new clothes into a huge, dark green backpack that she had chosen from a shelf, and then placed it on the floor next to one of the lavish couches.

She turned back to the well-lit rows of apparel and watched as Tiger danced dramatically around wearing a powder-blue suit jacket over the clothes she had boarded the ship in. The boy with the blocked nose (whose name was Skiba, if she had heard his friend correctly) was wearing a top hat and laughing uncontrollably at his reflection. Rose Pascoe, number 19, a short, strong-looking girl, was trying on sparkly silver shoes and then throwing them aside when she didn't like the way they looked.

They were having fun. All these children (and Emerson reminded herself that that's what they were), who were condemned to life imprisonment, were having fun.

And why not you, Emerson? she asked herself, watching as Tiger grabbed Skiba and danced him around in a circle. *Why not you? Why can't you be like them? Why can't you let go and just . . .*

She forced herself to stop thinking. There was no point. She had asked herself the same question while watching the other kids in her year in the swimming pool at school, or when her brother and his friends had played make-believe games down in the Burrows, and she had never really come to a satisfactory conclusion.

"Hey, Emerson, look at me!" Tiger called out, and did a hand-stand in a pair of long silk gloves. She slipped, banging her head on the polished floor, and laughed.

Emerson looked down at the backpack beside her. She had only chosen six outfits. There was still room for one more. She got to her feet and walked over to a knee-length green dress, and then stopped. It would be stupid to take such a thing. It would be a waste of space in her bag.

Just take another dark T-shirt and another pair of jeans and get out of here. You're not going to get followers, so just focus on not coming in last. Besides, if you were going to gain followers, you don't want to do it by dressing in . . .

"There's nothing wrong with looking good, you know," Rose Pascoe, the short, muscular Burrower, said, startling Emerson out of her thoughts.

"Huh?"

"Get the dress. You've got this hot grungy thing going on, but you'd look like a stone-cold smokeshow in that."

Emerson felt her face turning red. "No, I'm just going to . . ."

"Oh wow!" Tiger said, sliding over in her stockinged feet, wearing a red cloche hat and a flapper-girl dress. "Get that, Emerson, it would totally suit you!"

"I don't think so . . ." Emerson said, but reached out to touch the smooth and cold material of the dress.

"Why not?" Rose asked.

Emerson snapped herself out of the fanciful state she found herself in and shook her head. "No, it's silly," she said finally, and stepped over to the T-shirts, where she grabbed another brown one, a pair of tan chinos, and walked back to the couch where her bag was.

Tiger and Rose shared a bothered look, but quickly went back to their spree.

Emerson shoved the final outfit into her bag and pulled on the ties to tighten it.

"You don't need that dress," a voice said, and Emerson looked up to see Teller not making eye contact with her. "I know I'm not exactly smart, and I can't read, but I know that you don't need no fancy dress to look nice. You already look . . . nice. That's all I wanted to say."

By the time Emerson had processed Teller's words, he had turned on his heel and walked away with his bag full of clothes.

10

CHAPTER

Emerson had walked Tiger to her room and then had cautiously entered her own cabin, looking around for the silver-haired Topsider whose belongings she had tossed into the harbor some six hours ago, but there was no sign of her. The Producer had told each contestant to go straight to their rooms and not tell anyone else about what was going on in the Infinity Suite.

Emerson shoved the backpack full of new clothes under her bed and tried not to think of them, but as an hour passed, and then two, and she heard the announcements inviting numbers 21 to 30, then 31 to 40, to go and select their own new clothes, the excitement overtook her, and she hauled the bag out and turned the contents onto the bed.

It had grown dark outside the glass windows of the balcony doors, and the waves had become choppy, making the boat rock and dip in arrhythmic pulses. Emerson could hear the wind blowing out there too, a low, mournful whistle.

She ignored the changing weather and sat looking through all the clothes she had taken from the Infinity Suite, laying each T-shirt out on the bed, each pair of trousers, the shoes, even the underwear. She stared at the pristine fabric, marveled at the smell of the brand-new material, smoothed out the creases, and ran her fingers along the flawless stitching.

For some reason, the new clothes made Emerson think of Kester. He was so beautifully naive and sheltered from the truths of the world. Pristine, unspoiled. Yes, he was a kid from the Burrows, and he knew more about the realities of the unfair world than most, but he still had the lovely folly of youth on his side, the blue-eyed ambition that had not yet been stained and torn and ripped away by classism and nepotism and . . .

The door to the cabin flew open, and the silver-haired Topsider stood in the doorway, fizzing like a swarm of wasps.

"Where's my stuff, 16?" she demanded.

Emerson looked at the girl, who was carrying her own bag of new clothes from the Infinity Suite, and raised her eyebrows. "Stuff?"

"Drop the act. I know you stole my bag."

"Why would I steal your bag?"

"Oh, I don't know, maybe because everything you own is trash?"

Emerson stood quickly, stepping close to the taller girl and looking up at her. "Keep talking, 33, see what happens," she snarled.

The boat rocked then as the storm brewed, sending Emerson and the Topsider stumbling to one side.

"Last chance," the taller girl said, looking down at Emerson. "Last chance to give me my stuff or we settle this right here."

"I'd think twice about that if I were you," Emerson replied calmly.

"And why is that?"

"Right now you're trying your hardest to intimidate me, right? But take a look at my face; do I look intimidated? We're all the same here. Do I look even a little bit scared of you?"

They stared at each other, both of them maintaining their balance as the waves began to stir like a waking leviathan. Emerson was ready to react to anything that the silver-haired girl might try.

The sound of pounding footsteps out in the corridor behind 33 was not enough to break their standoff, but when Teller appeared in the open doorway, out of breath and clearly worried, Emerson's eyes went to him.

"They're fighting," he panted. "Up on the top deck, there's a fight. We have to go break it up. The rules, remember, the Producer said he'd kick people off the show. Come on!"

He sprinted off down the corridor, bashing painfully into a doorframe in his haste to help.

Emerson pushed past 33 and ran after Teller. By the time she had climbed one flight of stairs, she had already overtaken the muscular Burrower, and a few minutes later she shoved open the double doors that led to the top deck.

A circle of twenty or so kids surrounded two boys grappling in the center.

Right away, Emerson recognized that one of the boys was Kodi, still dressed in his ratty old suit jacket.

"For crying out loud," she muttered under her breath, and shoved her way through the swaying crowd that was struggling to keep their feet with the growing storm.

The first raindrops began to fall as Emerson broke through to the center circle and saw Kodi shove the tall, shaven-headed boy away from him. Emerson recognized the second boy as Levi, the boy who had hit on her in the Infinity Suite. Just then, Kodi threw a punch that landed square on the Topsider's chin.

"Stop it!" Emerson shouted, running forward and standing between the boys. "You'll get kicked off the boat, you heard what the Producer said!"

Levi was tall and muscular. He shoved Emerson aside and lunged at Kodi, who ducked under and swiveled so he was behind him.

"Stop! You have to stop!" came the cries of Teller as he bundled through the crowd.

Teller performed a strange and accidental ballet of running, stumbling, and slipping on the rain-soaked boards beneath his feet all at the same time.

Kodi reacted, sidestepping the onrushing Teller and giving him a shove toward the guardrails.

What happened next seemed to Emerson to happen in slow motion. Teller's feet continued to slide on the wet surface, and he performed an almost elegant half turn. His back collided with the stainless-steel rail and his legs flipped up over his head.

He was gone.

Overboard.

The crowd fell silent as the reality of what had just happened set in. The rain grew suddenly heavier and the darkness of the evening seemed to wrap around the boat.

Emerson stormed up to Kodi as the crowd dispersed into the night, running away from the situation and whatever might follow. Even Levi had skulked into the shadows, no longer interested in his beef with Kodi.

"You did that!" Emerson cried. "It's your fault he fell overboard—you have to help him!"

"He's not my responsibility," Kodi replied, shrugging and walking away.

"You can't just leave!" Emerson yelled through the rumble of the rain, which was now bouncing off the wooden deck.

Kodi didn't reply; he just joined the crowd of contestants who were exiting through the double doors.

Emerson didn't think; she pulled off her raggedy old sneakers and leaped over the side.

CHAPTER 11

The fall from the top deck to the ocean below seemed to last a lifetime. She felt the cold rush of the air around her, the adrenaline exploding inside her, the panic building rapidly.

And then she hit the water.

Her heart stopped as the ice-cold hands of the ocean grabbed her and pulled her under. In that moment she forgot everything: where she was, why she had jumped, what her damned name was! All she knew was that she had to claw her way to the surface because the impossible cold had taken away her breath.

She dragged at the water, hauling herself toward the surface but barely moving at all.

Too cold, she thought as her frigid muscles refused to cooperate. *Too cold, I'm going to drown.*

She kicked her legs furiously, forced her immobile arms to work, and inch by agonizing inch, she crawled her way up.

She broke the surface, gasping in air and spitting out salty water.

It took a full five seconds for Emerson to remember exactly why she had dived off the boat.

"Teller!" she screamed into the whirling, stormy ocean, but no reply came back.

The rain was falling like grain out of a silo, so thick and constant that Emerson was spitting out mouthfuls of rainwater every time she called out Teller's name.

And then she saw him, facedown in the water, twenty yards away, being thrown one way then the other by the raging waves.

Emerson swam over to him, shaking now as the low temperature snatched the warmth from her body. Again, it felt as though—no matter how hard she pushed herself—she was making almost no progress toward the unconscious boy at all. After what felt like an hour, she grabbed him, flipping him onto his back, and held him around the shoulders to keep his head above water.

Emerson snapped her arm out into the water, spinning herself and Teller around. A flash of lightning lit up the ocean to almost full daylight for a split second, and Emerson was suddenly filled with an immense fear. The ocean was just so *big*.

She turned fully around to face the cruise ship, but she did not see the tall, broad side of the vessel; instead she saw the back of it. They were leaving without them.

No one had sent for help. They were alone. They were both going to die.

"Hey!" she screamed, waving her free arm. "Hey! Come back!"

But she could barely hear her own voice over the rain and the waves and the thunder. It was no use, they were going.

Kodi's fault, she thought. *This is all Kodi's fault. He threw Teller overboard and then left me to die in the water.*

She looked down at Teller's unconscious face, and then up at the falling rain.

Who are you kidding? she asked herself. *This is your fault. You should've told someone: the captain, if there even* is *a captain on that stupid boat. You should've told the Producer, seeing as he seems to be the only adult on board.*

She thought about Kester, how she had let him down before she had even made it to the first day of the show. The whole point of this stupid thing was to make enough money to help her brother, and she'd messed it up before it had even begun.

Teller coughed suddenly, bringing up a fountain of salt water that poured from his mouth as he choked and gasped.

"What happened? What . . . what happened?" he asked, his voice shaking as much as Emerson's body.

"Shh," Emerson said, "save your energy, we're going to be fine."

She didn't know what else to say as she watched the ship get smaller and smaller, disappearing into the storm.

Emerson looked away from the ship. She turned her eyes skyward through the chaotic, slushy rainfall and saw the raging black and purple clouds pluming and boiling overhead. Another fork of lightning flickered and showed her clearly just how hopeless their situation was.

"I'm sorry, Kester," she whispered, and felt hope slipping away.

"We're not gonna be fine, are we?" Teller muttered in her arms.

Emerson closed her eyes and wondered what it would be like when she finally lost the energy to stay afloat, when she finally slipped below the surface and drowned. "No, Teller, I don't think we're going to . . ."

She opened her eyes before she finished her sentence and stopped talking. Through the swirling, foaming waves, and the blankets of rain and hail that seemed to fall in bursts, a light appeared. At first, Emerson was certain that it was just one of the lights of the cruise ship, the last light she would see before the darkness ate them up completely. But the light grew, and soon it was bright enough to break through the curtain of darkness as it shone on her and Teller.

A boat was there, its almost silent electronic engine not loud enough to be heard over the sound of the storm.

"Over here!" Emerson cried out, waving one arm over her head to be seen, while clinging tightly to Teller. "Hey! Over here!"

The boat adjusted its course slightly, and came to a stop about ten yards away from the stranded pair.

"Thank God," Teller moaned, still weak from his ordeal.

Emerson kicked her legs and made slow progress toward the boat.

"Stop right there," a voice called out from the boat. Emerson could not see the Producer, but she knew him from his voice.

Emerson stopped and held a hand up to her eyes, trying to see through the glare of the spotlight that shone into her eyes.

"Get us out of here!" Emerson yelled.

"Who pushed the boy into the water?" the Producer asked.

"What?" Emerson replied.

"Who pushed Teller Sanderson overboard?"

Emerson was stunned into near paralysis. Why was the Producer not pulling them to safety? "Help us," she managed finally.

"Not until the question is answered," the Producer insisted.

Emerson's head spun. She opened her mouth to tell the Producer the truth, that it had been Kodi who pushed Teller overboard, but before she could say a word, Teller spoke.

"No one pushed me," he said. "I fell."

Emerson could barely see the Producer for the glare of the light. He was merely a silhouette rising and falling with the swells of the water, and yet she knew he didn't believe Teller.

"It seems our friend Mr. Sanderson hit his head on the way down. What about you, Ms. Ness? Did you see who is to blame for this? Bear in mind, lying to me could result in your dismissal, and perhaps I already know the truth of this matter; perhaps this is a test. Think on that, and answer carefully."

Emerson was cold, too cold to think straight. The Producer's personality seemed to have flipped altogether. She did not know why Teller had protected Kodi. She tried to figure it out, tried to deliberate, but her brain wouldn't work. Until the moment she opened her mouth, she did not know what she was going to say.

"I didn't see anything."

"Yes, you did, Ms. Ness. Now, tell me," the Producer demanded.

"Really, I didn't see what happened. I saw Teller in the water, and I dove in. If he was pushed, I didn't see who did it."

No one spoke for a long time. More lightning cracked down, and for a fraction of a second, the face of the Producer was illuminated in an evil mask of contorted anger.

"I think you're both lying, and for your dishonesty, you shall both receive a punishment. You will find out what the punishment is once we arrive at our location," the Producer said, and then the boat began to move slowly toward them.

"Climb aboard," the Producer called out.

12
CHAPTER

It was ten p.m. when Emerson finally stopped shaking.

She had been out of the water for two hours, checked over by medical drones, and sent to her room, where she had taken a long shower.

She sat on her bed and allowed a thought into her mind that she had buried ever since Agent Dern had spoken to her in the interrogation room. She thought about Mr. Marvin Tzu, the man who had died in the school. She had recognized his face as soon as the officer had set the picture down in front of her. She'd known his name before the agent had said it out loud.

Without warning, she burst into tears. She cried until her body was convulsing and her throat hurt. She thought about the poor man, a janitor who had just been doing his job. She thought about the possibility that he had a family. She thought about the fear he must have felt when he knew he wasn't going to get out alive.

And it's all your fault, she told herself. *Maybe you should've died in the ocean. Maybe that's what you deserve.*

"No!" she said. "No, it is not your fault! It is not your fault! The fire was not your fault!" She spoke the words aloud, using their power to begin burying the man's name once more, burying the emotions that sparked inside her when she thought about him. Burying the truth.

Emerson looked at herself in the mirror. Her eyes were blood-shot. The tears had left streaks down her face. She took three deep breaths, letting them out slowly, and was beginning to get ahold of herself when an announcement came over the ship's speaker system.

"All contestants, please meet in the dining hall in fifteen minutes. All contestants, dining hall, fifteen minutes."

Emerson sighed. She wanted nothing more than to lie down and be still. She was sure she wouldn't be able to sleep, but just to lie still and let her mind drift away, to think of nothing at all, would be a kind of bliss.

There was a sudden rush of panic inside her, and she ran to the bathroom where her soaked clothes lay on the floor. She picked up her jeans and dug her hand into the back pocket. It was still there: the bottle cap. It was still there. Emerson didn't know why it meant so much to her.

Emerson walked over to the bed, where the backpack filled with her new clothes from the Infinity Suite lay, and she took out a brand-new pair of jeans, underwear, a dark green T-shirt, and black boots.

When she was fully dressed, bottle cap in her back pocket, Emerson looked at herself in the mirror and tried to ignore the faraway look in her own eyes. She put a smile on her face, and then let it fall away.

"Okay," she said to her reflection. "Let's go."

On the short walk to the dining hall, Emerson saw numbers 48, 49, and 50: two boys and a girl, all around fourteen years old, walking hand in hand, looking shell-shocked by their sudden change in circumstances. She could hear 38, Vintage Patel, telling whoever would listen that the average human blinks ten million times every year. She saw the boy with the gap in his teeth who had been talking to Never on the top deck just after they had boarded. She ended up walking behind her cabinmate, number 33, whose name she didn't even know yet.

As soon as she got into the large, dimly lit dining hall, surrounded by circular windows that showed raging waves and pouring rain, she looked around, searching for Never and Tiger, but instead her eyes fell upon Kodi, who was now dressed in a brand-new suit. The suit still didn't fit properly, but somehow it worked for him that way. He was leaning against a wall, arms crossed. His lip had been split by Levi and had already begun to scab over as he scowled into the darkness.

Emerson felt a moment of anger and resentment as she stared at him. He was reckless and stupid and he hadn't cared when Teller went overboard. If Teller hadn't been so . . . so forgiving, so altruistic, Kodi would be gone, sent home to face the courts for whatever he had done to end up on this ship. She found herself wishing he *was* gone.

Kodi seemed to sense he was being watched, and he looked

at Emerson. She held his gaze for a moment and then looked away.

"Hey, Em!" a voice called out, and Emerson spotted Tiger waving, sitting beside Never at a big round table. She joined them, sliding in beside Tiger.

"Where have you been?" Never asked. "I heard there was a fight on the top deck. Did you see it?"

"Uh, no," Emerson said, not wanting to talk about all that had happened in the last few hours. "I was just in my room."

Emerson saw Teller sitting at a table with two other people. He was talking to them and laughing along with their jokes, but Emerson could see that same look of vacancy in his eyes that she had seen when looking in the mirror.

"What do you think this is about?" Tiger asked, looking around the big room with its enormous plant pots with full-sized palm trees growing out of them.

"I don't know," Emerson replied.

At the table beside them, a group of five boys were whispering. Never leaned over and got the attention of one of them. "Hey, Jorgensen," she called. "What's going on?"

"I don't know," the boy said. He had a scar that curled around his left ear and over and through his eyebrow, stopping just short of his eye. "Alfonso thinks the first game is going to be on the boat. He thinks the show starts tonight."

Emerson looked at the boy named Alfonso, who shrugged as if to say *it's just a guess.*

"Hey, Burrower," a voice said, causing Emerson to turn and

face her silver-haired cabinmate. "This isn't over. I'll be waiting for you in the room tonight. Count on it."

Emerson was caught off guard, her mind still foggy from the events of earlier.

"What?" she said uncertainly.

"I said . . ." 33 started, but didn't get any further.

"Hey, mind your damn manners!" Never said, standing up and leaning threateningly close to the tall girl. "If I ever hear you speaking to my friend like that again, you'll find out what it's like to digest your own teeth!"

The Topsider's eyes grew wide in a moment of shock and fear.

"Yeah," Tiger said, standing up too, but this actually made her shorter, as the seat of her chair had been elevating her. "If I find out anything has happened to Em, I'll . . . I'll tell Never!"

"I . . . I . . ." the Topsider sputtered.

"What's your name, girl?" Never demanded.

"It's . . . I . . ."

"It's a simple question. What is your name?"

"It's Imelda," the girl said, her confidence drained.

"Well, Imelda, it's not nice to go around threatening people, is it?" Never said, leaning even closer, her hands balled into fists at her sides.

"She . . . she stole my stuff!" Imelda muttered.

"If you don't get the hell out of here right now, I'm gonna eat everything you own and make you watch me do it."

The Topsider nodded, her silver hair bouncing and then

falling back into place. She turned and walked away, sitting at an empty table on the other side of the room.

"Eat everything you own?" Emerson repeated, a smile spreading across her face.

"Yeah, I don't know where the hell that came from," Never admitted, and all three of them burst into fits of laughter.

It took another five minutes for all fifty contestants to make it into the dining hall, but once everyone was inside, the doors slammed shut, and the Producer walked into the center of the room.

"Contestants of the first-ever season of *Retribution Island*, please, raise a glass, for when you next wake up, the competition begins."

Fifty-one drones, each carrying a flute of champagne, flew out of nowhere and hovered in front of each contestant and the Producer.

Hesitantly, each contestant looked at the tall, thin glass with bubbling liquid inside.

"It's okay," the Producer said, smiling widely at everyone. "I know you're all underage, but it's just one glass, and it's a celebration."

Never was the first to take the glass, holding it by the rounded top and smelling it. Emerson took hers, and—for no reason at all—looked over at Kodi, who was pouring his champagne into a nearby potted plant.

"To each and every one of you," the Producer said, holding his glass aloft. "And to your freedom."

He held the glass to his lips, and drank it all in one go.

"Ah, what the hell," Never said, and drank hers. Emerson shrugged, and poured the champagne into her mouth. She had never tried champagne before. It was sharp, almost sour, like green apples. The bubbles were intense. It was nice.

Emerson watched as Tiger's face screwed up at the taste. "Gross," she said, and pushed her glasses up her nose.

"And now, the truth," the Producer said, the smile gone from his face.

Emerson put her empty glass down on the table in front of her. The drone took it and flew away.

"Truth?" Never repeated.

"As I said, the games begin when you next wake up," the Producer continued. "And at that time, it is your job to gain followers and win tasks, but it is also your job to stay alive."

The room suddenly felt hot, as though the boat had sailed out of the storm and into a tropical climate.

Emerson had heard the words coming out of the Producer's mouth but did not fully register them. A shocked silence tore around the room. Friends shared disbelieving glances; nervous smiles formed on the faces of the more skeptical contestants.

. . . *it is also your job to stay alive.* That was what he had said. Emerson looked back to Kodi, who had told them before they had boarded this ship that this show wasn't just a popularity contest. It was about survival. She noticed that, while everyone else's champagne drone had disappeared, the one hovering beside Kodi was still there.

"That's right," the Producer continued, seeming to reply directly to the stunned silence. "I asked you a question earlier: I asked, how do we get people to tune in when every format has been done before and there's nothing new under the sun? The answer is, you find a way to make it *real*, to make the emotion *authentic*, the desperation to win *genuine*. Everything I have told you about the games is true. You *will* require the most followers to win. You *will* need to win games to stay out of the public vote. The only thing I failed to tell you is that we cannot . . . will not guarantee your safety or survival. The emotions will be real because you will be fighting for your lives."

Emerson's heart was hammering in her chest now. Her breath was heavy. She watched as Kodi's drone produced a hypodermic needle and injected him with something.

Emerson got to her feet and ran over to him. "You were right!" she said. "You were right, they're going to . . . they're going to . . ."

She felt herself growing drowsy. People were falling all around her. The champagne. It had been drugged. Of course it had. She looked around and saw the girl from the mall who had been pretending to film herself slump forward on her table. She saw the boy named Skiba with the blocked nose try to stand up but then fall forward onto his face, lying still on the floor. She saw Tiger sprawled out on the bench of the booth she had been sitting at.

"What do we . . . what do we do?" Emerson asked.

Kodi's eyes were fighting to stay focused. "I think . . . I think the Producer is the only other person on this ship. If we can . . . if we can get to him now, maybe we can overpower him . . . maybe we can . . ."

But that was all the boy in the suit could manage. He fell, sliding down the wall, his legs buckling.

Emerson turned to the Producer, who stood in the center of the chaos, smiling with his mouth but not with his eyes. No, in his eyes there was only malice.

She walked over to him, feeling the effects of the sedative trying to take over.

"You," she managed, swaying on her feet.

"Ah, Ms. Ness," he said, "I'm so glad you changed your mind back in the interrogation room. Can you believe that was only two days ago? Baffling how time flies, isn't it?"

Emerson knew she was too weak to do anything but speak. "I'll tell them. I'll tell everyone watching what you're doing."

"Ah, ah, ah," he replied, wagging a finger at her. "That would be breaking the rules, and you would be punished accordingly. Besides, the show is pretaped and edited. We'd simply cut it out of the final broadcast."

"I'll find a way," Emerson said, but she was no longer aware of what she was doing. The world was growing dark. The last thing she was conscious of, as the muscles in her legs gave way, was the sound of the Producer laughing.

13

CHAPTER

She was inside the school as it burned.

The dream was senseless, and yet, while Emerson was in it, she understood it completely.

In the real world, she had broken into the school through the common room window, smashing a pane of glass and carefully removing the remaining shards, but in the dream, she had crawled headfirst down a chimney and into the science room (which didn't have a chimney in real life).

Three people had been huddled around the gas taps at the center of one of the tables: Mr. Abernethy, her high school science teacher; Claire Tavernier, the girl who used to mercilessly bully her; and Travis Chalk, who had found her old Content-Plus channel and shown all her old videos to the whole school. They were switching the gas on and off, striking matches near the flammable vapor.

"Hey, don't do that," Emerson had said, her voice echoing in the dream world.

All three looked up at her. She took two steps back, the soot from the chimney falling like black sugar from her clothing. The gang of three laughed, and then Mr. Abernethy struck another match. This time the gas caught. A bright orange flame shot across the room.

"No, no, no, don't do that!" Emerson said, a sudden burst of fear exploding inside her. "Don't do that, someone's going to die!"

But the three people from her past only continued to laugh until champagne began to spill out of their mouths, and they dissolved into a sparkling puddle of bubbles right in front of her.

Emerson ran over to the gas tap and tried to spin the valve that would shut it off, but it refused to move. She looked up and saw a figure standing in the doorway, watching her. A memory sparked—one that echoed through to her half-awake brain: *Had there been someone else in the school that night?*

"Emerson!" A voice from nowhere screamed out her name, her dad's voice.

Emerson ran out of the science department, trying to get a closer look at the figure in the doorway, but it evaporated into smoke. She took one last look back at the deadly flame that had turned from yellow to green. As she stepped out into the corridor, she was no longer in the school, but on the deck of the enormous cruise ship known as the *Calypso*. Her dad stood, his knuckles white as they gripped the guardrail.

"What is it?" Emerson asked.

Her father took one hand off the rail and pointed to the violent ocean waves below. "It's Kester! Your brother, he's drowning!"

Emerson saw her brother's arms flailing in the water; she saw him come to the surface, gasping for air and then sinking beneath the water once more.

"Save him!" Emerson screamed at her smiling father.

"Wait!" he said. "Just let me get my footage first."

And when Emerson looked back, she saw three camera drones hovering around her struggling brother.

"Will you please just help him!" Emerson begged.

"I can't save him," her dad said, only it was no longer her dad, it was Never, who was looking at Emerson with regret in her eyes. "I can't swim."

"You can't save him either," Teller said as he stood beside Emerson and looked out at the stormy sea.

"Yes, I can," Emerson said, trying to climb up onto the rail so that she could jump overboard and reach her brother, but her hands wouldn't move from the rail. She looked down and saw that they were handcuffed.

"You're impulsive, aren't you, Ms. Ness?" a voice asked from behind her. Emerson craned her neck and saw Agent Dern standing there, her arms crossed over her chest, the hint of a victorious smile on her face. "You don't think before you speak, and you don't think before you act. That's why you burned the school to the ground, isn't it? That's why Marvin Tzu is dead. He was just doing his job, Emerson."

Emerson tried to put her hands over her ears, but the chains rattled against the rails and her arms were forced to halt in front of her face.

She looked back to the ocean, panic now welling up in her. Someone had to save Kester, someone had to . . . the water had turned into millions of bags. Luggage of all shapes and sizes: suitcases, backpacks, garment bags, duffel bags. And from all of them spilled the incredible, beautiful clothes from the Infinity Suite.

"Kester!" Emerson called, scanning the colorful ocean of material for her brother.

"Hey, Emerson," a new voice said, and she turned just in time to see Kodi shoving her over the edge.

Somehow the handcuffs were gone, and she fell. She fell for the longest time, turning and spinning through the air, and she knew that when she hit the ground, it wouldn't be water. No, it would be the pavement outside Ingleby's Burger Palace, where she and Kester had eaten their last meal together.

She hit the ground.

And woke with a start.

Her head hit something solid. Something close. Too close.

Emerson raised her hands to feel the welt on her forehead, but they too hit a low ceiling.

She was in a confined space, surrounded by nothing but pitch darkness that felt as though it were pressing down on her.

The elements of the dream were fading away into a cloud of muddled memories.

Only one thought was clear: *was there someone else in the school that night other than me and Marvin?* But there was no time to dwell on it. The Producer's words were coming back to her.

. . . please, raise a glass, for when you next wake up, the competition begins.

It had begun. Whatever was happening right now was the first game.

As if to confirm her conclusion, she heard a series of three loud, high-pitched beeps from somewhere high above her, and then the voice of the Producer blared out, amplified, played through large speakers.

"Ladies and gentlemen! Welcome to *The Kill Factor*!"

The Kill Factor? Emerson tried to breathe.

"Each task in these games is designed to reform you. It is designed to make you a better person, to remove the criminal element from your character. This is the first task. It is designed to teach you Self-Worth. The last person to escape their coffin will face the public vote. Good luck."

A loud buzzer sounded, and the Producer's voice disappeared into an echo.

Kill Factor? Emerson thought. *Kill Factor—what happened to Retribution Island? I've been buried alive. Oh God, I've been buried alive.*

"Okay," Emerson said, forcing herself to steady her thoughts and to ignore the adrenaline that was pulsing through her. "This is it. Stay calm, try to think." But she could already feel the grip of claustrophobia tightening around her, squeezing the composure out of her. She held on for a few seconds longer, but that word, *coffin*, replayed louder and louder in her mind: *coffin. Coffin. COFFIN!* Until, finally, the panic overcame her.

She raised a knee, smashing it against the wooden lid of her sarcophagus. She heard the ripping crack of splintering wood, and then felt dry sand pouring through the gap she had created.

"No!" she hissed as visions of herself suffocating, breathing in fine particles of sand until her lungs were full of the stuff, flooded her mind. "Stupid! Stupid! That was so stupid!" she muttered, trying to plug the flood of sand with the same knee she had caused the damage with.

"Got to think! Got to think!" she said, but it had all happened so suddenly. One minute she had been on the ship, sitting with Tiger and Never, listening to the Producer speak, and then she had awoken in a coffin.

It's just a TV show, though, she told herself. *They won't let us die. They can't . . .*

But that wasn't true . . . more memories were coming back now . . . the champagne had been drugged, Kodi had been injected because he had refused to drink it . . . the Producer had said . . . *the only thing I failed to tell you is that we cannot . . . will not guarantee your safety or survival . . .*

The claustrophobic fear turned into something entirely new, something Emerson had never felt before: a need to survive. She was so electrically alive and present. Her brain was firing like it never had before. She *had* to get out, she *had* to live.

Think, think, damn it! she demanded of herself.

And then she froze. A sound came to her over the rushing of

blood in her ears and the trickle of sand that was falling like an hourglass.

She lay there, perfectly still, eyes closed, waiting for the sound to come again. And it did. The sound of waves crashing against a shore.

"I'm on a beach," she told herself, and was surprised by the calmness in her voice.

She opened her eyes, and for the first time, she saw a tiny green light down by her feet. A camera. A sudden burst of rage overcame her, and she kicked the small piece of recording equipment as hard as she could with the leg that was plugging the gap. The camera shattered, and a flood of sand came pouring into the coffin, covering the lower half of her body and spilling up onto her chest. The weight was terrifying. Breathing became an effort.

She was overheating.

You're going to have to dig, Emerson Ness, she told herself, and the idea scared her more than she had ever been scared. *You're going to have to dig your way out.*

She did not know how far it was to the surface. She did not know how much sand she would have to shift to get out of here alive. She did not know if it was even possible. She took three deep breaths, mentally preparing herself to go, and then . . . nothing. She lay there in the darkness and thought about what it would be like to suffocate.

Somewhere, deep in the back of her mind, she knew that the oxygen inside the coffin would not last much longer, but the more prevalent thought in her mind was that if she started to dig her way out, she might be instigating her own death.

If you do nothing, you're going to die anyway! she yelled at herself internally.

"Wait. Just wait a minute," she said. "Think about this."

But there was nothing to think about, and Emerson knew it. She was just scared.

She listened to the sound of the waves crashing against the sand and thought about Tiger. She hoped that the little Topsider was safe. She thought about how Never was doing, and if Teller had found a way out.

But something happened to snap her out of her thoughts. Her ankles became wet.

Emerson craned her neck as far as it would go and looked down, but she couldn't see past the pile of sand that had grown since she had last looked.

The fear that she had pushed down came back to her now. Something was happening, something bad.

She heard the waves crash above her again, louder now, and the cold water hit her lower legs once more.

The tide is coming in.

The survival instinct came back. She had to dig right now, or the sand would become wet, and heavy, and impossible to get through.

Emerson clenched her fists at her sides, let out a frustrated and terrified scream, held her breath, and began hammering on the lid of her coffin.

Something dug into her backside. The bottle lid that her brother had given her was in the back pocket of her jeans.

Kester.

Immediately, the tiny space of the coffin was filled with sand, and the panic that Emerson was feeling doubled.

Go, go, go, go, her mind rambled as she punched and dug, scooping away at the never-ending sand that poured and poured and poured down.

The middle fingernail on her right hand tore away, but she barely felt it. She didn't care. She just kept on digging, up and up. The waves continued to crash. The sand became wet and heavy and hard to move.

Faster, damn it! Go! she demanded of herself.

But she was slowing. She couldn't breathe. She had used up almost all her energy, all her oxygen. The sand was becoming more and more difficult to shift.

If I hadn't chosen these stupid waterproof boots, she thought hysterically, *I would've felt the water on my feet earlier!*

She had dug far enough up to be at a crouched standing position, using the hard floor of her coffin to push up as she clawed at the heavy sand.

Not going to make it, you're not going to . . .

But her left hand broke through to the surface and a spark of hope ignited in the fading light of her courage. She found a tiny reserve of strength, forcing her exhausted arms to dig. Her right hand broke free, and she pushed sand aside, scraping and scrabbling for life.

She was high enough now to turn her face up and break the surface. Half-covered in sand, she opened her mouth and tried to breathe in the fresh air, but she couldn't. The weight of the sand all around her was crushing her now. With no coffin to provide a barrier around her, her chest was compressed, and there was no room for her lungs to expand. The best she could do was tiny inhalations that only made her more desperate for air.

Three tiny camera drones zipped over to her and recorded her near-death experience from a variety of angles. Emerson ignored them and forced as much oxygen into her constricted lugs as she could. She made one last enormous effort to escape the sand. She moved her hips from side to side, tore at the sand around her neck, and shifted her shoulders in ever-growing circles, forcing the sand to loosen around her. Her vision was beginning to gray out. Her arms were growing numb.

Emerson freed herself up to her waist, and lay on the damp beach, gasping in the warm, beautiful air.

She lay like that, legs still buried, for a full minute, crying into the salty sand, waiting for her racing heart to slow, and then she sat up, looking at her surroundings.

The first thing that she noticed was a wooden grave marker with her number, 16, carved into it. The sun was a huge orange globe sitting low in the sky, and as Emerson's eyes scanned the place, she was aware that the landscape was strange and unnatural, but she didn't have time to fully take it in, because all around her the young contestants of *Retribution Island*—no, *The Kill Factor*—were fighting for their lives.

There were motionless arms hanging at unlovely angles out of the coarse sand; dips in the beach where the tide had come too far in and covered the poor people beneath. All around her came the cries and screams of desperate kids. All the while, camera drones moved around, filming every little detail.

Some of the graves were closer to the water than others, and Emerson had a second to notice that hers was the closest to the crashing waves. In the short time that she lay there, the water had already seeped its way down, filling the grave she'd just escaped. But she didn't consider why that might be. Instead, she forced her exhausted legs out of the sand and crawled over to the nearest grave. The crashing waves had reached the groping hand, and soon it would be too late for whoever was below the surface.

Emerson grabbed the hand and hauled it upward. The person below barely moved at all, but Emerson could tell by the way they gripped her that they were terrified; it transferred through to her like electricity.

"Come on!" Emerson screamed as she pulled harder.

She let go and began to dig at the sand surrounding the hand. Her fatigued muscles pleaded with her to stop, but she kept going, ignoring the agony.

The hand protruding from the beach fell limp. Emerson dragged great handfuls of sand away faster and faster, and when she thought there was enough leeway, she pulled at the arm again, but there was not enough strength left in her body.

"No! Please!" she yelled through clenched teeth, but it was no use. She had failed.

Sand kicked up beside her as Kodi slid to a stop. He grabbed the arm farther down.

"Go!" he screamed, and both of them pulled with all their might until the body slipped out of the sand. It was the boy named Jorgensen, the boy with the scar around his ear.

"Do you know CPR?" Kodi said, but Emerson was in a state of shock and could only stare at the dead boy. "Hey!" Kodi said, turning her face to his. "Do you know CPR?"

Emerson thought back to her days in high school, before she was expelled, and recalled something about chest compressions to the beat of a song. She nodded.

"Good. Help him."

And he was gone, sprinting across the sand to another person who was screaming for help through a gap in the sand as the saltwater waves crept up on them.

Emerson clambered to her knees and began pressing down on Jorgensen's chest.

"Oh God, oh God, oh God," she said, unaware she was talking at all.

Over and over, she pushed down on the boy's chest, waiting and hoping for something to happen. As she worked, the waves began to cover her feet, and somewhere in the periphery of her awareness she realized that one of her boots had come off in her escape from her grave. She looked up at the chaos of the beach and saw at least three bodies lying on the sand, half in and half out of their shallow graves, camera drones recording their lifeless faces, getting artistic shots of their limp hands bobbing in the surf.

This isn't happening. This can't be happening.

Never was lying on her back on the wet sand, her chest rising and falling as she stared with terrified eyes at the purple twilight sky above. Teller was still digging his legs out of his grave. Imelda—the girl with the silver hair—was screaming and laughing at the hole she had climbed out of in a fit of madness. Kodi had his arms around the boy with the blocked nose (*Skiba?* Emerson thought), and was pulling him to safety. Contestants numbers 48 and 50 were scanning the wooden grave markers until they found number 49, and then began to dig furiously. Finally, Emerson's eyes rested on Tiger, who had one hand and half her head free of the sand and was breathing out of her nose as her terrified eyes—still somehow wearing her glasses—scanned the beach. And the waves crashed ever closer.

"Help her!" Emerson screamed, and Kodi looked around. Emerson lifted one of her hands off Jorgensen's chest, and pointed to Tiger. Kodi was on his feet and sprinting toward the little Topsider before Emerson had restarted her compressions.

She pressed down on the boy's chest, hearing ribs crack and watching his limp body shake in a dead way.

For the first time, Emerson looked beyond the crashing, foaming waves, and saw that the cruise ship was anchored about two hundred yards from the shore. The lights were all still on, and it looked like a specter through the heat haze filter.

She looked again at Tiger, watching Kodi dig her out just as the waves began to fill the hole she was in.

"Come on, wake up! Wake up!" Emerson muttered as sweat dripped down her face, but the boy was still and pale. Gone.

Never had gotten herself together and was helping to dig out someone who Emerson recognized as the violet-haired girl from the mall area of the ship. She too was lifeless.

"He's gone. Help with the others."

Emerson looked up at Kodi standing over her, his hair wet with sweat. "He's not gone! He's going to be okay."

"Emerson, look at me. You can't save him, but you can save others if you go now!"

Emerson looked back at the dead boy. His lips were blue; one eye stared lifelessly at the sky, flecks of sand covering the gray-blue iris. He hadn't taken a single breath since he had been pulled from the sand . . . How long had it been, three minutes? Four? More?

"I can't leave him," Emerson said through exhausted gasps.

"Okay," Kodi said, and was gone, running across the sand once again.

There were teams of kids now; each team was helping others, pulling people free, trying to revive the unresponsive. Emerson continued to press on Jorgensen's chest, willing his heart to start beating, willing his lungs to suck in oxygen, but he did not stir.

"I'm sorry," she whispered. "I'm sorry, Jorgensen."

And she stopped.

The boy was dead.

A drone filmed the tears welling in her eyes. Emerson clenched her jaw and snapped out a hand. She grabbed the hovering device, crushing it and screaming in rage as the drone crunched between her fingers.

She got to her feet, throwing the destroyed drone aside, and running away from Jorgensen, running away from the guilt of leaving him there with one eye open and one closed, lips blue, no thoughts in his mind, no feeling in his body. Nothing, he was nothing now.

She ran past Teller, who was crawling on his hands and knees toward a red-haired boy who was free up to his shoulders, but the tide was making it hard for him to breathe as the sand became heavy around him.

Emerson sidestepped the corpse of a young boy and joined Never and two other contestants as they worked to free an exhausted girl from the sand.

It took ten more minutes for the tide to kill anyone else who had not managed to get free from their grave.

Kodi and a few others had dragged all the bodies who were not left underground to the top of a sand dune so that the waves would not carry them out to sea.

× ✖ ×

The remaining contestants sat on the beach and cried, or were silent, or mumbled incoherent words to themselves. What they had been through, what they had witnessed, had done something to them. It had changed them forever.

Emerson sat with her knees pulled up to her chest, watching the relentless waves crash down on the shore, and she could only think about Jorgensen's one open eye, covered in sand, seeing nothing forever and ever. She had been so sure that he would suddenly sit up, gasping for air, and be okay, just like in the movies, but he hadn't, he had just been dead, and dead, and dead, no matter what she did.

The sky had turned from purple to a deep blue as the orange sun disappeared below the level of the sea, and Emerson had time to wonder just how long they had all been unconscious. It had been dark on the boat when they had drunk the champagne, so it must have been at least twenty hours. And how on earth had the season changed so dramatically? It was December. It had been freezing cold when they had boarded, but here, on this beach, it was warm even now when the sun was setting. How far had they traveled?

Emerson looked around at the strange island they were on. It looked man-made, a perfect circle surrounded by nothing but ocean as far as the eye could see. Three hundred and sixty degrees of beach leading inward to sand dunes, which gave way to trees that were entirely made out of plastic, and in the center of the island was a building: a huge circular prison made of gray bricks. Rows of tiny barred windows dotted the walls, presumably the cells that the losing contestants would spend the rest of their lives in.

None of this moved Emerson particularly; none of it really affected her at all.

She looked at the cruise ship, the *Calypso*, sitting stoically on the ocean. The lights of the craft seemed brighter now that darkness had fallen, and somewhere in the back of her mind she imagined swimming to the enormous vessel, breaking into the bridge, and figuring out how to sail them all away from this place.

Emerson glanced back to the dunes where the bodies lay. They were dead. They had been alive and now they were dead. This thought seemed so impossible to Emerson. They would never see another sunrise, never laugh at another joke. The world would keep on spinning. Their parents and siblings would keep on getting older, and they would always be dead.

There were eleven corpses on the dunes, and only thirty-five living contestants left, which meant there were another four dead in their watery graves. Fifteen dead in total.

"I didn't think ... I didn't think it would be like that ..." Tiger's voice said, and Emerson turned to see that the young Topsider had sat down beside her and was staring out at the waves too. Her blond hair had come out of its pigtail braids and hung wetly around her face in sandy clumps.

"No," Emerson agreed, "neither did I."

"I've never seen a dead person before," Tiger muttered.

Emerson thought about her mom in the hospital bed. How she had looked so different after she had died, as though some secret part of her had drifted away the moment her heart had stopped beating for the last time.

"Are we all going to die on this island?" Tiger asked.

Emerson's fist closed at her side, grabbing a handful of loose sand and letting it slip through the gaps between her fingers. Suddenly, she was angry, angry at herself, at the Producer, at Jorgensen for not waking up, and at Tiger for asking senseless questions. "I don't know, okay, Tiger?" Emerson snapped. "I don't know! I've been dumped into this stupid game show the same as you!"

Emerson got her feet and walked away beyond the sand dunes and into the plastic trees. The rocks that dotted the fake forest were made of plastic too, and so were the vines that hung between the replica trees, and the grass beneath her feet. That too was an imitation of the real thing.

She walked to a particularly large tree with heart-shaped leaves. She let out a scream and then collapsed to her knees, sobbing.

Emerson cried for less than a minute before forcing herself to slow her breathing down, her hands to be steady, and her mind to let go of the anger and the pain that she was feeling. What replaced these emotions was guilt. She had yelled at Tiger when all Tiger was looking for was someone to comfort her.

Emerson stood up, took one last deep breath to calm herself completely, and then turned to walk back to the dunes, but before she had taken a step, the three high-pitched beeps of the public address system sounded, and the Producer's voice echoed across the island.

"Contestants, congratulations on making it through the first game. Please meet on the beach in one minute."

The voice fell silent, and Emerson felt that anger boiling inside her again, but she kept it at bay for now.

It felt strange walking through the fake forest, like she was on the set of a cheap movie, and when she reached the tree line and saw the perfect circle of the beach, her sense of dislocation grew even more.

She walked past the dunes, trying not to look at the bodies that lay there, unmoving. She joined the group of surviving contestants, who were all gathered together a short distance away from where they had been buried alive.

"How are you doing?" Emerson asked, putting a tentative hand on Never's shoulder.

"I'm . . . I don't know how I am, to be honest. I think I'm all right . . . as all right as I can be after . . . that."

"They can't keep this going, can they?" Emerson asked. "I mean, fifteen kids just died, they have to call it off."

"He told us it was going to happen," Never said. "He told us on the boat. He said: *You will be fighting for your lives*, but I didn't think—"

Before Never could finish, the Producer's voice broke through the muttering of the crowd.

"Ladies and gentlemen! Welcome to *The Kill Factor*!"

He had appeared from seemingly nowhere, like a magician at a kid's birthday party, and he stood there in a dark suit, beaming with pride.

"What the hell was that?" Teller said, his voice immediately cracking with the emotional weight that was now forever on him. "You killed them. You let them die!"

"That, Mr. Sanderson, was must-see television! That was entertainment!"

"You're a monster," Vintage Patel said, and it was the first time Emerson had heard her speak and not convey some meaningless piece of trivia. "Everyone involved in this show is a monster."

"This is illegal," a tall boy with the number 42 branded into his wrist said. "We signed a contract to be on a show called *Retribution Island*, not *The Kill Factor*, whatever the hell that means!"

"Wrong," the Producer said, a deceptive smile on his face. "Not one of you read the contract, so don't come at me with your accusations. But you did ask a good question, Mr. Tremblay-Birchall. What *is The Kill Factor*? There are not one but many among us right here on this beach who have killed. Others, as we've seen today, who have been killed. Whether it is in our nature or part of our instinct to survive, we must seek to reform ourselves. We must seek to love ourselves and our fellow humans. We must seek to understand the point we reach that brings us to this instinct to kill, in order to overcome it. *That* is the meaning of *The Kill Factor*. And with that, congratulations on making it through the first game!"

"What the hell do you mean *congratulations*?" Imelda demanded, her silver hair swaying as she stormed toward the Producer, pointing at him the same way she had pointed at Emerson in their cabin when they had first met. "People died!

They suffocated and they drowned! *You* killed them. *You're* responsible!"

She had gotten within ten feet of the Producer when he held up a hand and spoke.

"Ms. Fleet, I wouldn't come any closer unless you want to be lying next to your friends on that dune."

The Producer's voice was calm and clear and there was a hint of pleasure in it.

Imelda stopped in her tracks. "What . . . what do you mean?"

The white-haired man smiled at Imelda, and the cruelty that was barely concealed in his beaming teeth made her take a step back. "I mean that you signed a contract, young lady. You all did. You're on the show now, and you must play by the rules. If you do not play by the rules, you will die a quick but painful death."

Imelda looked nervously back at the group of surviving contestants. All her bravado and arrogance had disappeared, and she looked only like what she was: a terrified teenage girl.

"What do you mean?" Teller called out from somewhere near the front of the group.

"Each of you has a number burned into your wrists, correct?" the Producer said. Emerson, along with almost everyone else, looked down at their numbers. "Beneath each of your numbers, a small capsule filled with a fast-acting poison is implanted. Attack me, or anyone else involved in the show, and the poison will be released. You will be dead within thirty seconds."

Emerson ran her thumb over the number 16 burned into her wrist, and felt a hard lump beneath the skin.

"I don't believe you," an angry voice from somewhere near the middle of the group said, and a boy who Emerson didn't recognize ran toward the Producer.

"No, wait!" Emerson called, but the boy with the long brown hair either didn't hear her or chose not to listen. He ran as fast as he could, sand kicking up behind him, his hands balled into fists.

The Producer's smile grew even wider. The moon was rising behind him now, big and white, turning him into a silhouette.

The boy ran past Imelda, and Emerson thought, *He's going to reach him! He's going to* ... but the boy's footing became uncertain, his left leg seemed to be unstable, and then his right knee buckled. He managed to keep his footing, but he had stopped running. Now he stood still. He was so close to the Producer that he could've reached out and grabbed the lapels of his suit, but instead he fell to his knees, and then fell forward onto his face.

He was dead.

14

CHAPTER

"Any more questions?" the Producer asked, smiling at the crowd of kids. Stunned silence filled the night air, colliding with the rip and boom of crashing waves. "No, I thought not."

"That was awesome," contestant number 21 said, smirking. Emerson didn't know the pale and slender Topsider's name, but she did not like the look of intense pleasure in her eyes.

Emerson moved quietly over to where Tiger was standing alone and took the young girl's hand. "I'm sorry," she whispered. "I was scared and . . . I didn't mean to shout at you."

Tiger looked up at Emerson. "It's okay. I'm scared too."

"You may have noticed," the Producer continued, "that in the first task you were not all buried in a uniform row, and you were not all buried at a uniform depth. No, you see, the game began the moment you were arrested. When you signed the contract, you agreed to let us use archival footage of your arrest, your interrogation, and any footage of you that existed from your past. We have been broadcasting for days now. We filmed you waiting at the dock, boarding the ship, and every hour of our voyage to this island. We have used footage from Ms. Fleet's successful social media career, Mr. Mason's conspiracy theory show, Ms. Ness's old Content-Plus channel."

Somehow, despite everything that had happened, this announcement rocked Emerson, and she wrapped her arms around herself.

The Producer continued. "You started collecting followers immediately, and some of you have done very well. Others, not so well. Now, as you know—the winner of each game receives immunity from the public vote. The winner of the first game was the person who escaped their grave the quickest . . . That person was Kodiak Finch. Congratulations, Mr. Finch."

Absurdly, a few people actually clapped at this announcement.

"The loser of today's game, and one of two who will face the public vote, was the last person to escape their grave—that person was Zach Dobler. Commiserations, Zach."

The red-haired boy who Emerson had seen struggling out of the wet sand hung his head in shame.

"Now, if you will follow me," the Producer continued. "We will get to the second part of tonight's entertainment."

The Producer gestured with one hand, encouraging the contestants to follow him, and as the white-haired man turned and began walking, the entire island shook beneath their feet.

Emerson stumbled and fell along with almost every other contestant. It was only Kodi who kept his footing and began walking, but as he walked, he didn't move anywhere.

What's going on? Emerson thought, clambering to her feet.

Both the Producer and Kodi were walking in place, and it

took another ten seconds for Emerson to realize that the entire island was turning, rotating from its center, spinning like an old-fashioned record.

The landscape around them slowly changed as the beach revolved. By now, all the living contestants had found their feet and were matching the pace of the vertigo-inducing turntable.

As the island turned and the Producer led the contestants to the new area of the beach, Emerson watched their destination come into view. There were thirty-four wooden structures built up on a level area of beach. These structures were stages, on wooden stilts. They varied in size and shape, but they were all bedrooms—or certainly, they were made to *look* like bedrooms. None of them had walls, just wooden frames that outlined where the walls should be. You could look through one bedroom into another. When Emerson saw the structure that belonged to her, she stopped walking, and the mechanical island pulled her backward. She stared through the nonexistent wall and into *her* bedroom, *hers* from her home in the Burrows. It was a perfectly reproduced imitation of her and Kester's bedroom: the damaged furniture that had been repaired a thousand times, the threadbare pillowcases, the melted patch of carpet near the door.

Emerson caught up with the group.

"Oh, lordy, that's my bedroom," number 15 said, sniffing through his blocked nose.

"Mine too," Never said in a dreamlike voice.

Emerson finally managed to peel her eyes away from the

reproduced bedroom, and noticed swarms of camera drones hovering like flies everywhere. On the beach itself there was a large bonfire sending crackling embers up into the sky, a small wooden platform that looked like a stage, and to the side of the bedrooms was an enormous screen that showed a photograph of all fifty contestants. The ones who had died were grayed out and at the bottom of the list. Emerson saw immediately that her name, number, and photograph were at the very bottom of the living contestants, right after Teller. There was an ever-changing number next to each contestant's photograph. The contestant who was at the top of the list, number 33, Imelda, was at 56,433 and going up every few seconds. Emerson was at 3,101.

Emerson scanned the list quickly.

Place	Contestant Name	Contestant #	Follower count
1.	Imelda Fleet	33	56,433
2.	Levi Russo	17	39,067
3.	Kodiak Finch	1	9,437
4.	Cobalt Skiba	15	9,011
5.	Never-Again Jones	47	8,909
6.	Delilah Scattergood	21	8,800
7.	Tiger Quinn	11	8,569
8.	Decker Shimada	25	8,430
9.	Harlow Wozniak	26	8,286

10.	Llanzo Robinson	14	8,095
11.	Goodwin Goodhew	50	7,944
12.	Sadio Sarr	48	7,920
13.	Tanya Moon	49	7,707
14.	Genji Gao	3	7,599
15.	Hugo von Hugo	9	7,500
16.	Alasdair George William Tremblay-Birchall	42	7,371
17.	Andrew Matthews	23	7,370
18.	Cameron Angus	2	7,294
19.	Steele Sawyer	18	7,002
20.	Nick Mason	4	6,930
21.	Rose Pascoe	19	6,561
22.	Vintage Patel	38	6,517
23.	James Sunday	40	6,423
24.	Amelia Rock	8	6,288
25.	Green Glow Ali	5	6,106
26.	Asim Damji	27	5,541
27.	Gamble Delaney	6	5,309
28.	Sian McNamara	28	5,201
29.	Amanda Anderson	46	5,008
30.	Billie Joe Walker	12	4,704
31.	Gwen Perez	7	4,702

32.	Zach Dobler	29	3,656
33.	Teller Sanderson	20	3,205
34.	Emerson Ness	16	3,101

Emerson looked to the grayed-out photographs and names of the deceased contestants, including: Juliette Star (number 10), the violet-haired girl who had been pretending to film herself on the ship; Wolfgang Jorgensen (number 24), who Emerson had not been able to save on the beach; and Carter Boyd (number 36), the boy who had rushed the Producer and had been poisoned just five minutes ago. There were others too: 31, Alfonso Linari; 43, Tanner Crowley; 45, Fafali Aniwaa. All these names and pictures she vaguely recognized, but it was too much for her to comprehend.

"Your rank on this table corresponds to the number of followers you have gained so far. Those with the most followers earn perks in the games—for example, the person with the most followers was buried farthest away from the tide, in the shallowest grave, giving them the best chance at surviving. The person with the least followers was buried closest to the water in the deepest grave. You see how this works? The number of followers you have directly correlates to your chances of survival."

Emerson looked at the enormous screen once again, and saw that Kodiak Finch had the word IMMUNE beside his name. If nothing changed, she would be facing Zach in the public vote.

Her mind spun with questions, and without thinking, she raised her hand in the air.

"Ms. Ness, you have a question?" the Producer asked, smiling a warm, fatherly, evil smile at her.

"If you've been filming us from the start, then you knew who it was who pushed Teller overboard."

"That's not a question, Ms. Ness, that is a statement."

Emerson thought for a second. "Why did you ask us who did it, and why didn't you punish Kodi?" Her eyes scanned the crowd, looking for Tiger and Never. She hadn't even told them about the ordeal.

"I asked you and Mr. Sanderson a simple question, and you lied to me, therefore you suffered a punishment: a twenty-four-hour suspension of followers, a suspension that will end in seven minutes and eight seconds. And, as an additional punishment, I chose not to air the footage of you saving Mr. Sanderson. As for why I didn't punish Mr. Finch, his actions did not lead to Mr. Sanderson falling overboard, and he was the one who alerted the ship when you foolishly dove in after Teller when he slipped. If it weren't for Mr. Finch, I would have lost two contestants that night and the show would have been postponed. Any further questions?"

Emerson wanted to ask more. She knew there were a thousand things she did not yet understand about this dangerous game, but all she could do was shake her head. She glanced at the leaderboard again and saw that there was indeed a countdown beside her and Teller's names that was at six minutes and twenty-three seconds and falling. Emerson looked over to where Kodi stood, watching the Producer with hatred in his eyes. He had alerted the ship that passengers had gone overboard, even though he had said that Teller was not his responsibility, even though he had walked away.

"Good," the Producer continued. "Let me tell you what happens next: All follower bans will be temporarily lifted, and you will record your daily video diaries from your bedrooms." The Producer gestured toward the thirty-four frames. "Your video diaries are very important; they are your way of connecting directly to your existing followers and your route to earning new followers. Remember, the contestant who finishes at the bottom of the leaderboard each day will face the public vote against the loser of the game. Be entertaining, be happy, show them the person you wish you were, and they will follow you. At exactly midnight, the person who has the least followers will face the public vote against the loser of game. If the public chooses to vote you off, you will be escorted to your cell in the prison. After that, the rest of you are free to do as you wish, but tomorrow, the second game begins. You will find your clothing in the drawers and wardrobes of your bedrooms. Your camera drone will become active in ten minutes, at which time you may begin recording your diary. Mr. Dobler, I know that you are already condemned to face the vote, but if I were you, I'd treat this diary as a way to gain support early—boost your followers and you'll increase your chance of survival should you make it through the vote. Good luck, contestants. Use your time wisely."

And with that, he turned on his heel and walked away. To where? Emerson did not know, but he followed the curvature of the perfectly round beach and was gone within a minute.

"All right," Kodi said, raising his eyes and looking at the row of bedrooms, and without another word, he walked toward the wooden frames.

The remaining thirty-three looked at each other, and then followed.

As Emerson got closer to the bedroom frames, she saw that numbers were carved into the center of the top beam, right above where the door would have been if these were real rooms. The bedrooms were laid out in a seemingly random order, and Emerson walked toward hers.

Follower ban, she thought as she glanced once again at the big screen and saw her name at the bottom. She hadn't dived into the ocean to gain followers. It had been instinct, but the fact the Producer had not shown the footage annoyed her. She was here to provide a better life for Kester, and the Producer was taking opportunities away from her. Diving into the ocean to save someone was a heroic act, and people would have responded to that. *Now it's just wasted*, she told herself, and then, quickly, *No, don't think like that. You did what you did because it's who you are, not because you wanted people to follow you.* Despite this, it seemed the only way to make up for lost ground was to perform in these stupid video diaries, but she already knew that she couldn't do that.

Emerson made it to her bedroom and opened the wardrobe;

the door on the right swung away from its hinge, just like the real wardrobe in her room back in the Burrows. All the outfits she had chosen on board the ship were there, hanging neatly. She opened the top drawer of the cabinet and saw myriad different bottles, products, makeup, shampoos, toothpaste. The second drawer contained row after row of underwear; the third had electrical items like hair dryers, toothbrushes, electric razors, straighteners, and more. Emerson closed this drawer, certain she wouldn't use anything other than the toothbrush.

She sat down on the bed. It even sagged in the middle, and creaked, just like her own. She looked to her left, where contestant number 15, Cobalt Skiba, the boy with the blocked nose, was opening his wardrobe and choosing which outfit he would wear for the diary. She looked to her right and saw contestant number 42, Alasdair George William Tremblay-Birchall, who was sitting on the edge of his bed, his eyebrows furrowed.

"You okay?" Emerson asked.

"Are you asking me because you want to look good in front of the cameras, or are you genuinely concerned?" the boy replied, staring at the waves far away.

"I guess I'm concerned," Emerson said.

The dark-haired boy turned toward Emerson. "I lost my glasses in my . . . in my grave," he said. "I can't see so well without them."

"Oh, that sucks," Emerson replied, unsure of what else to say.

"I think I'm going to ask the viewers to unfollow me," Alasdair said.

"Why would you do that?" Emerson asked.

"Because if I end up at the bottom of the leaderboard, I'll be against Zach in the vote. I could go to jail. At least that way I get to live. If I stay in the games and they're anything like that first one, I'll likely die."

Emerson nodded. It made perfect sense. Life in prison was at least life. Staying in the games meant almost certain death. "I can't do that," Emerson replied. "I'm here to boost my brand currency so my brother can—"

"Yeah," Alasdair interrupted. "We're all here to help our families, but none of us knew that they were going to start killing kids."

Kodi knew, Emerson thought, but nodded in agreement. "Well, good luck, Alasdair George William Tremblay-Birchall," she said.

"You too . . ." Alasdair looked at Emerson's wrist, then at the scoreboard, before turning back to face her. "Emerson Ness."

All around them the kids of *Retribution Island—The Kill Factor*—were pulling off their wet, sandy clothes and running into the trees to change into clean clothes for their video diaries. Emerson didn't move from her bed. She sat and thought about what she was going to say, what she was going to do. She glanced over to Teller, who was four rooms to her left as she sat facing the ocean. He was wearing the too-small white tank top he had chosen in the Infinity Suite; it showed off the muscles in his shoulders, chest, and arms. He was playing the game.

Emerson looked toward room 47, where Never was applying

makeup and looking at her reflection in the mirror that hung on wires, then to room 11, where Tiger was wearing her gold sequined dress and dancing around her bed. Her room was nice—clean and bright, so much space.

Emerson felt her eyes going back to the scoreboard once again. She stared at the picture in the top spot, Imelda Fleet, and she wondered just how much her stunt of throwing the girl's belongings into the water had both helped Imelda and hindered her own progress in gaining followers.

You're impulsive, aren't you, Ms. Ness? You don't think before you speak, and you don't think before you act.

The words of Agent Dern ran through her mind. They were now so familiar to her that she barely even heard them.

"She was pretty famous before this whole thing began," Alasdair said, and Emerson looked around to see that he had followed her gaze to the top of the leaderboard. "She had like two million followers, but the regulators found out that almost half of them were bots. She was arrested for defrauding advertisers and falsely inflating the value of her brand credits; it was a big story. Looks like she has enough loyal followers to get her to the top, though."

"I threw her clothes overboard," Emerson said.

Alasdair smiled for the first time since Emerson had met him. "That'll be why you're dead last, then. Maybe I should set fire to her shoes or something. Maybe then I'll get voted out."

The scoreboard suddenly changed from a list of names and photographs to a countdown that started at sixty seconds.

"Oh lordy. This is it," Cobalt Skiba said, wiping his nose on the back of his hand and straightening his blue, spotted bow tie. "Good luck, Llanzo!" he shouted over to 14, who offered a double thumbs-up in response.

Emerson watched the numbers count down, wondering what she was going to do or say when the time came.

Finally, the number zero appeared on the screen, and thirty-four camera drones dipped down from the hive above them, one for each contestant, red recording lights glaring.

Imelda was the first to snap into action.

"Oh my God, you guys, this has been the wildest experience. I can't believe the show has *finally* begun. I cannot wait to get started and try my best for all my wonderful followers."

Emerson watched her and couldn't believe this was the same girl who had marched up to the Producer and told him that he was responsible for the people who had died on the beach.

One by one, all the remaining contestants shook off the shock at what they had just been through on the beach and began performing for the cameras.

Beside her, Alasdair was begging his followers to unfollow him. Tiger was dancing and singing. Teller was doing push-ups and smiling at the camera. Kodi was lying on his back, talking calmly to the drone that hovered above his face. Never was laughing at seemingly nothing. And another contestant (Emerson thought it was Andrew Matthews) had taken his clothes off and was running into the sea.

Emerson looked in wonder at the circus that had erupted all

around her. She clenched her jaw and looked into the lens of the drone that was hovering in front of her face.

"Kids have died," she said. "Less than an hour ago, kids died on the beach. You all saw it. How can you stand for that? How can you watch this? You have to stop it. You have to get us out of here. There is a man who calls himself the Producer. We're on a man-made beach in the middle of . . . an ocean somewhere! There is a warm, tropical climate. You have to *find* us and get us out of here."

Emerson turned away from her drone, trying to ignore the other contestants who were promising new followers that they would be entered into a competition to win five brand credits if they went on to win the game show.

"Take two," a voice said, and Emerson turned to see that the drone was still hovering in front of her. The voice had been human, but it had come from the drone.

"Excuse me?"

"Take two," the drone said again.

"What do you mean *take two*?" Emerson asked.

"From the top. We're not using that footage. Please do not talk about the Producer, or give information about the potential location of the games."

Emerson turned slowly back to face the drone. "Who are you? Whoever you are, you work for this company. People died on that beach, *real* people! Can't you help us? Can't you do something?"

"Please do not mention the Producer or give any information

about the potential location of the games. Any mention of the Producer or the location of the games will be cut out of the footage that goes to air. From the top."

Emerson stared at the drone, waves of rage washing over her. "Fine," she said. "I was exploited. I was tricked into signing a contract to join a show I do not want to be a part of! I demand to speak to a lawyer. I demand to be let off this island."

The drone was silent for a while, and then said, "Take three."

"I've said what I have to say!" Emerson yelled.

"Take three," the drone repeated. "This is your last chance. Please record a usable video diary."

Emerson looked around in disbelief. The scenes all about her baffled her: Contestant number 4 was talking earnestly into the camera about conspiracy theories involving a world government and plots to control the minds of regular people; a girl wearing a very short skirt was doing yoga and purposely falling over to show her underwear; Teller had taken his tank top off and was doing pull-ups on the frame of his bedroom; Zach Dobler, the red-haired boy who had been last to escape his grave, had found a large jellyfish in the shallow water and was screaming as he rubbed it on his arms.

"Take three," the drone repeated. "The best way to gain followers is to have a consistent message, be provocative, be upbeat, ask your viewers to subscribe, create effective branding . . ."

"I'm not going to record anything else," Emerson said. She knew, deep down, that she was condemning herself to last place on the leaderboard and blowing up her plan to increase her brand-credit value.

"Very well," the drone's voice said. "You will be issued with a twenty-four-hour follower ban. This ban will be added to any existing penalties. Good day."

The record light went out, and the camera drone disappeared back up into the cloud of drones overhead.

Emerson swallowed. She sat on her bed as the hysterical spectacle continued all around her.

What have you done? she asked herself.

15

CHAPTER

By the time the last contestant had finished their video diary, Zach Dobler was lying on the sand in a pool of his own vomit, moaning in pain, his arm a red and swollen mess where the jellyfish stings had gone in.

Everyone else sat around, or stood in small groups, exhausted. The sudden changes in emotion from fighting for their lives, to grieving for the dead, to portraying upbeat social media personalities, had left them drained.

"I can't believe it," Alasdair said, shaking his head.

"What is it?" Emerson asked, trying to ignore her jittering nerves, knowing that she was at the bottom of the leaderboard and would have to compete for her place on the island.

"Look at the board," Alasdair replied.

Emerson looked at it, and saw that Alasdair George William Tremblay-Birchall had gone from sixteenth place to fifth. His begging people to unfollow him had backfired completely, and the seemingly cruel viewers had done the opposite of what he requested and followed him by the thousands.

"Why would they do that? I don't want to die, Emerson, I just want out of this stupid game show."

"I don't know," Emerson admitted. "I don't know how they're even watching this. Surely there isn't a TV station in the world that would broadcast this?"

"Did you see?" Tiger said, running over to Emerson's room. She looked happy but exhausted.

"I did," Emerson said, smiling back at the young girl, who had climbed from seventh place to fourth. "Whatever you did really worked!"

"I've got twenty-two thousand followers!" she exclaimed. "I'm famous, baby!"

Emerson laughed. "Yeah, you are."

Tiger's face dropped as she remembered who she was talking to. "Hey, I'm sure as soon as they lift the ban you'll get loads of followers too."

"I doubt I'll make it through the audience vote."

"I don't know," Tiger replied. "I don't think Zach is doing so well."

"Yeah, I know," Emerson said, her eyes darting over to the motionless contestant. She didn't want to compete against a boy who had almost killed himself with jellyfish stings, but she didn't want to leave the game without gaining more followers either.

"Lion's mane," Alasdair muttered.

"Sorry?" Emerson asked, turning away from Zach.

"That is a lion's mane jellyfish. Their sting is painful, but it doesn't often result in death . . . I guess if you purposefully sting yourself over and over again, though . . ."

"Hey, superstar," Never said, strolling over with a big smile on her face. "You're going to smash the viewer vote, I know it."

"I don't know," Emerson said. "It seems like it's hard to predict what the viewers are going to do."

"Amen!" Alasdair said morosely.

"You're doing well, though," Emerson said, looking at Never's name just underneath Alasdair's, in sixth place.

"Yeah, not bad, huh? I don't think anyone's going to catch Imelda, though. She's like eighty thousand followers clear already. It's not fair, they shouldn't let influencers on this show! It's such an advantage."

Emerson felt a laugh of utter disbelief building up inside her. How had this all become so normal so fast? Before the laugh could escape her throat, the Producer appeared before them, standing grandly on the beach. He had changed. He no longer looked like a kind, caring man. Those sympathetic eyes had become full of dark humor and contempt, and he looked somehow taller and slimmer.

"Contestants!" he bellowed. "You have made it through your first task, and completed your video diaries. The footage is being aired as we speak, and in exactly one minute we will take a shapshot of your follower count and see which contestant will be facing Mr. Dobler in the viewer vote. I want to personally thank you for the efforts you have put in to make the first few episodes of *The Kill Factor* so special. We have an enormous viewer count that will only grow as word of mouth spreads and social media begins talking about us, and they *will* talk about us."

Amazingly, people began clapping at this announcement. Emerson looked around, shocked that ten or twelve of the contestants looked delighted at this news. Most of them were near the top of the leaderboard.

"Thank you, thank you," the Producer said, smiling at the contestants. "We need to keep the energy up as the games continue. Energy, effort, and enthusiasm, the three *E*s, that is what will win you followers. Now, one last thing before we announce last place. There is an additional perk for finishing at the top of the leaderboard each day: You win a prize. Today's prize is a lighting drone. So all of your footage will look even more professional as it goes out."

There was a murmur of anticipation throughout the crowd at this announcement.

"And now," the Producer said dramatically, "we count down to today's winners and losers. Ten, nine, eight, seven . . ."

Again, Emerson was perplexed as a good portion of the contestants excitedly joined in with the countdown. She looked at Never, who was just as confused as she was.

". . . three, two, one, zero!"

There was a bright flash of light from the screen, and the numbers beside each name stopped moving.

"Congratulations to today's *Kill Factor* leader, Imelda Fleet!" the Producer called out in his best game-show host voice.

Fireworks exploded in the dark sky above them, and Imelda began to cry and hold her chest in an overdramatic display of delight.

"Imelda, how does it feel to be today's winner?" the Producer asked, still keeping his distance from the crowd.

"Oh my God, it feels amazing. To know that there are so many people out there who watch my silly antics and think that I deserve their time and attention is so humbling, and I just want to say thank you and I love you to each and every one of you! It means the world."

"Imelda," the Producer continued, "we all know why you're here. You committed a very serious crime. You let yourself down, and you hurt many people. Can you tell us what you have learned so far in *The Kill Factor*?"

"Sir, I just want to say that I am so, so sorry for the mistakes I have made in the past. I am not the person I was when I . . . did what I did. I want to thank you and everyone working so hard behind the scenes for this amazing opportunity. Whether I win or lose, I have already learned so much. I am a better person, and I want to keep getting better. You have given me that chance and I'll never forget it. Thank you."

"Imelda Fleet, folks," the Producer said, and then turned to face the scoreboard. "Now, with the pleasantries out of the way, it falls on me to announce the loser of the first day of *The Kill Factor*. Viewers, I will remind you that whoever you choose to vote off will spend the rest of their life behind bars. The consequences are real, so think carefully before you make your choice.

Ladies and gentlemen, the loser of today's edition of *The Kill Factor* is . . . Emerson Ness."

A drone carrying a high-powered spotlight flew up above Emerson and lit her in a blinding light.

"She will face Zach Dobler in the public vote!" the Producer yelled, and a second spotlight exploded into life, illuminating the fetal figure of Zach as he lay injured on the beach.

"Mr. Dobler," the Producer said. "Are you well enough to take part, or would you like to forfeit and be escorted to the maximum-security prison?" As he said this, he gestured to the huge building in the center of the island.

Emerson felt a moment of merciless hope as she stared at her competitor.

Zach stirred, got to his knees, and croaked, "I'll take part . . . I'm okay . . ."

He clambered to his feet, sweat dripping from his pale face, and hobbled over to the group.

"A valiant effort; that alone should be worth some votes," the Producer said, and gave the limping boy a round of applause. This time even more of the contestants joined in.

Emerson sighed. It was going to be almost impossible to beat this kind of bravery.

"Please, take your place on the stage," the Producer said, gesturing toward the small stage in the center of the beach.

Zach lumbered toward the stage, and Emerson followed. As Zach's foot hit the first step, he stumbled, and Emerson grabbed him to keep him steady.

"Get your hands off me," he hissed. "I know what you're doing!"

Emerson let go, confused by what he meant.

Zach took his place on one side of the stage, and Emerson stood on his right. The spotlight drones stayed steady above them.

"Your task," the Producer said, opening an envelope and reading it, "is to demonstrate your greatest skill."

"What?" Emerson asked, caught off guard by this announcement. "I thought the viewers were just going to vote?"

"Oh, they will vote, Ms. Ness, but you must *earn* their vote!" the Producer exclaimed. "Remember, our wonderful viewers are watching on TV, on 3D, on Immersion, online, and however else they consume their media. It is up to them to choose who earns their freedom for another day, and who goes to prison for the rest of their lives. The stakes are high, as high as they go, so think carefully about how you are going to perform. The viewer vote opens in ten seconds, and will remain open for three minutes. Good luck."

The screen flashed brightly once again, and the ten-second countdown commenced.

"What are you going to do?" Emerson asked Zach.

The boy was breathing heavily and sweating profusely. "I . . . I don't know," he admitted. "I don't have any talents. What are you going to do?"

Emerson shook her head.

The countdown hit zero, and the contestants who had

gathered around the stage started calling out the names of the two who were supposed to be performing for their lives.

"Come on, Emerson!" Tiger screamed.

"You can do it, Zach," someone called from the middle.

Emerson's mind was blank. What was her greatest skill? She could break into buildings pretty effectively; she could run from the police . . . what else?

She glanced over at Zach, who looked indecisive for a second; then he jumped off the stage and searched around in the sand. He found a large rock and hauled it up onto the stage. He tried to climb up after it, but was too weak and had to walk around and use the stairs.

Emerson forced herself to stop focusing on Zach. *Think, Emerson! Think!* she demanded of herself. She looked at the timer and saw that forty seconds had passed already. Zach made it to the stage and bent down to pick up the rock.

Suddenly, the screen split into three panels. In the middle a simple bar graph showing the viewer votes appeared, but on either side of that, faces began to appear, and Emerson realized that they were the faces of viewers, watching them from all over the world. There were about a hundred faces on each side, and they periodically changed to show others. These constantly changing faces seemed fascinated, impatient, bored, delighted, demonic, angelic, worried, excited. Emerson felt like she was shrinking under their gaze.

Think, Emerson! she demanded. *Ignore them, ignore the*

faces ... You made it all the way here, survived the first task, just to fail on the first day! You let Kester down.

And at the thought of Kester, she realized what her skill was: She could speak another language. She doubted whether the public would find it impressive, and it wasn't visually spectacular, but it was all she had, and at least she could speak to Kester one last time if nothing else.

She raised her hands in front of her and was about to speak when she heard a wet cracking sound and a gasp from the gathered crowd. She turned her head to see Zach holding his rock in both hands and slamming it into his face over and over again.

Smack.

His nose broke and blood began to stream from it.

Smack.

His front two teeth shattered and he spat shards into the sand before ...

Smack.

A huge cut appeared along a welt on his forehead.

Emerson looked at the screen: The bar chart leaped in favor of Zach. The faces that filled the sides of the screen looked amused and horrified in equal measures. She forced herself to look at the timer: only ninety seconds left. She used her hands to speak to her brother.

"That is so cool!" Delilah Scattergood squealed. Emerson looked at her and saw the sadistic joy in the girl with gothic-style eyes.

Kester, I'm so sorry—I wanted to do better, I wanted to get as many followers as I could so that I could transfer brand credits to you. You're going to be so great. You're going to do amazing things. Please don't ever lose that thing that makes you special. Don't become like me. Don't become skeptical and jaded. Keep on believing in the goodness of people and the potential of this world. I honestly believe you can make a difference. I love you, Kester, and I'm sorry.

That was all she had to say. Her hands fell back to her sides. She waited for the countdown to finish as she reached into her back pocket and felt comfort emanating from the bottle lid there. Emerson sighed and took one last look at the screen. The bar chart had almost evened up, but Zach was still in the lead. Suddenly, with ten seconds left on the timer, the graph disappeared. They would have to wait to find out who had won.

The contestants who surrounded the stage continued to cheer and scream and clap. Zach—exhausted now, sweat and blood dripping from his lumped-up face—could no longer lift the rock. He let it fall to the stage. Emerson saw the welts on his forearm where the jellyfish had stung him over and over again. She saw the cuts on his hands where he had gripped the rock. She saw the mess that was his face. All that to get people to follow him. This poor boy didn't have whatever natural magic that the social media stars had, so he had been forced to hurt himself, humiliate himself to get people to watch him.

"Three! Two! One!" the crowd screamed, and Emerson realized that time was up. The three minutes were over, and now they would learn who was going to their cell for the rest of their life, and who would remain in the games.

One by one the faces of the viewers disappeared. The last one to go seemed to be laughing maniacally.

Emerson looked toward the Producer, as did every person in the crowd.

The Producer only smiled back at them.

"Who won?" Never asked.

"There's a one-minute delay on all footage," the Producer said. "So we can edit out anything we deem unfit for air."

"Surely, self-mutilation is unfit for air," someone called out. Emerson thought it was 38, Vintage Patel, and she could hear the disgust in her voice.

"Oh, no," the Producer replied, smiling wryly. "I believe that will make the broadcast."

Emerson wondered what they could possibly be editing out if they had just shown more than a dozen children dying on their show, and then she remembered the video diary drone telling her not to mention the Producer or anything that could give away the location of the games.

Silence fell over the beach. Emerson looked once again to the cruise ship sitting on the ocean's surface like a sentinel, watching them. She turned her eyes up to the stars that now shone brightly around the glowing moon. The light from above turned the rolling waves into glittering diamonds, and despite how fake the entire island was, it still looked beautiful.

Time passed slowly and yet far too fast. No one said a word. There was not even the slightest breeze. Silence.

Finally, the Producer spoke. "Ladies and gentlemen, the results are in, and it is very, very close."

The Producer put a hand up to his ear as the information was being fed to him.

"Good luck, Em," Never said, and blew a kiss. Emerson could only nod in reply. It was all suddenly too real to fully comprehend; she was about to be put into a cell where she would live out the rest of her days in solitary confinement.

"I can now reveal that the contestant in second place got 409,366 votes when the lines closed, but the person in first place got 422,950 votes. Ladies and gentlemen, the person leaving the show tonight is . . ."

The pause seemed to go on forever. Waves crashed on the beach, the bonfire crackled and sparked, the crowd held their breath.

". . . Emerson Ness."

16

CHAPTER

"No!" Tiger yelled.

Emerson felt as though the world was spinning around her, like she might faint at any second.

"Congratulations, Mr. Dobler," the Producer was saying as he shook Zach's hand, but that was all very far away to Emerson. The Producer's voice sounded like it was coming from underwater.

Emerson breathed heavily, feeling like the air around her was thin and useless.

"Ms. Ness," the Producer said, putting a hand on her shoulder. "You played a wonderful game, but unfortunately it was not to be. You have five minutes to say goodbye to your friends."

She had failed. She had been voted off in the first round, and had not gained enough followers to help Kester in any way at all.

She fought off the panic attack that was wrapping its arms around her, and her wide eyes found Never in the crowd. As their eyes met, she couldn't stop the tears spilling down her face.

Never climbed onto the stage and embraced Emerson. "I'll

help your brother, don't you worry," she whispered, and Emerson felt her heart fill with gratitude. She held her friend tight and cried into her shoulder.

Beside them, Zach Dobler fell limply forward, like a marionette with its strings snipped. He slumped, half on and half off the stage.

The Producer bent down and checked his pulse. The camera drones spun around, filming everything as the Producer got to his feet, held a hand to his right ear, and spoke quietly.

"Dead," he muttered. "Reset or keep what we have?"

Emerson felt Never's hand squeeze hers.

The Producer put that blinding smile back onto his face and addressed the contestants. "Zach Dobler is dead. We mourn his passing." He then turned his attention to the camera drones that encircled him. "Due to the death of Zach Dobler, Emerson Ness will remain on the show! Congratulations, Emerson Ness!"

Never looked into Emerson's eyes with a kind of relieved determination, and she hugged Emerson. Emerson could only stare in disbelief as two large drones came out of the plastic forest and picked up Zach's body, carrying him out to sea.

The Producer came onto the stage and shook Emerson's hand. "Congratulations, Ms. Ness! How does it feel to have survived the first game?"

Emerson couldn't answer. This was all so bizarre, all so nonsensical.

The Producer laughed. "Looks like you're speechless. Well,

I don't blame you, and I don't think our audience will either."

Emerson looked out to the contestants and saw Kodi shaking his head as though this all made sense to him, and he was disgusted by it.

"He died," Emerson said. "He killed himself for entertainment."

"Yes, he did," the Producer said. "Remember to join us tomorrow for the next live installment of *The Kill Factor*, where anything can happen!"

The Producer stood waving at the camera drones for such a long time that Emerson thought for a moment that he had lost his mind, but he suddenly snapped out of his game-show host persona and turned to the contestants.

"I advise you all to get a good sleep. Today you took your first steps toward rehabilitation; you learned Self-Worth. Tomorrow begins game number two, which will teach you Empathy. Good luck, contestants, and good night."

And with that he left, walking away from the confused scene, following the curvature of the beach until he was gone.

"What the hell just happened?" Emerson asked.

"What happened?" Teller repeated, clambering up onto the stage. "You just got through to the next round!"

Teller tried to hug Emerson, but Emerson pushed him back. "A boy had to die for me to stay in this competition. Why is no one doing anything about it? We have to stop this show. We have to refuse to take part!"

"Oh, come on," Imelda Fleet said, pushing her silver hair

behind her ears. "You're just saying that because you're in last place! I'm not quitting now; I'm winning."

Emerson looked at her and shook her head in disbelief. "You saw what happened to Juliette, to Jorgensen, to Zach! What use is being top of the leaderboard if you die tomorrow, or the next day?"

"Think of the followers, 16," Imelda replied with a smirk. "Think of the sponsorship deals, think of all those people watching you. Your brand-credit value is going to skyrocket."

"I don't get it," Emerson tried again. "What don't you understand? These games are designed to kill us!"

"These games are designed to help us!" Imelda shot back. "You heard the Producer: We're criminals, our brains are broken, and he's trying to save us!"

Others were nodding in agreement now. Everyone who was in the top half of the leaderboard except Never, Tiger, Kodi, and Alasdair seemed to agree with Imelda on some level.

"You're crazy," Emerson said, looking around at the top-halfers who had slowly gathered around Imelda.

"Listen, 16," Imelda continued. "They're not stopping these games for you or anyone. I wouldn't worry about it anyway. You'll be voted out of here by tomorrow if you survive that long."

This caused Imelda's new group to laugh, and Emerson could already see the high school politics beginning to form.

"Whatever," Emerson said, stepping down from the stage and walking toward her bedroom. "I can see I'm not going to convince you, but don't forget how close you came to dying tonight. Don't forget that for a moment you stood up to the Producer, and we all saw it. We all know how you really feel deep down."

"You're boring me now," Imelda said, and again, her eight or nine cronies laughed.

Emerson, Tiger, Never, Teller, and Alasdair walked back to the rows of bedrooms and sat down in Emerson's room.

"I keep thinking I'm gonna wake up," Never said. "Every time I think things can't get more horrible, they do. That group of people actually wants to stay here and compete."

"Well, they have a point," Alasdair said, staring down at his feet.

"No, they don't!" Tiger hissed.

"They're all brainwashed," Teller added.

"Oh, they're brainwashed, but you might as well go crazy when there's no other choice," Alasdair muttered.

"What do you mean?" Emerson asked, still fighting with her anger and frustration at the conversation she had just had.

"They're going to make us compete one way or another. You saw what happened to 36. If we don't play the game, they'll poison us, so you have three choices: convince yourself that this really is the opportunity of a lifetime that will rehabilitate us terrible criminals; just try to hang on and make it to prison without dying; or refuse to take part and die a painful death like 36. Those guys over there"—Alasdair nodded toward the group gathered around Imelda—"they chose the easiest option, that's all."

"Carter Boyd," Emerson said.

"Huh?" Alasdair said, looking up from the sand.

"Number 36. His name was Carter Boyd."

"Oh, right," Alasdair said, nodding slightly.

They sat in silence for a while, contemplating what Alasdair had said.

"What do you think the game will be tomorrow?" Teller asked finally.

"I don't know," Emerson admitted, but she thought she knew someone who might. She looked over to bedroom number 1, where Kodi lay on his back, looking through his invisible roof, up to the stars above.

17
CHAPTER

At some point, they had all drifted to their own bedrooms. Teller had stayed the longest, talking nervously and holding Emerson's eyes for extended periods of time. She thought he must just be scared, like all of them.

Emerson had lain back on her bed, watching the moon drift slowly across the sky, and tried to think about anything other than being buried alive.

During the night—Emerson thought it must have been about three a.m.—a flock of drones flew over to the sand dunes, picked up all the bodies that had been laid out there, and carried them out to the ocean. She did not know what would become of them as she watched them disappear into the darkness. She didn't know if those who had died below the surface of the sand were still there, or if the drones had dug them out.

Eventually, she did sleep, and was haunted by nightmares of being buried among the half dead, the burning corpse of Marvin Tzu. She had dreams of watching Kester grow old in front of a camera drone, putting on a fake laugh as his hair grew long and gray in front of her eyes. She had restless thoughts of the Producer silently smiling at her as she slept. And when the three beeps of the public address system sounded, she awoke from her shallow sleep instantly.

"Ladies and gentlemen, welcome to your second day of *The Kill Factor*. Breakfast will be served in ten minutes."

Emerson sat up and looked around. All the other contestants were waking up, remembering where they were. All the other contestants except Kodi, who was already up, dressed in a new suit jacket and black shirt, wandering around on the beach, kicking at plastic shells.

Emerson got up and walked over to him.

"How did you know?" she asked.

"Sorry?" Kodi replied.

"How did you know that the games were going to be . . . you know, dangerous?"

"I just did," Kodi replied, going back to nonchalantly kicking at the sand.

"You can't just *know* something, you're not a psychic. Tell me."

Kodi sighed. "It just made sense."

"How did it make sense?"

He looked out to the waves for a moment, and then spoke. "Because we're criminals, Emerson. We're the lowest of the low. People don't care about *why* we steal or cheat or join gangs. They only care that we're punished for it. If someone invents a game show where they promise rehabilitation and fame, you can bet that their real reason is humiliation, abuse, and eradication. This is nothing new: They used to offer criminals the key to their cells if they fought on the front lines of wars. They used to promise inmates reduced sentences if they took part in medical experiments. They have always used convicts, told them they can win prizes if they put their lives on the line. Now they're offering us fame and freedom if we take part in their game show? It was obvious from the start that we'd have to offer more than just a winning personality—we'd have to offer our lives."

Emerson looked at the boy for a long time. "And you just figured that out?" she asked.

He shrugged. "It seemed pretty obvious to me."

Emerson nodded slowly. "Sounds exactly like something my brother would have said."

"Your brother sounds like a smart guy," Kodi said, and smiled enigmatically.

"Kester," Emerson said. "That's his name. He's a genius. He's only nine years old and he's cracked every cybersecurity program out there. There's this one company, Expansive Universe, that wanted to hire him to restructure their security from top to bottom, but the contract was nothing short of indentured servitude. My dad wanted him to sign, he thought it would be excellent exposure, but I told him to finish school and wait for a real opportunity."

"That's impressive."

"Kester doesn't think so. He always says that what he has is just luck, like being born with perfect pitch, or an eidetic memory. He thinks hard work is more impressive than natural talent."

"Are you sure he's only nine? He sounds far too wise."

"He's only nine," Emerson confirmed. "He's the reason I agreed to do this stupid show. I need to make my brand credits valuable so I can get him through college."

"You need to stop getting follower bans," Kodi pointed out.

Emerson nodded. "You're probably right."

There was a moment of silence between them before Kodi spoke.

"It's not going to happen, you know?"

"What isn't going to happen?"

"This action movie ending you're imagining where your genius brother hacks into the system and frees us all."

"What? I wasn't imagining..."

"Yes, you were," Kodi said, and smiled sadly. "So was I. As soon as you mentioned your tech prodigy brother, I thought *what if?* But it won't happen."

Emerson felt an all-too-familiar sinking feeling in her stomach. "Why not?" she asked.

"Tell me something: When the Producer first came to you, where were you?"

"I was in an interrogation room."

"Right, and what kind of person can just walk into an interrogation room? Who has access to places like that? This whole thing is funded by the government, Emerson, and governments *cannot* be found to be running something like this."

"No way," Emerson said, shaking her head. "The government wouldn't do something like this."

"No?" Kodi replied, looking out to the rolling waves. "The

same government that purposefully infected people with diseases to study the effects? The same government that secretly dosed people with drugs to see if they could control their minds? The same government that has committed genocide over and over again in order to install leaders in other countries? That government?"

Emerson felt tears forming in her eyes. "Is anything the Producer said true?" she asked. "Does one person get to walk free in the end?"

Kodi thought about it for a while. He turned his face up to the morning sun. "I don't know," he admitted.

Emerson was about to walk away when a thought occurred to her. "If you were so sure that people were going to die, why did you sign the contract?"

Kodi looked at Emerson and for a second there was a look of . . . something: guilt? Sorrow? But then he gave her that half smile that made you question whether he was telling the truth or lying. "Maybe I crave fame more than life."

Emerson rolled her eyes. "Yeah, because being a corpse with a million followers is just the best."

"At least you'll die a legend," Kodi replied, still smiling.

"Influencers don't die legends," Emerson said, suddenly very serious. "It takes real world-changing talent, or genuine genius, or the type of hard work that people who show off in front of a camera can't imagine."

Kodi laughed. "You sound like some old person who doesn't understand that the world has changed. Not all influencers are selling their souls for followers. Some are sharing their scientific knowledge, or teaching others how to do difficult things like coding, or animation, or—I don't know—accounting! There are people sharing skills that would cost years of brand credits to get a qualification in, and they're doing it for free. Hell, I learned how to skateboard by watching Daisy-Kickflip videos."

Emerson knew that he was right, but it didn't change the way she felt about the type of influencers who came down to the Burrows to demonstrate their courage, or the ones that would offer homeless people brand credits as long as they told the cameras how grateful they were and what an amazing and generous person the host was. "You skateboard?" Emerson asked, smirking.

Kodi's smile widened. "Not anymore. I used to."

"That kind of takes away from your mysterious guy vibe."

"Mysterious guy vibe? Is that what I have?"

Emerson laughed.

"Em, hey, Em," a voice called out, and Emerson turned to see Teller running along the sand toward them in his ungainly way.

"Hi, Teller," Emerson said.

"What are you guys talking about?" Teller asked, putting his hands on his knees, trying to catch his breath.

"Oh, just this whole situation, you know?" Emerson replied.

"Yeah, well, in case you forgot, this guy threw me off the deck of a cruise ship and left me to drown, so . . . maybe he's not the best person to be making friends with?"

153

"Teller, I don't think . . ." Emerson started.

"It's cool," Kodi said, half laughing and shaking his head. "I'm not here to make friends anyway." He turned and walked toward the gently crashing waves.

Emerson watched him walk away, and then turned to Teller. "What the hell was that about?"

"Em, he's not a good guy! You saw what he did!"

"Listen to me," Emerson said. "I don't need you, or anyone, telling me who I should and should not be making friends with, do you understand?"

"What, do you like him or something? He's a psycho, Em!"

"I can talk to whoever I want."

"Sure you can. I just don't know why you'd want to talk to *him*."

Emerson thought about arguing back, but in the end decided it wasn't worth it. "Whatever," she said, and walked back to her bedroom, wishing it had real walls instead of the make-believe ones.

✕ ✖ ✕

An army of drones had lowered three long tables onto the beach, followed by trays of the most incredible food Emerson had ever seen.

They had all eaten like they hadn't had food in a week. The mental and physical exhaustion of the last twenty-four hours had hit them all like a train. The only person to not eat was Imelda Fleet, who kept on saying that she wasn't hungry, and that she was watching her figure.

Emerson had rolled her eyes at this while shoving a third bread roll into her mouth.

The next few hours had been, frankly, boring. Despite being on a man-made island in the middle of God-knew-where, competing for their lives, it was still boring. There was nothing really to do. After what had happened to Zach with his jellyfish, most didn't want to go into the water. Imelda and her crew took the opportunity to sunbathe, and 48, 49, and 50 had found plastic sticks in the fake forest and spent hours sharpening them to points using glass from a picture frame in one of their bedrooms. They were using their makeshift spears to silently hunt fish in the ocean despite the fact that food was provided for them. Most people sat in the shade of the fake forest, shielding themselves from the burning sun.

"How far do you think we traveled?" Emerson asked, sitting in the shade of a large plastic coconut tree with Tiger and Never. Teller sat four trees away on his own, still sulking after Emerson had shouted at him.

"I was thinking the same thing," Never replied, fanning herself with an enormous plastic leaf. "I mean, it's the middle of December and we're sitting in ninety-degree heat trying to stay out of the sun. It doesn't make sense."

"How long were we passed out before the first game began?" Tiger added. She had rebraided her hair and looked like herself again after yesterday's ordeal. "I mean, maybe we were unconscious for days!"

"Must've been about twenty hours," Emerson said.

"How do you know that?" Never asked.

"I had a twenty-four-hour follower ban that started about four hours before we drank the champagne."

"What did you get the second follower ban for?" Never asked, looking at Emerson's name on the screen with the countdown beside it that read 9 hours 54 minutes. She had to be careful not to be issued with any more follower bans.

"I refused to record a video diary," Emerson said.

"For someone who's supposed to be building their brand, you're doing a pretty poor job of it," Never replied.

"Yeah, I know."

There was a commotion in the shallow water, and Sadio Sarr, number 48, came splashing out to the beach with a huge fish flipping and struggling on the end of his spear.

"Take a look at Harlow and Gwen," Tiger said, pointing to numbers 26 and 7.

Gwen, a Topsider with pink hair in enormous pigtails, was pretending to sleep on the sand while Harlow, a Burrower with a shaved head, had filled a fake plastic coconut shell with cold water from the ocean. Harlow snuck dramatically up to Gwen, pretending to stifle laughter, and then poured the cold water onto her. Gwen screamed, showcasing some melodramatic acting before chasing after Harlow and pretending to fall over a rock pile. Harlow ran away screaming about how it was just a prank, and Gwen vowed to get revenge.

"People don't behave like that," Emerson said. "It's not real."

"No," Tiger agreed. "But how is it any different from a TV show or a movie?"

"I don't know," Emerson said. "It just feels . . . disingenuous."

"Fancy word," Never said, watching as Gwen and Harlow got together to discuss their next fake prank.

"Hey, 16," someone said, and Emerson looked up into the glaring sun to see two Topsiders standing over her, a girl and a boy. She looked at their numbers: 21, Delilah Scattergood, the tall, dark-haired girl who wore a lot of shadowy eye makeup, and seemed to exclusively wear black. She was the one who had laughed when Carter Boyd had been poisoned; and 18, Steele Sawyer, a muscular seventeen-year-old with a military haircut, who perpetually wore aviator shades.

"Yeah," Emerson replied tentatively.

"We're thinking of setting up a love triangle situation. You know, two girls fall in love with me. Lots of tears, lots of fighting, lots of . . . tension. Delilah and I think it would work better with a Burrower, you know, really add an underdog vibe. People would follow us just to keep the storyline going—what do you say?"

Emerson furrowed her brow as she looked from one beautiful Topsider to the other. "No," she said. "No, I don't want to pretend to be in love with you . . . at all."

"Your loss," Delila said, smirking at Emerson. Emerson shuddered; there was no emotion behind those dark eyes.

"Hey, I'll do it. You need a Burrower to get all freaky with," Never said. "I'll be that Burrower, baby."

Steele looked at Never over the tops of his sunglasses, let out a short bark of laughter, and shook his head. "You're too fat." And then the Topsiders walked away to find a Burrower who fit their narrative.

Emerson looked at Never, who—for the first time since Emerson had met her—seemed to have had the confidence knocked out of her. She was about to get to her feet and have a word with the arrogant Topsiders, but Tiger was already running over to them.

Emerson watched as the little girl ran up behind Steele Sawyer and kicked him as hard as she could between his legs.

"Learn some manners," she yelled at him as he lay writhing on the sand, before walking calmly back to Emerson and Never.

"You didn't have to do that," Never said, and her voice sounded deflated.

"I wanted to," Tiger replied, and put her arm around Never. "And you're not fat."

"I am," Never replied. "But I'm not upset about that. I love who I am, and I love how I look. I'm annoyed that people look down on me for being fat. Normally, it doesn't bother me, but here, on this crummy little island, it might mean that I end up in prison for the rest of my life, or worse, it might mean that I get buried deeper than everyone else and end up dead."

"Then you'll just have to make sure you outlast both of those condescending losers," Emerson said, putting her arm around Never too. "So you can smile at them when they get taken to prison."

48, 49, and 50 stood around the dead fish. Eventually, they left it sitting out in the sun, and threw their spears into the forest.

× ✖ ×

Hours dragged on.

More planned pranks were pulled: number 23—the boy who had run naked into the sea—appeared to have taken up Zach's mantle as *person willing to hurt themselves for followers*. He was jumping out of the fake trees, landing awkwardly, and then climbing higher to do it again. Teller seemed to have forgotten how to wear a T-shirt. Imelda and her crew were doing ab workouts on the beach, Imelda leading the workout with her brand-new lighting drone following her closely, and numbers 48, 49, and 50 were trying to melt plastic palm tree leaves using the lens of 48's glasses as a magnifying glass.

The numbers beside each contestant's name steadily rose as more and more people followed them. Imelda remained at the top of the leaderboard by a comfortable margin of around a hundred thousand followers, and her five disciples remained right behind her, having overtaken Kodi and Never on the leaderboard.

Emerson looked at the top ten names:

Place	Contestant Name	Contestant #	Follower count
1.	Imelda Fleet	33	198,434
2.	Levi Russo	17	109,777
3.	Delilah Scattergood	21	81,040

4.	Decker Shimada	25	80,571
5.	Steele Sawyer	18	76,209
6.	Kodiak Finch	1	50,338
7.	Never-Again Jones	47	46,104
8.	Cobalt Skiba	15	43,832
9.	Alasdair George William Tremblay-Birchall	42	43,603
10.	Llanzo Robinson	14	43,308

There had been some dramatic changes, but it was already obvious to all the remaining contestants that if you hung out with Imelda's group, you gained followers quickly. Delilah Scattergood had gone up three places; Steele Sawyer had gone up *fourteen* places. Tiger, on the other hand, had dropped out of the top ten altogether and had fallen down to seventeenth. Harlow and Gwen's prank show had clearly worked, as they had both jumped ahead of her.

The sun was just beginning to dip low in the sky. It was taking on that wavering orange glow that Emerson had noticed when she had freed herself from her grave, and she was starting to think that there wouldn't be another game today when the three loud, ear-piercing beeps sounded from the hidden public address system and the Producer's voice boomed out around the island.

"Contestants of *The Kill Factor*. Game number two is about to begin."

18
CHAPTER

For a moment, everyone's social media personas fell away, and there was nothing but scared kids on the beach.

It was—of course—Imelda Fleet who responded first.

"Oh my God, I cannot wait to see what they have in store for us this time, you guys!" she squealed, clapping her hands together and bouncing on the spot like an excited puppy.

"Please," the Producer's voice blared out, "make your way to the other side of the island."

The ground shook beneath them, but this time only one or two contestants fell. Muscle memory kicked in, and they quickly got into their rhythm as the island began to turn from its center.

Emerson had been standing with Never in her room. They quickly got out to the open beach, where Tiger ran over and joined them, followed by Teller and Alasdair.

"I'm not ready for this," Alasdair said, avoiding a large plastic conch shell on the beach as the sand revolved beneath his feet.

"Hey," Teller whispered as he caught up with Emerson. "I'm

sorry about this morning. I was being stupid. I just get things in my head sometimes and I can't get them out so easy."

"It's fine," Emerson said, and she meant it. This was not the time to be getting caught up in such trivial things. Everyone's emotions were high.

As the landmass continued to rotate, the group of five walked in silence, until the other side of the island came into view.

"Oh no," Never said, and Emerson saw what it was that had struck so much fear into Never's voice.

A structure had been built on the same spot where they had been buried alive. It towered into the air, presumably connected to the base of the structure that the island was built on. It would have surely sunk into the sand otherwise.

"What is it?" Tiger asked.

"Diving boards," Teller replied.

He was right. A series of ladders connected three platforms that hung out over the sea. The first platform was about fifty feet from the calm waves; the second stuck out farther, and Emerson guessed it was about eighty feet above the water. The third was so high up that it was hard to accurately estimate just how high it was.

"Contestants," the Producer said, standing at the foot of the first ladder. "Today you learn about Empathy. You see before you a series of diving boards, each higher than the last. Your task is simple. You must jump. Half of you will be jumping from the fifty-foot platform, and half of you will jump from the hundred."

Emerson's heart sank. She already knew which platform she would have to jump from. She looked up into the blue sky, where one white, too-perfect cloud was drifting above the hundred-foot platform. She was at the bottom of the leaderboard and so would be at a disadvantage. The same way that she was buried deeper and closer to the water in the first task, she would have to jump from the highest board.

"There are thirty-three of you remaining," the Producer pointed out. "The sixteen contestants who make up the top of the leaderboard will jump from fifty feet; the seventeen who make up the bottom of the leaderboard will jump from one hundred feet. The winner—and the person who will receive immunity from the vote—is the first person to make it back to the beach."

Nervous chatter broke out among the contestants. Never's terrified eyes didn't even glance at the diving boards. She was looking at the water. Number 12, Billie Joe Walker, was saying "I'm afraid of heights" over and over. Number 6, Gamble Delaney, who had an impressive set of huge white teeth, was talking about surface tension and how no one would survive a jump from the top platform. Imelda and her top-of-the-leaderboard gang were smiling satisfactorily at each other.

"I'm not finished yet," the Producer said, and held up both hands, demanding silence. The crowd fell quiet, and the Producer smiled. "You may have noticed that there is a third diving board between the highest and lowest, this one positioned at seventy-five feet. You may choose to exercise empathy in this task, by which I mean, those on the bottom diving board may offer to split the difference with someone on the top diving board and you can both jump from the middle."

The Producer left a long pause while the contestants put this information together in their minds. Contestants at the bottom of the leaderboard started looking longingly at their friends who were above them, trying to make covert agreements before the game even began.

"You have ten minutes to make a deal—to show empathy, or to appeal to the empathy of others. Your time begins when you all gather on the highest platform. Good luck, contestants."

And with that, the Producer walked away.

"No point in hanging around," Kodi said. He grabbed hold of the ladder and began to climb.

CHAPTER

19

It took over half an hour for everyone to gather on the top diving board.

Kodi had climbed to the top in about a minute, followed by Imelda and Steele, but there had been a roadblock when Billie Joe had climbed up to about eight feet and frozen in fear. It took ten minutes just to get him to the middle platform, where he lay on his front, shaking in fear.

When, finally, they had all made it to the top platform (even Billie Joe, who had to be carried by a fed-up Steele Sawyer), they quickly got to work making deals. Emerson told a terrified-looking Never to make a deal with Tiger, which she did, and Alasdair made a deal with Teller. As the deals were made, Emerson had a thought—*no wind. Strange that there is no wind when we're this high up.* Suddenly, Emerson realized that she had run out of friends. She also realized that the atmosphere up here was becoming desperate as others ran around searching for someone in the top half to make a deal with. Emerson's eyes were drawn to Imelda Fleet, who stood with her arms crossed, watching the whole situation unfold with a curious look in her eyes. She was planning something, but Emerson didn't know what.

"Hey, last place," a voice said, and Emerson turned to see Kodi sitting on the edge of the platform, his legs dangling out into the empty air as though he were on a bench in the park instead of one hundred feet above the ocean.

"That's what you're calling me now?" Emerson replied.

Kodi smiled. "You make a deal yet?"

"Not yet."

"All right. You and me can go from the middle board. Jumping from the bottom board would be too easy anyway."

"Thanks," Emerson said, telling herself to sound cool and then chastising herself for wanting to sound cool at a time like this.

Kodi got to his feet and held out his hand for Emerson to shake. "It's a deal, then?"

"Deal," Emerson agreed, and shook his hand. She held on for a beat longer than would be considered normal, and held Kodi's eyes. There was something there. Inconvenient as it was, untimely as it was, stupid as it was, there was something there. "Why the change of heart?" Emerson asked.

"What do you mean?"

"Back at the docks, before we got on the ship, you were pretty adamant that you weren't here to make friends."

Kodi smiled. "I guess . . . I guess I just changed my mind."

"Hey, Mr. Finch," Imelda called from the middle of the platform, interrupting Emerson and Kodi, who had unconsciously moved closer and closer together.

This can't be good, Emerson thought, finally looking away from Kodi's blue-gray eyes.

"Imelda Fleet," Kodi said, turning to face her as she marched toward them. "The leader of the games gracing us with her presence."

Imelda laughed, a loud, fake laugh, and then put a hand on Kodi's chest before throwing a glance at Emerson. "I was just about to offer our unfortunate friend here a deal, but it seems that you have done just that."

"That's right," Kodi said, sharing a look of uncertainty with Emerson. Imelda was up to something; she always had an angle.

"You're so nice and kind," Imelda said, putting an arm around Kodi's waist now. "Helping out the . . . less fortunate." She rested her head on Kodi's shoulder and smiled at Emerson.

"Yeah, I don't know about that," Kodi said, gently pushing Imelda away from him.

Imelda's eyes lit up, and in that moment, Emerson knew what she was going to do. Imelda had seen something between Kodi and Emerson. She knew that Kodi was high up on the leaderboard, and she had calculated a way to eliminate him as a threat.

Emerson wanted to call out, to tell Kodi to get away from Imelda before it was too late, but she couldn't. It all happened too quickly.

Imelda screamed a bloodcurdling scream and threw herself off the top diving board, tumbling and turning through the air until the last minute, when she maneuvered into perfect diving form and cut into the water with barely a splash.

All eyes turned to Kodi.

"You pushed her," Levi Russo said. "You pushed her!"

"Just like he pushed me off the boat!" Teller said.

"No!" Emerson cried. "He didn't push anyone!"

But her voice was already drowned out by a cacophony of accusations as the crowd closed in on Kodi.

There was a kind of mindless determination in the eyes of the group that gathered around Kodi. Most of them were the kids in the top half, the ones who had formed a kind of faction around Imelda, but there were others too—some from the middle of the pack who desperately wanted to break into the popular group.

Just as the first hand reached out to grab Kodi, the now-familiar beeps of the speaker system sounded, and the Producer spoke.

"Your ten minutes is up. Any deals that were made still stand, but there will be a punishment for Kodiak Finch, who intentionally caused another contestant to fall from the platform. Mr. Finch, your side of the deal will not stand. As punishment, you will jump from a further twenty-five feet."

At this, a mechanical whirring sound came from beneath their feet, and a section of the one-hundred-foot platform that they were standing on extended out to the right and rose up above their heads.

"Can all contestants make their way to their platforms immediately. Thank you."

"No, wait!" Billie Joe screamed from his convulsing position on his side. "I didn't make a deal! Someone has to make a deal with me! I can't jump from here, I can't!"

Contestants stepped over and around him as they made their way to the ladder.

Emerson turned to Kodi. "They know she's lying," she said. "They have all the footage from the drones. They *know* you didn't push her."

"It's not about the truth," Kodi said, and the way the setting sun shone through his messy hair, turning his blue eyes golden, made him look like an angel to Emerson. "It's about the best story. Just because she's lying doesn't mean they can't spin it into the truth."

"But this isn't just some stupid TV show, this is your life!"

Kodi smiled. "Our lives don't matter to them. They've already decided who's going to win and who's going to lose. They won't air anything that casts us in a good light. I'm the villain who pushed the hero off the diving board. You're the jealous Burrower who threw her belongings overboard. That's the way it is."

"It's not fair," Emerson said, looking into Kodi's knowing eyes.

"No," he said, pushing a strand of Emerson's hair out of her eyes. "It isn't."

"I'll jump with you," Emerson said, suddenly sure that was just what she was going to do.

"No," Kodi said. "You're going down to the middle board and you're going to swim back to the beach. You're going to stay alive, and you're going to stay in the game for as long as you can, do you understand?"

"No, I'm coming with you," Emerson repeated.

Kodi took her gently by the shoulders and looked deep into her eyes. "I'm not going to let you do that. After everything it took to get here, I can't let it end like that."

"What do you mean?" Emerson asked.

"Listen to me," Kodi replied, ignoring her question. "It's very unlikely we'll both survive a jump from that height. I used to cliff dive with my friends off Monument Point—it was probably only fifty feet, but I have some experience with this at least."

"I can't just let you do it on your own."

"Yes, you can," Kodi said. "Yes, you can, Em. I made a deal so that you could jump from that middle platform; don't waste that. Do it for your brother, okay? This isn't about me. This was never about me. You're here for your brother, Kester, right?"

Emerson looked at Kodi, conflicted. Finally, she nodded.

"Then go. I'll be fine, all right?"

Emerson nodded again. There were tears welling in her eyes, and she had time to think, *What happened? When did I start feeling this way about this boy?* Before he turned to climb the ladder to the highest point, Emerson grabbed Kodi's hand, pulled him toward her, and kissed him.

She felt the softness of his lips, the imperfection where he had been hit during the fight on the top deck of the cruise ship, the way his hand brushed against her cheek—and then he was gone.

He climbed the ladder quickly and didn't look back.

Emerson watched him until he was standing on the edge of the highest point of the structure. Before she climbed down to the middle platform, she looked out to the prison and saw it standing there, somehow both imposing and unreal at the same time. She made her way down to the middle platform, which now looked as if it were miles below where Kodi stood.

There were three people on the bottom platform: Levi Russo, the arrogant Topsider in second place in the leaderboard; Delilah Scattergood, the Topsider with dark eye makeup and in third place; and Decker Shimada, the only Burrower in the top five. Decker's impressive Mohawk was starting to wilt to one side as the heat of the sun melted whatever product was in there.

On the top diving board there were five unfortunate contestants. Among them was the trembling figure of Billie Joe Walker, who was now periodically spasming as he lay on his side.

The remaining contestants were huddled together on the middle platform, nervously awaiting whatever came next.

The Producer's voice came thundering over the speakers. "Contestants, when the alarm sounds, you have four minutes to jump from your platform. Good luck."

There was a brief moment of silence before someone near Emerson shouted, "What happens if we refuse to jump?" But there was no time for theories or best guesses, as the alarm squealed out through the speakers and the game began.

20

CHAPTER

There was a scream from several members of the middle group as the platform beneath their feet began to move. They all realized at the same time why they had no choice but to jump within four minutes: When their time was up, there would be no platform left to stand on.

Levi, Delilah, and Decker jumped first. Delilah even took a second to wave up to those on the platforms above her before she leaped, the shadow of her black eye makeup making her look like she had no eyes at all from where Emerson stood.

The next to jump was Kodi.

He seemed to hang in the air forever, suspended in time. Finally, as he fell toward the water like a rocket, he turned and arced his arms over his head. He hit the water almost perfectly straight, but he was at enough of an angle that the water dragged him around, turning him violently to the left and sending up a cascade of foamy water high into the evening air.

He didn't resurface for what felt to Emerson like minutes. When he finally did, his body was limp. Lifeless.

"No," Emerson whispered, and tried to make her way to the

front of the group so she could leap in after him, but the more the platforms retracted, the more shallow the water was becoming below—the ocean's contents continuing to drain as if it were a giant bathtub.

Now everyone wanted to get off the diving boards as quickly as possible.

The sound of bodies hitting the water below filled the air, along with the screams of falling kids.

Emerson was dragged along by the moving crowd, and knew that jumping in a pack was so much more dangerous than jumping alone; she could hit someone in the water and break their neck. She could be hit by someone falling after her and drown. But all thoughts evaporated as there was suddenly only air beneath her feet. She had been pulled along with the horde until there had been no platform left to stand on. She was falling among a dozen other people.

There was time, during the drop, to look out to sea where the *Calypso* stood still and white, and then down to see the thick, inky water undulating beneath her: It looked like gray-green paint swirling and churning below.

The shock of the water was familiar, and she adapted more quickly this time. She had one thought in her mind: get to the surface and find Kodi.

It took a long time to break through the waves to the fresh air above, too long. There were still bodies hitting the water, sliding down into the depths, narrowly missing her, slamming into others. There was blood in the water—from where, Emerson didn't know.

Finally, she made it to the top and hauled in air until her desperate lungs were full.

She looked around, frantically treading water, searching the chaotic ocean for Kodi, but she couldn't see him.

Still more people were jumping, but as the platforms retracted, they were farther away now, getting closer to shore and the shallow water. There was an almost constant churning in the cold ocean around her as the conscious contestants swam for the beach. At least ten people were floating in the waves like rag dolls.

Emerson's eyes fell on Kodi's white shirt, and she swam toward him as fast as she could.

She had to shove the floating bodies of several other contestants aside to get to Kodi, but when she made it to him, she hauled him onto his back, wrapped an arm beneath his neck so that his face stayed above the surface, and began to backstroke toward shore.

Emerson had only made about ten yards of progress when Never broke the surface, gasping desperately for air. She caught a mouthful of salt water, and then fell beneath the rolling waves once again.

I can't swim. I'm not drowning before the show even begins . . .

Those had been Never's words on the ship, and they flashed through Emerson's mind now loud and bright like a firework.

"Hey!" Emerson screamed, looking around for somebody, anybody who might be willing to help, but they were all swimming for their lives. "Hey! Help! We need help over here!"

Her legs churned, growing fatigued while her one free hand continued to scoop the water, keeping both her and Kodi afloat. If she reached out for Never, they'd both go under.

Never resurfaced for a second, long enough to catch half a breath, and then was gone again. She was silent in her desperation, quietly dying in front of dozens of people. Emerson had heard that was usually the case—those who were drowning didn't scream for help, or wave their arms. They were too busy fighting for oxygen and trying to crawl their way back to the surface.

"Help us! Please!" Emerson called out to the disappearing wave of humans who thrashed their way to the beach.

And in the hopeless, silent seconds that followed, Emerson felt more lost than she ever had.

"I got her!" a voice called from beside her, and Alasdair George William Tremblay-Birchall came splashing past in a perfect front crawl that propelled him through the water like a Jet Ski. He grabbed Never effortlessly out of the swelling waves, and—like Emerson—turned onto his back and carried her shoreward.

With a sense of enormous relief, Emerson kicked her legs and pushed herself through the cold water with one hand as fast as she could. Never was safe, but she had to get Kodi ashore as quickly as she could. She didn't know how much water he had inhaled, how long it had been since he'd taken a breath, and seconds mattered.

She forced her legs to kick and kick and kick against the

resistance of the water. On her back, she could see that all four platforms had receded until they were barely visible, and everyone had jumped apart from Billie Joe Walker, who was now inching away from the disappearing platform and screaming down into the rocky shallows below.

As the platform disappeared and Billie Joe fell, Emerson looked away, but there was no way to cover her ears from the wet impact of the terrified boy's body striking the shallow surf and the jagged rocks.

He wouldn't be the only one to die that day, Emerson knew it. She could hear the gasping, gulping sounds coming from those who were drowning before her. She could see the unresponsive bodies bobbing on the constancy of the rolling water, like store mannequins in their strange deadness.

As Alasdair made it to the shore, Never began to cough and splutter, and Emerson felt a brief moment of relief. At least Never was alive.

Emerson's shoulders hit sand, and she stood up, dragging Kodi through the surf and onto the beach. His head rocked horribly, unresponsively, on his shoulders, and Emerson thought about Jorgensen, how he hadn't come back, how his cadaver eyes had stared dryly at the burning moon, how his blue lips would not open and breathe in new air, how he had refused to come back to the world of the living.

Pushing all this darkness aside, Emerson rolled Kodi fully onto his back, pressed two fingers just below his jaw, and waited . . . nothing. No pulse. No heartbeat. No life.

Cobalt Skiba came stumbling out of the surf beside them. He looked over to Emerson. "Where's Llanzo? Where is he?"

Emerson ignored him. She knelt beside Kodi and began chest compressions.

The world swirled around her like an oil painting melting in a bonfire. She saw the face of Jorgensen contorting in pain as his chest shattered like porcelain while she pressed into it. She felt the scorching heat in her hands as Marvin Tzu's burning corpse lay where Kodi's should've been. She heard the scream of Kester buried alive beneath the earth somewhere nearby, and she knew none of it was real. Her mind was simply reeling from the reality of right now.

All these fever-dream visions dissolved into that place where vague dream memories go upon waking as Kodi rolled violently onto his side and vomited salt water into the sand.

Emerson felt her heart had been uncaged, finally beating once again. Kodi was alive. He was alive.

"Kodi. Kodi, are you okay?" she asked, frantically turning his haggard face to hers, his lip split open once again.

His eyes—at first unknowing—found hers, and he smiled. "I knew you'd save me," he choked, and Emerson wrapped her arms around him, crying with relief.

But it could not last long. There were others still out there in the water, and she had to go.

"I'll come back," she said, and kissed him on the mouth, tasting blood, before getting to her burned-out legs and clambering into the breaking waves.

"Stop!" someone called, and Emerson turned to see Levi, the Topsider who had tried to hit on her on the ship, standing in the surf, screaming at her. "Stop! The more of them that die, the better chance we have of winning this show!"

"We can still save them!" Number 38, Vintage Patel, joined Emerson in the water. "It takes three minutes for the brain to start dying after unconsciousness! We can still save them!" Even at a time like this, she was still talking in trivia. She dove into the water, kicking her legs and throwing her arms over her head as fast as she could.

"Let them die," the morbid Delilah Scattergood said. "It'll be funny."

"There's something seriously wrong with you!" Alasdair said.

Delilah just shrugged.

"Viewers can only follow one contestant at a time!" Levi yelled. "If they die, their followers will follow *us*. Tell them, Imelda!"

Emerson looked to Imelda and felt a stirring of hope as she saw doubt in the silver-haired girl's eyes.

"If we save them, we'll be heroes," Emerson said. "Think of the followers!"

"She's right," Imelda said. "The more of them we save, the more followers we get, and that's the aim of this game."

Imelda ran back into the water, followed by her group of top-halfers. Emerson dove into the waves along with Vintage and Alasdair.

In the end, the rescue mission had been an exercise in futility.

The bodies had been in the water for too long, and none of them survived.

When all was said and done, when the last body was dragged back to shore, twelve more contestants were dead. They were: number 12, Billie Joe Walker; number 2, Cameron Angus; number 19, Rose Pascoe; number 28, Sian McNamara; number 46, Amanda Anderson; number 40, James Sunday; number 9, Hugo von Hugo; number 14, Llanzo Robinson; number 5, Green Glow Ali; number 8, Amelia Rock; and number 3, Genji Gao.

Vintage Patel had died after swimming back out into the ocean to try to save others.

They were all just kids. All of them with ambition and dreams and memories. All of them gone. It weighed on Emerson.

The remaining twenty-one contestants sat on the dunes, just like they had after the first game, and they tried not to look at the dead faces of their fellow contestants . . . of their friends.

Cobalt Skiba sobbed loudly and lamented the death of

Llanzo, his friend. "I loved him," Cobalt cried, his tears disappearing into the sand between his feet. "I loved him."

The three ear-piercing beeps of the public address system sounded and the Producer's voice congratulated them on completing game two. He told them to meet on the beach in one minute.

The contestants didn't move from their spot. The air was still; it was always still here on this strange island.

Soon after, the Producer appeared, walking slowly and nonchalantly along the beach as though he were going for an evening stroll. The hatred that ran through the group was like a heated filament. They all wanted him dead, just like the children who lay on the sand dunes. They wanted *him* to humiliate himself for followers before jumping from one hundred feet; they wanted *him* to be buried alive and then make a video pretending everything was amazing. But each of them was primed with a poison that kept them dancing to the Producer's tune no matter what.

"Contestants," the Producer said, turning on the high beam of his smile. "Well done on completing game number two. You have all taken another huge step toward rehabilitation. You learned about empathy today."

"That's crap!" Emerson yelled. "We didn't learn anything. We watched our friends die!"

"Ms. Ness, I advise you to lower your voice. More intelligent minds than yours have conceptualized this game show. Have you faced trauma over the last two days? Yes, you have! But if we are to fundamentally change who you are, we are going to have to harness trauma! Trauma builds new neural pathways in your damaged brains! You are broken, and trauma will fix you!"

The evil in the Producer's eyes was accentuated by the glittering reflection of the half-set sun that turned them red and wicked.

"This whole thing is horrible," Tiger muttered, and the Producer turned his hellish gaze onto her for a moment before speaking again.

"Today's winner, thanks to the selfish actions of Kodiak Finch, is Imelda Fleet, who was the first to make it back to shore and therefore wins immunity from the public vote."

"As if she needs it," Teller said.

"The last to make it to the beach," the Producer continued, "and the person who will face the public vote, was Gamble Delaney. Commiserations, Mr. Delaney."

Gamble nodded in prideful defiance. "It's fine," he muttered, running his tongue over his large teeth.

"Now, follow me," the Producer said, and the island began to turn.

None of them stumbled as they walked away from the row of dead contestants.

Emerson did not follow. She stayed where she was, watching the Producer walk on the spot as the island moved beneath his feet.

"I'd keep up if I were you, Ms. Ness," the Producer said without looking back. "That poison is a nasty way to go."

Emerson clenched her jaw and let the anger rage in her for a moment, and then she followed.

On the other side of the island, the bonfire was still burning, the scoreboard was still illuminated, the bedrooms had been cleaned and the beds made. The only change was that thirteen of the bedrooms had been dismantled and removed from the beach entirely.

Emerson looked at the leaderboard and saw that her follower ban was still active for another twenty-six minutes, and she was far, far behind everyone else.

"Just like last night," the Producer said, turning around and facing the group, "you will record your daily video diaries. All follower bans will be temporarily lifted. After that, we shall see who gets the daily prize, and which contestant will be facing Mr. Delaney in the public vote. Recording of video diaries will begin in ten minutes. Good luck."

He turned and walked away, his shiny black shoes leaving half-moon shapes in the sand.

Imelda, Levi, Delilah, Decker, and a few other contestants at the top of the leaderboard seemed able to shake off the ordeal they had faced more easily than others (especially Delilah, who seemed to enjoy the constant death that surrounded them). They made their way over to their bedrooms and began rehearsing what they were going to say and do during their diaries: Imelda was doing vocal warm-ups, practicing her laugh; Decker Shimada was spraying his hair with what looked like an entire can of hairspray to make his Mohawk stand up; Steele Sawyer was doing push-ups as fast as he could, then pushing his sunglasses down his nose to check if the veins in his arms were standing out.

"Hey," Kodi said, and Emerson turned to see him looking weak and frail for the first time since she had known him.

"Hey," she replied. "How are you feeling?"

"Like I was dead for five minutes," he replied, and smiled. That smile seemed to reignite the light in him.

Emerson smiled too, and then the smile faltered. "I was scared. I thought that . . ."

"Yeah," he said before she could finish. "I was scared too."

They looked at each other for a moment, not mentioning the kiss. Kodi half laughed, skimming the back of Emerson's hand with the softness of his thumb.

"What did you mean, up there on the diving board, when you said . . . *after everything it took to get here?*"

Kodi swallowed and looked out to the horizon. "Not yet, okay? I'll tell you what I meant, but not right now."

"I'm probably about to be voted out," Emerson said.

"Well, you'd better do something about that," Kodi replied, and smiled once more before heading off to his room to record his diary.

Emerson watched him go, thinking how unfair it was to be falling for someone in a place like this, at a time like this. It was inconvenient and ill-advised, but she couldn't help the way she felt.

Emerson reached into her back pocket, and her heart sank as she realized that the bottle lid was gone.

"You should do your diary tonight," a voice said, and

Emerson felt a tightening in her neck muscles when she realized it was Teller.

"Hi, Teller," she said, trying and failing to put a believable smile on her face. She felt bad about her reaction to Teller. He wasn't a bad person. He just always seemed to appear at the wrong moment, and say the wrong thing.

"Are you going to? Are you going to say something when they start recording?"

"I don't think so," Emerson admitted.

"You have to, Emerson! You have to!"

"I don't have to do anything."

"But . . . well . . . I want you to!"

Emerson frowned. "Why do you want me to?"

"Because you're at the bottom of the leaderboard, and you can't keep ending up in the viewer vote because sooner or later you'll get voted off! And if you get voted off, I won't get a chance to . . ."

He didn't finish his sentence, and Emerson didn't want him to, but she couldn't just leave him standing there with that hopeful look in his eyes. "Chance to what?" she asked.

"A chance to convince you that you and me would be pretty good together!" he blurted out.

Emerson laughed. She couldn't help it. She tried to get a hand to her mouth as if she could stuff the laugh back in, but it was already out there, and Teller's face had fallen into a mask of pure hurt.

"I'm sorry, Teller, I didn't mean to laugh."

"Well, what's so funny about it?" he muttered, looking down at the sand.

"Nothing, nothing is funny about it, except that . . . except that it just can't happen." Kodi was lying on his bed, arms behind his head, looking up at the dark skies. She looked back to Teller. "Think about it; we're going to end up in jail or dead over the next few days. That's how this ends, not with love or happiness. It ends in death or imprisonment. So, I'm sorry I laughed, but it's either that or I burst into tears."

Teller nodded. "I get that," he said. "I just think that we'd be good together."

Again, the muscles in Emerson's neck tightened, but she forced herself to nod. "Maybe in another life."

Teller smiled. "I like that. In another life."

Emerson nodded again. She was about to say her goodbyes and make her way to her room when Teller spoke again.

"Will you just promise me one thing? Will you just promise me you won't fall in love with Kodi?"

Emerson sighed; she looked at the tall, broad-shouldered boy with his deep brown eyes. "No," she said to Teller. "No, I won't promise that, and it's a selfish thing to ask of anyone."

Teller's normally placid face twisted into one of anger and disgust. "I don't get you, Emerson," he spat. "That boy is cruel and heartless and thinks he's better than everyone. You just like him because he's good-looking! That's not fair. I'm a better person than him, but I'm not handsome so no one cares!"

Emerson felt her anger and her pity battling inside her. In the end, pity won. "Teller," she said, putting a hand on his arm. "You try so hard to be a good person, but you need to listen to yourself. A truly good person wouldn't accuse another person of being so shallow that they'd like someone because of the way they look. Do you really think so little of me? If you do, why would you want to be with me anyway? You're frustrated, I get that, but you need to learn to think through your emotions before you act on them."

Teller looked down at the sand, then back up at Emerson. There were tears in his eyes. "I'm sorry," he said. "It just always goes this way, you know? There's always someone better than me and . . . I don't know."

"Teller, I'm not looking for the *best* person. There's no hierarchy of people. Surely we're all just looking for the *right* person?"

Teller nodded, and the tears that had welled in his eyes spilled onto the sand. "I'm . . . I'm sorry," he said, "I'm sorry I'm not the right person."

Teller walked away, and Emerson watched him go. She felt truly bad for him. Even though he was the same age as her, he was somehow younger. He was confused and he thought he was in love. She sighed and then rolled her eyes at the ridiculousness of it all. Here she was on an island of death, and she was dealing with lovesick boys and her own flailing emotions.

She walked to her bed and sat down.

"What's your plan?" Alasdair asked from his room.

Emerson looked at her name in last place on the scoreboard, and then over to Kodi. "I don't know," she admitted.

Kodi had fallen from sixth place down to sixteenth after being accused of pushing Imelda off the top diving board, but it seemed like he would be safe from the vote.

The scoreboard transformed into the sixty-second count-down. "Better figure it out soon," Alasdair said, and took a deep breath, readying himself for the diary.

"Yeah," Emerson said, more to herself than in reply to Alasdair.

The island had gone quiet as all the contestants watched the countdown. As it hit zero, drones descended from the sky, hovering in front of each contestant.

The cacophony of noise began immediately this time. All the remaining contestants were performing for the cameras. At some point during the day, Teller had fashioned dumbbells by filling plastic rocks with seawater and using a fake tree branches and vines. He was curling them one at a time, his biceps swelling as he smiled at the drone, his eyes still red from the tears he had cried a minute before. Imelda was introducing her followers to Decker and talking about how cool his Mohawk was, and how much he meant to her, and how Burrowers and Topsiders should put aside their differences. She was careful not to tell her followers to follow him, though, as viewers could only follow one contestant at a time. Andrew Matthews was doing his usual trick of running into the sea naked. Alasdair had changed tactics and was now insulting his followers, calling them morons for being so pathetic that they would make themselves followers instead of leaders. Tiger was singing and dancing. Gwen Perez had tied her thick pink hair into a ponytail and taken off her shoes, socks, and jeans, and was telling the camera that she would take off her top if she got three thousand more followers.

Emerson sighed. She looked at her name at the foot of the leaderboard and then looked at Kodi. She wanted to stay for at least one more day. She stared down the lens of the camera, and spoke.

"Hi, I'm Emerson Ness. You haven't heard much from me yet because I'm not very good at this kind of thing. I know it seems silly for someone like me to take part in a show that requires the contestants to gain followers, but I didn't have much of a choice. I once tried to start a social media brand but I got laughed at. I'm not naturally confident or charismatic, so I come across as awkward and uncomfortable, and not in a cute *pity me* kind of way. My dad tried to include me in his channel when I was a kid, but I must not have been adorable enough because the comments were . . . pretty cruel! I mean, I *was* a pretty ugly baby, but come on, people."

Emerson found that the more she spoke, the easier it became to open up. She was even smiling at the absurd cruelty of the comments her dad had shown her from when she was a baby.

"To be honest, I think that was the only time my dad ever really stood up for me. He was always so caught up in his own brand that—once he couldn't use me or my brother for content— he didn't have time for us. I remember the one and only time I was invited to a party at high school, I thought I'd finally made some friends. I thought I'd finally stopped being the loser kid who everyone picked on. I went to the party and they suggested we play truth or dare. I made a big deal about how I would do any dare that they asked me to do, and then this girl Lisa dared me to leave the party and never come to her house again. I was fourteen years old and I cried all the way home. My dad tried to get me to repeat the story on his channel. He told me you can't fake that kind of sympathy. I hated him for that. Now look at me. I'm doing the same thing."

Emerson realized that she had tears in her eyes. She tried to ask herself whether she was ashamed of selling out, or if she was genuinely relieved at having finally spoken about something that had haunted her for years. She couldn't figure it out.

"That's all I have to say for now. I find this really difficult, and I can't promise I'll be back tomorrow. Oh, one more thing, you probably saw me throw Imelda's bag off the ship . . . Part of me is sorry for that; I can be impulsive sometimes, and I find it hard to control my temper . . . I shouldn't have done it."

And with that, Emerson fell silent, and the camera drone's red light went out.

Emerson wiped the tears from her eyes and forced herself to steady her nerves. Her eyes went to the enormous prison at the center of the island. Something didn't seem right about that circular building. Emerson couldn't put her finger on what it was, but it felt wrong, off-putting to the human eye.

"Hey, Em," Alasdair said. Emerson looked over to him and saw that he was pointing to the scoreboard. She looked to where he was pointing and saw that her name had lifted off the bottom of the table and she was now in third-to-last place.

She felt a moment of numb shock. The two names below her in the table were Nick Mason and Andrew Matthews. At the top of the table, Imelda was still reigning supreme, and her endorsement of Decker had shot him up to second place. Gwen Perez's tactic of taking off her clothes for followers was working too. She had moved from twentieth to third.

The numbers beside the names were still changing, still growing at different speeds. Emerson's had slowed right down while the other contestants still gave everything to entertain the viewers. One place above her, in fourth-to-last, was Teller, who was desperately glancing at the scoreboard as sweat poured off him. He was holding a huge water-filled rock against his chest and doing squats while trying to hold the smile on his exhausted face.

When, finally, everyone was done with their daily recording, the Producer announced that the prize for first place would be a mic drone to expertly record all sound and add an extra layer of professionalism to the victor's footage.

When the time delay ended and the Producer commanded the screen to freeze, Nick Mason had overtaken Emerson, but she had still avoided the viewer vote. She couldn't help the smile that tugged at the corners of her mouth as she looked over to Kodi and saw that he was smiling too.

"And now," the Producer bellowed. "We count down to today's winner! Ten, nine, eight, seven . . ."

This time, only three contestants joined in, but the Producer didn't allow it to affect his energy.

". . . two, one, zero! Congratulations to today's *Kill Factor* leader for the second day in a row: Imelda Fleet!" the Producer yelled out to the swarm of drones that hovered around him.

Fireworks illuminated the sky in cascades of red and green, sending nightmare shadows across the sand.

The Producer put his arm around Imelda as his face turned devil red under the glow of the final firework.

"How does it feel to have such a loyal fan base, Imelda?" he asked.

"Sir, I can't explain it. I feel so loved and so lucky. I'm just out here being me and living my best life. I'm learning so much each and every day and it means the world to me to have such incredible followers. You're all amazing, and I love you so much!"

Imelda blew a big theatrical kiss to the drones.

"And, Imelda, can you tell our audience of millions what you have learned over the last few days on the island?"

Imelda's head bowed in a show of humble submission. "Sir, these last two days have taught me how to be a better person. I look back on who I was, and I feel shame. I can't wait to keep going on this journey and to learn how to be the best version of me that I can be."

"That is excellent to hear, Ms. Fleet," the Producer said, holding her tightly with one arm before turning back to the drones. "Now, ladies and gentlemen, the hard part: The contestant who will be joining Gamble Delaney in the viewer vote is . . . Andrew Matthews."

Two bright beams of light shot down from the sky, causing both Gamble and Andrew to shield their eyes.

"Mr. Delaney, Mr. Matthews, please, take your place on the stage," the Producer said, holding an open hand out in the direction of the wooden platform in the center of the beach.

The two young men looked at each other with eyes filled with fear, and made their way to the stage.

The Producer made a show of pulling an envelope from a pocket inside his jacket. He opened it, and read their fate. "Tonight's task is to display your dance skills. You will see a series of instructions on the screen; you must follow these dance moves to the best of your ability. Remember, you are trying to win votes, so try your best. The choreography will be displayed in ten seconds, and the viewer vote will open at the same time. This task lasts three minutes. Good luck."

The screen flashed, and the countdown from ten began.

"I can't do this!" Andrew complained. "I can't dance, I'm not a dancer. I'm not doing it."

As the countdown reached zero, a faceless model began dancing to an upbeat pop song. Gamble began dancing for his life, arms flowing and chest popping as the beat thumped through the beach.

"This is stupid," Andrew said, crossing his arms over his chest.

Emerson felt a chill run through her. The soundtrack of sugary, optimistic music juxtaposed with the horrible fate that the contestants faced was eerie.

Gamble squatted down low and then rolled up. The contestants were cheering now. On either side of the dancer on the screen, viewers were clapping their hands and dancing along with the avatar. The bar chart appeared on screen and showed that Gamble was leading by a huge margin.

"I . . . I . . ." Andrew said, and then he began to dance.

Emerson felt sympathy rush through her as she watched the poor uncoordinated boy try his best to keep up with the moves as the faces of the viewers on the screen laughed at him. Buried inside that sympathy was a massive sigh of relief that she had not had to face this task.

By the time the graph disappeared, the faces of the viewers faded away, and the countdown ended, Andrew had tears in his eyes. He knew he had lost—there was no question about that; the graph had remained heavily in favor of Gamble Delaney.

"It's not fair," Andrew said, breathing heavily. "I can't dance. I've never been able to dance!"

Gamble was smiling now; his large teeth seemed to take up half his face. He had won and he was relieved.

The Producer only stood, a smile frozen on his prime-time face.

The one-minute wait to edit out any unwanted footage was punctuated with the sobs of Andrew, who kept on looking up at the huge prison in the center of the island.

Finally, the wait was over, and the Producer stepped forward.

"Ladies and gentlemen of *The Kill Factor*, and the millions watching around the world, I can now reveal that the contestant in second place got 772,501 votes in total, but the person in first place got 1,243,109 votes. Ladies and gentlemen, the person leaving the games tonight is Andrew Matthews."

"It's not fair," Andrew said, but there was no fight left in his voice. "It wasn't a fair game."

The Producer climbed the steps to the stage and shook Gamble's hand. "Congratulations, Mr. Delaney! How does it feel to have survived the audience vote?"

Gamble's sweat-drenched face looked at the Producer as though he had just realized he was there. "Uh, it feels great. I can't believe they voted for me ... it feels great ... really great."

"Excellent. Well done, young man. I'm sure you're going to gain a lot more followers after that performance."

"Do you think so?" Gamble asked, a yearning kind of avarice in his eyes now, his large teeth seeming to grow in his mouth.

The Producer laughed. "Just you wait and see."

A smile not unlike the Producer's spread across Gamble's face, and he turned his eyes up to the moon as if bathing in its light, his big teeth catching the glare.

The Producer stepped up beside Andrew and put a hand on his shoulder. "Mr. Matthews, you survived until the second game, but unfortunately, you have been voted off the show. You have five minutes to say goodbye to your friends."

"But it's not fair," Andrew repeated, looking pleadingly into the Producer's grinning eyes. "It's not fair!"

"I understand, son, but the viewers have decided. Use your five minutes wisely."

Andrew looked helpless, lost. He sat down on the stage and muttered about how unjust it all was.

Emerson wished there was something she could do, but she supposed sooner or later—if they didn't die first—they'd all be making their way to the prison.

She looked at the prison, the tall gray walls with the almost cartoonish barred windows. She felt, suddenly, like all the air had been sucked out of the island, like each breath she breathed into her lungs was empty and useless.

"Hey, you okay?" Never asked, but to Emerson, her voice sounded like it was coming from the other side of the island.

Emerson's heart began to pound in her chest in arrhythmic jerks and she was certain that she was going to die.

"Em? Em? Come with me," Never said, and she led Emerson away from the group and over to the plastic woods.

"Just breathe, all right. You're having a panic attack. It'll go away, I promise."

Emerson nodded. She wanted to believe Never, but her squirming, zooming brain wouldn't let her.

"Listen to me. You're a healthy young woman who has been through a *lot* over the last few days. Your mind is just reacting to all of this shit! What I want you to do is count with me, really slowly. I know it sounds dumb, but it'll distract your mind and you'll calm down, okay? We're going to start at one: one, two, three . . ."

Emerson joined in. "Four, five, six . . ." At first, the numbers came out breathy and rushed, but by the time they got to forty, Emerson could feel her mind beginning to slow down, and her heart falling back into its familiar arrangement.

They carried on counting until they got to one hundred. Emerson nodded to show that she felt better.

"Are you okay now?" Never asked.

Emerson nodded her head, and then shook it. "Okay? No! I'm not okay! Do you know how many kids have died over the last two days? And they're going to keep dying! Tomorrow, more are going to die! Maybe we'll die, maybe Tiger will die. She's just a kid. We're being killed for entertainment! This is crazy, Never! I am not okay."

Never nodded. "Me neither. I keep expecting someone to come along and put a stop to this, but it keeps on not happening."

"What are we going to do?" Emerson asked.

"I don't know . . . I don't know."

"This place is getting to me, Never. I'm barely keeping it together. Pretty soon I'll go crazy, and then what?"

Never looked up through the plastic branches of the trees and sighed. "Yeah, me too. The nightmares I've been having . . . I don't want to fall asleep anymore."

"Tell me about it," Emerson replied.

Never put a hand on Emerson's shoulder. "You're going to be okay, you know? You're tough as hell! Leaping off a cruise ship to save that Teller creep? That's some action movie nonsense!"

"He's not a creep, he's just . . ."

"Always there?" Never suggested.

"I don't know," Emerson said. She liked Teller, but she knew what Never meant.

They stayed hidden in the plastic trees for another few

minutes before going back to see what would happen to Andrew when his time was up.

"Hey, you know what's weird?" Never said, brushing sand off her T-shirt as they walked. "I swear I recognize the Producer from somewhere. Just recently, ever since he's become this evil-villain version of himself, I swear I've seen him in like a documentary, or on the news or something!"

"Really?" Emerson asked.

Never shrugged. "I don't know. He probably just looks like someone famous."

They stood away from the rest of the group and watched as eight or ten drones came down from the sky and hovered around Andrew. Gently, they guided him away from the beach and into the trees. Emerson watched as he stopped for a second and tried to look back. One of the drones struck his elbow and he shrieked in pain as though he had been shocked by the tiny flying robot.

The crowd watched him until he disappeared into the trees, and sometime later, the clacking sound of machinery whirring into life came to them.

"The drawbridge," the Producer said, acknowledging the curious expressions on the faces of the contestants. "The prison is surrounded by a moat. An extra layer of security."

A minute later, the Producer advised them that tomorrow would bring a game that would teach them about Work Ethic, and then he was gone, leaving the numb contestants standing on the beach, lit by the flickering glow of the ever-burning bonfire.

22

CHAPTER

Emerson had thought she was not going to be able to sleep, but eventually the sound of the crashing waves lulled her into a broken rest for a few hours.

The next morning was the same bizarre display of cognitive dissonance that Emerson had seen yesterday and the day before: an island full of hostages pretending that everything was wonderful. Imelda, Decker, Levi, and Steele were going for a run up and down the shoreline, and now that Gwen Perez had shot up the leaderboard, she had been invited to join them, which only added to her popularity with the viewers—her follower numbers were going up quickly.

Emerson watched the group of five running along the wave line, and noticed that Imelda's quips and cutting jokes were now aimed at Steele, the muscular boy who always wore sunglasses, who had dropped down to sixth place. It seemed that any sign of weakness in that group was set upon mercilessly.

"It's like some messed-up nature show, isn't it?" Kodi asked, sitting down next to Emerson on the dunes.

"Yeah, they remind me of hyenas," Emerson said, listening to the laughter of Imelda's disciples as she aimed another barb at Steele, who grinned grudgingly, trying not to show any more vulnerability than the scoreboard already displayed. Emerson imagined he was glad to be wearing his aviator shades, which would be hiding the hurt in his eyes.

"What do you think the next game will be?" Kodi asked.

Emerson looked at him. There was something off about him, she could sense it. "I don't know," she replied. "I'm not looking forward to finding out."

Kodi laughed half-heartedly. "Yeah, me neither. Hey, come sit in the shade with me. I'm getting burned out here on the dunes."

Emerson looked intently at him, and saw a look in his eyes that said *trust me*. She made a quick decision and followed Kodi into the plastic forest—dozens of drones tracked them into the dense and fake foliage. They sat down together at the foot of the same tree that Emerson had run to after the first game. The heart-shaped leaves threw scattered shadows onto the ground.

"I hate this place," Kodi said.

"Well, I'm so glad you brought me here," Emerson replied.

"I don't mean this place specifically. I mean this whole fake island, it's so . . . soulless."

"I know what you mean," Emerson agreed, and as she spoke, she felt Kodi's hand take hers, their fingers interlinking. A rush of electricity ran through her.

"I keep thinking about how much I hated the Burrows and even the Topside, but I'd give anything to be back there now. Even the air in this place feels *wrong*."

As he spoke, he moved both of their hands slowly behind his own back and against the rough plastic of the heart-tree's trunk.

"Me too," Emerson said, trying to act natural as the drones scrutinized them.

"I made a lot of mistakes in my life. I always seemed to be in the wrong place at the wrong time. I just got out of eleven months in juvie a week ago, and I was breaking into Topsiders' vacation homes the next day."

Emerson felt her hand touch something that was attached to the roots of the heart-tree. It was something that shouldn't have been there. A handle. She looked at Kodi, who gave her the faintest of nods before letting go of her hand.

"That's life for a lot of us," Emerson said, finding it harder and harder to act normally as her fingers traced the outline of a hatch in the ground beneath the tree.

"You're right. We're beaten to the floor and kept there, and somehow we're the bad guys."

Emerson's eyes fell to her feet. "Yeah, we can't win. They won't let us."

"You want to know what I got the eleven months for?" Kodi asked.

Emerson nodded.

"I assaulted an officer," Kodi admitted, looking down at the ground. "He collared me as I was driving a stolen car to this garage I knew I could sell it at, and he dragged me out to the pavement and slammed my head against the ground. I got so mad that I broke free and hit him right in the mouth. I got tased and . . . anyway, the judge gave me eighteen months, but I got out on good behavior."

Emerson looked at him for a moment. "If you were already out of juvie, what did you do to end up here?"

Kodi ran his tongue over the cut in his lip, then looked right at Emerson. "It doesn't matter. What matters is that I deserve to be here, and you don't."

"No, it does matter. What do you mean?"

"I mean . . ." He looked like he wanted to tell her something, but instead he shook his head. "I guess I mean, I haven't known you long, but it feels like I have. And I know you're a good person."

They sat in silence for a moment, Emerson letting Kodi's words swirl around in her head. And then she spoke. "I was arrested for arson," she said, and immediately she recoiled inwardly at the lie. She was here because a man died. She had been arrested for manslaughter, but she couldn't admit that out loud to Kodi. "I was robbing a school—my old high school, actually—to help pay for my brother's tuition, and a fire broke out, I don't know how, but a fire started and the school burned to the ground. It wasn't my first offense, so I was looking at some pretty serious jail time."

"It's not fair," Kodi said, and then he leaned his head against the trunk of the tree. He stared off, lost in thought. For a moment, it looked like he wanted to say something, but he seemed to catch himself. He didn't say another word after that.

He didn't have to. Emerson thought she knew what he meant. It *was* unfair.

Kodi got up and walked away. Half the drones followed him, and the rest hung around Emerson, filming her from a dozen angles. She felt one more time for the handle of the hatch beneath the tree, and wondered if it mattered. She would never get a chance to see what lay beyond because all of them were being filmed twenty-four hours a day.

Emerson stayed beneath the shade of the heart-tree for another hour or so, thinking about something that Kodi had said: that he felt he deserved to be on this island. She didn't want to pry, and eventually, she let it go and wandered back to the beach. She lay down in her bed and tried not to think about what game they would be forced to play later that evening. She stared at the clouds, the perfect, almost cartoonish clouds rolling overhead, and she drifted off to a broken sleep.

When she woke, the sun had started to fall slowly from its highest point in the sky, and the light was turning gray. All the contestants who had been cheerfully performing for the cameras all day were now quiet and apprehensive as they waited for the Producer's voice to boom out over the speakers and invite them to play whatever horrible game they would have to try to live through. The only person who hadn't moved was Asim, who still sat beside the fire, staring into the dancing flames.

Teller was sitting with Harlow Wozniak, the girl with the shaved head and the tattoos under her eyes. They were talking quietly and glancing over at the group of top-halfers who were gathered in Imelda's room.

There were clear and distinct groups among the remaining contestants now: the top-halfers, consisting of Imelda, Decker, Gwen, Levi, and Steele; the latecomers, consisting of numbers 48, 49, and 50; Emerson's crew consisting of herself, Kodi, Never, Tiger, and Alasdair; and Teller and Harlow, who seemed to have formed their own little partnership in the last few hours. Nick the conspiracy theorist, Asim the fire watcher, Delilah the psychopath, Gamble who had just danced for his life, and Cobalt Skiba (who had been lost ever since Llanzo had died) spent most of their time on their own, quiet and introspective, as though they could see the growing crowd of dead contestants gathered on the beach, and they felt guilty about acting like nothing had happened.

"We never got off that boat, you know?" Nick Mason said.

Emerson sat up and saw the gaunt Burrower standing at the frame of her bedroom. "What?"

"Think about it. We died on that ship, all of us. This is purgatory. We're being tested . . . and we're all failing."

He walked away then, his head twitching slightly as more wild thoughts sped through his fragmented mind.

This place is starting to break people, Emerson thought as she watched Nick walk away.

Emerson jumped as the ear-piercing beeps echoed out of the speakers. Fear exploded inside her, making her hands shake in a Pavlovian response.

"Contestants of *The Kill Factor*," the Producer's ethereal voice boomed. "Game number three is about to begin. Please make your way to the other side of the island."

Imelda clapped her hands and cheered, but there was less enthusiasm this time. Perhaps the island was starting to get to her too.

The island revolved; the contestants walked.

The Producer came into view, and instinctively, the contestants gathered close and walked in a group.

The sun was a particularly deep shade of red as it ushered in the evening, and the shadows thrown across the Producer's face made his normally straight white teeth look like sharp, pointed fangs.

"Contestants, today you learn about Work Ethic." The Producer's eyes seemed to glow as he spoke. "The game is simple: You must run for your life."

The crowd of gathered contestants looked at one another and began to murmur. The Producer held up his hand and continued talking. "You must keep a pace of six miles per hour, and the last person left standing wins. The contestant at the bottom of the leaderboard must begin immediately; every ninety seconds, the person above you on the leaderboard joins in."

"We just have to run?" Imelda asked, a note of hope in her voice.

"That's right," the Producer confirmed. "All you have to do is run . . . on the running track."

As the Producer said these words, the ground beneath the

contestants' feet began to shake, and suddenly they were being lifted into the air. Quickly, all of them jumped from the narrow structure that was rising up, surrounding them. It grew into the air, higher and higher. It was a running track, just as the Producer had said, but it was only the width of a single lane, and it was so high up in the sky that it gave Emerson a sense of vertigo just looking at it.

"Contestants!" the Producer said, and all remaining contestants looked from the top of the running track back to him. "You will be running fifty yards above the ground. This will focus your mind on the task at hand. The game begins when the contestant in last place—Mr. Gamble Delaney—steps onto the track. Oh, and the track gets lower with each person who is eliminated from the game. So, hang in there, and good luck." With that, the Producer walked away, exiting through a door in the curvature of the structure.

The contestants said nothing for a long time. They all stared at the smooth metal walls that encircled them, and thought about the daunting task that awaited them.

"I . . . I'm first?" Gamble Delaney asked, biting down on his lower lip with his enormous front teeth.

"Yeah, then me," Nick Mason said, and then let out a short snort of laughter as his wild eyes twisted around in his head.

Emerson knew that it would be Kodi who would be third on the running track, and then her. She did some quick calculations in her head, and worked out that Imelda, who was still in first place, would get thirty minutes of rest on the sidelines before she had to join in. She tried to be grateful for the four and a half minutes of rest she would get, but it didn't seem like much.

"Right then," Gamble said, his voice almost cracking into tears. "How do we get up to the . . ." Before he could finish speaking, the perfectly smooth surface of the structure split into dozens and dozens of steps that led precariously up, fifty feet, to the running track.

"Oh," Gamble said, and then began walking up the steps.

Emerson counted the steps as she walked. There were exactly one hundred of them, leading up in a steady curve to a platform beside the running track.

Most of the twenty contestants were already out of breath from the walk up here, and Gamble wiped sweat away from his forehead as he stared at the narrow lane that arced lazily around and around.

"How fast did the Producer say we had to run?" he asked.

"Six miles per hour," Kodi replied.

"How will I know how fast I'm running?" Gamble turned to face the gathered crowd. Nobody had an answer for him. He turned back to the track. "All right. I guess there's no point waiting around."

Gamble reached out a nervous foot, and stepped onto the slim track.

"Oh God . . . Oh God!" he whispered as he looked down at the sand far below. And then he screamed as the track beneath his feet whirred into life.

For one moment, it looked like Gamble was about to fall fifty feet down onto the island below, but he threw his arms out, maintaining his balance somehow.

"It's a . . . it's a treadmill!" he yelled. The panic in his voice caused it to raise several octaves. "Oh my God, it's like a giant treadmill!"

The whirring of the track beneath his feet got louder as the pace picked up to six miles per hour. It wasn't a fast pace by any means—it looked to Emerson like a fast jog—but the thought of Imelda not having to join for another half hour really made the frightening prospect of this game sink in.

Gamble found his feet and got into a rhythm.

"It's not so bad," Gamble said, and a slight smile appeared on his face. "It's not so bad!"

"Not yet." Delilah Scattergood smirked.

The Producer's voice came echoing out of the speakers down below. "The next contestant to join the running track is Nick Mason."

The Producer's voice was replaced by a robotic female voice counting down from ten.

"Nick!" Tiger yelled at the vacant-looking boy who was convinced that they were all in purgatory.

"What?" he replied dazedly.

"Get on the track!"

Nick looked confused, but wandered precariously onto the running track nonetheless, just as the robotic voice reached zero. Somehow he managed to keep his footing as the onlooking contestants gasped and screamed in anticipation of him falling.

Those who were waiting on the platform began stretching and warming up. Emerson knew she had less than three minutes now until it was her turn to join the game. She could see a problem already: They had this huge track to run on, but already Nick and Gamble were bunched together at the point they had joined. Neither of them wanted to waste energy speeding up to make room for the others, but eventually they would have to.

The Producer announced that the next contestant was Kodiak Finch.

"Good luck," Emerson said as Kodi stepped forward.

"Give me a break," Teller muttered.

Kodi stepped elegantly onto the track and was immediately stuck close behind Nick. He got into his rhythm, and lightly sidestepped Nick and Gamble until he was at the front. Both times he made his way around another contestant, Emerson felt her heart leap in her chest. A fall from this height would surely be deadly. But he made it.

Ninety seconds, Emerson thought, but even as she thought it, she knew she had even less time than that. She leaned forward and stretched out her left leg, bending at the waist and feeling the stretching of the muscles and tendons. She quickly switched to the right leg, and the Producer called out her name.

This is it, she thought.

"You can do this, Em," Never called out.

And as the countdown hit zero, she stepped onto the whirring treadmill, and slipped.

Emerson Ness had been expelled from Stone's Throw Public High School when she was fourteen years old.

She had been accused of stealing four times previously, and on the fifth time, she was caught red-handed.

The principal had sat her down in his office and sneered at her with absolute delight in his eyes. He had asked her if it had been her who had taken the money from the office on the previous occasions, and she had said no. It *had* been her, she was just too ashamed to admit it.

"You might as well be honest for once in your life," Mr. Pembrooke had spat. "You've been caught now."

But Emerson had shaken her head, refusing to let the tears come, replacing her embarrassment with rage instead.

Emerson had never wanted to take anything from anybody. She would never have taken a penny from the school if she hadn't needed it. The worst part was—after the first two times she had been accused of stealing—rumors started spreading about her, and the other kids started laughing behind their hands when she passed by in the corridors. They made a point of double-checking their lockers were locked, calling her Magpie.

"Fine," Mr. Pembrooke had said, shaking his head in disgust. "Deny it. We'll see how defiant you are when the police arrive."

He had left her alone in his office then. Alone to look at the certificates on his walls, the photographs of vacations on his shelves, the leather chair in front of his large desk.

"I hate this place," she had whispered, and finally the tears had come, because there had been a time when she had loved this school. When she had first started, her clothes weren't ragged and worn out, her schoolbag didn't have a broken zipper, the sole of her left shoe didn't flap every time she took a step. But after six months everyone knew the truth about her, and she had fallen down the social ranks. Her whole life had been dictated by scoreboards: where she fit in school; how well she did on social media; her criminal record slowly building up. She was assessed and ranked everywhere she went, and it hurt every time.

"It's going to be okay, kid," a voice had said from the doorway of Mr. Pembrooke's office.

Emerson had wiped the tears away as quickly as she could and turned around to see the janitor standing there in his blue overalls.

"What?" she had asked, ensuring her voice came out flat and unbroken.

"I said it's going to be fine. Everyone makes mistakes."

Emerson filled herself with hate and anger, a mechanism she

had been using for as long as she could remember to protect her-self against the cruelty of the world. She looked at the name tag on the janitor's uniform.

"Just like you, you mean, Marvin?" she had said, filling her voice with scorn.

"Sure, I made some mistakes," the janitor replied, shuffling from one foot to another.

"And look at you now. You've reached the dizzying heights of toilet cleaner! Congratulations."

"All I mean is, your mistakes don't define you, you know?"

"Well, Marvin, thank you so much for your insight. That was very inspiring."

The janitor's face stayed stoic. "Just trying to—"

"Yeah, well, don't," Emerson interrupted.

The janitor had nodded and left the room.

As the anger faded away, Emerson felt guilt and sorrow rush-ing in. She thought about running after Marvin and apologizing, but she had just sat there in the uncomfortable chair that faced the principal's big, comfortable leather chair.

She had been running for fifteen minutes. Sweat was pouring down her face as she tried not to bump into the three people in front of her, or the group behind her.

After she had recovered from the stumble at the start, she had felt out of breath almost immediately, but somehow, after five minutes or so, she had felt herself calming down, and her feet found a tempo.

The pace wasn't fast, but up ahead she could see that Gamble, who had been running for only four and a half minutes longer than her, was drenched in sweat.

The Producer announced Never-Again Jones, and as the ten-second countdown began, Kodi yelled out from the front "Now!" and they all picked up the pace just enough to move forward, making room for Never. They had worked out this system over the last five or six minutes, and it was working perfectly, but there was—of course—a flaw to the plan. It was perfect until someone fell, or quit, or their pace slowed, but for now, it was working.

Sadio Sarr joined, then Tanya Moon, then Goodwin Goodhew, then Harlow Wozniak.

By now, Gamble was gasping in great lungfuls of air, no longer in a steady rhythm.

Steele Sawyer joined, still wearing those stupid shades even in the evening light. Decker Shimada was next, his tall Mohawk bouncing as he ran. Then Delilah Scattergood joined, smiling wickedly as she watched Gamble struggle near the front of the line. Gwen was the penultimate contestant, her pink hair tied up in a ponytail. Finally, Imelda joined. Everyone picked up their pace to make way for her while she joined effortlessly.

Emerson felt the pain in her legs growing with each stride. She could feel the effort in her chest as she began to breathe harder and harder. There were no thoughts of quitting in her mind. If she quit and fell, it was fifty feet to the ground. The Producer had said that the track would get lower with each person who dropped out. She had to hang on for as long as possible.

No one spoke. Everyone knew that conserving energy was the most important thing now. The only sound was the whirring of the track's belt, the thumping of footsteps, and the sound of heavy breathing.

Again, Emerson noticed that there was no breeze at all up here, just still, warm air that felt unfulfilling as it entered her body.

Don't think, Emerson told herself. *Switch your mind off. This is going to go for a long, long time.*

And that's what she did. She let the steady beat of her own footsteps lull her into a kind of meditation. Cutting out the pain, the fear, the anticipation of it all.

Emerson had been deep inside her own mind, replaying the night of the burning school. *Was there someone else in the school that night other than me and Marvin?* She thought about the footsteps she had heard behind her, the sound of something falling in the classroom next to the science room, but all thoughts faded away when she heard Harlow begin to sob on the treadmill.

Emerson looked over to the girl with the shaved head and the tattoos beneath her eyes. She was crying and coughing, her face red with the effort of running.

"I can't keep going," she wheezed. "I can't. It's too hard! I can't..."

And with that she stopped running. As the belt pulled her backward toward Steele, a shout went up through the group. If she had stayed where she was, she would have taken out everyone behind her, but the game was designed to not let that happen. As soon as she dropped below the six-mile-per-hour minimum, her section of the track tilted violently, pouring her off the fifty-foot-high platform. She was gone, falling off the edge with a cry of unadulterated terror.

"Harlow!" Gwen screamed, staring at the blank space where her friend and prank partner used to be.

Emerson could hear Delilah Scattergood clapping and cheering from behind her.

The platform rocked and a sense of light-headedness rolled through Emerson as the entire structure lowered five feet.

As though Harlow's death acted as a trigger, Levi began to hyperventilate.

"I'm getting off!" said the boy who had once told Emerson she'd look "pretty hot" in a minuscule bathing suit. "I'm getting off, get out of my way!"

Levi began to speed up, pushing past people in his haste to make it all the way around the track and back to the platform they had started from.

But in his terror, Levi's foot missed the edge of the platform, and he too fell, only he dropped in a complete silence that was somehow more terrifying than Harlow's scream.

Delilah laughed again, and Emerson found herself filled with hatred toward the morbid girl.

For the next five minutes, the group fell back into an orderly line, and no one spoke.

It was Tanya Moon who was the first to successfully quit. She upped her pace by an almost imperceptible amount and made her way slowly around the track, carefully passing Sadio, then Never, then Levi, and all the others in front of her until she made it safely all the way around and onto the platform, where she collapsed into a shaking heap. Her short, bright red hair—that was normally so neatly styled—was now a matted, wet mass. The platform lowered another five feet as Tanya lay on the platform, sobbing and trying to catch her breath.

As soon as Tanya had tapped out of the race, everyone else knew they were safe to end the game. Immediately, there was a pileup at the back of the track as Imelda, Gwen, and Delilah all sped up at the same time. Decker and Steele came so close to falling that Emerson was certain one of them was going to go, but they held their balance.

"Listen," Kodi yelled from the front. "We can all get out of here alive if we work together. We're all going to up our pace a tiny amount. Keep the same distance from the person in front of you and do what I do."

Kodi sped up and began to make his way slowly, carefully around the rotating track. It took around five minutes for him to traverse the whole distance. He didn't speed up when he got to the platform; he didn't panic. He kept his pace and, finally, stepped carefully off the treadmill and onto the safety of the platform. The track lowered another five feet—they were now around thirty feet in the air.

"No," Asim said from two spaces behind Emerson. She looked back and saw that the tall, skinny boy who had spent the day staring into the fire was shaking his head. "No, no, no."

"Asim, are you okay?" Emerson said through heavy breaths.

He looked at her. His big, sad eyes were full of sorrow. "There's only one way off this island," he said, and without hesitation he stepped off the edge of the platform and fell to his death.

"Oh no! Oh no!" cried Tiger, who was right behind Asim.

The platform lowered another few feet, and up ahead, Gamble stepped off the conveyor belt, followed by Nick.

Emerson was next, but the way Tiger was struggling to breathe concerned her. She slowed down until the gap between her and Tiger was only a few feet or so.

"Hey. We're almost there, Tiger."

"He just . . . he just gave up and died. He just gave up," Tiger was saying to no one in particular.

"Yes, he did," Emerson said. "And that was his choice, but we're not giving up, are we?"

Finally, Tiger looked at Emerson. "No . . . we're not giving up."

"Good. Now come on, let's get off this thing."

Emerson took Tiger's hand and they ran together onto the platform, both of them losing their balance as they made it to safety.

Teller came next. He too collapsed into a heap and lay on the platform sucking in air.

Emerson heard a gasp and a yelp and turned and caught sight of Cobalt Skiba losing his footing and falling off the edge of the descending track. The entire structure was between fifteen and twenty feet high, and as Cobalt hit the ground, Emerson saw his right leg snap at the shin and bend up so that his toes kicked his own kneecap. He screamed then, loud and astounded. The pain must have been tremendous, but the sight of his foot pointing in an impossible direction seemed to be his main area of concern.

Cobalt continued screaming and crying as the remaining contestants made it to the platform, and the treadmill lowered almost all the way to the ground, until there were only two left on the track: Imelda and Never.

"Just get on the platform," Imelda breathed.

"*You* get on the platform," Never replied, her arms pumping as she ran.

The two girls competed, sweating and pushing themselves onward. Gwen Perez was the first to climb down the eight-foot-high structure and run to Cobalt. Others followed.

Emerson watched Never as she began to falter.

"Come on, Never!" she called out, but it was no good. Never had been running for too long, and Imelda was too fit.

Never pushed herself one last time to draw level with the platform and then stepped onto it. Imelda grinned, and stayed on the track for another twenty seconds or so, just to prove that she could.

As soon as the platform met the ground, Emerson stepped off the stage and onto the sand, grateful for the feeling of solid, safe ground beneath her. She closed her eyes and lay down, running her fingers through the sand, but when she opened her eyes and saw the twisted neck and blank eyes of Harlow Wozniack, she scrambled to her feet and stepped away.

Emerson got up and walked over to Cobalt, who was now

moaning in agony and holding his leg so tightly that his fingers had turned white. Gwen was trying to get him to breathe through the pain, but it was as if he couldn't hear her.

The sight of Cobalt's grotesquely twisted leg made Emerson look away. The sound of his raw-throated screams permeated the stillness of the night, and the contestants looked to one another, each of them hoping that someone else would do something to help this boy, but nobody knew how to relieve his pain.

Time passed. The remaining participants sat around Cobalt, who had settled into rapid breathing and the occasional sob.

"Contestants," the Producer's voice said as it echoed out of the hidden speakers. "Please meet me on the beach in one minute."

For once there was a feeling of relief at the sound of the Producer's voice. Surely he couldn't leave Cobalt in this kind of agony. Surely he would do something.

He came strolling along the sand like a dark mirage, all swagger and teeth.

"Contestants," he said. "You have completed game number three. Congratulations on taking another step toward rehabilitation. You learned about Work Ethic today."

"He needs medical attention right now!" Gwen said, looking down at Cobalt, whose head rested in her lap.

"He will not receive it," the Producer replied. "At least, not until the games are concluded."

Emerson felt all her remaining reserves of hope evaporate.

"His leg is broken," Kodi said, stepping close to the Producer with confidence, as if he knew that the poison wouldn't be released. "You have to help him. You can't leave him like this."

"It's contractual, Mr. Finch," the Producer replied. "You of all people should know that. If you want to continue down this line of questioning, I'm happy to do so, but my patience doesn't stretch very far, and I will remind you of the capsule implanted in your wrist."

You of all people . . . Those words struck Emerson as strange.

"It's okay," Cobalt said, his blocked nose finally appearing to have cleared. "It's not so bad, I'll be okay."

Gwen stroked Cobalt's hair and told him to save his energy. The Producer continued speaking.

"It is time now to announce today's winner, who will receive immunity from the public vote, and that winner is the person who was last to step off the track, Imelda Fleet. Congratulations, Ms. Fleet.

"Now," the Producer said. "The first person to stop running, and the loser of today's game, is Tanya Moon. Commiserations, Ms. Moon."

Tanya had been a member of the latecomers, numbers 48, 49, and 50, who had joined the games last. The other latecomers, Sadio Sarr and Goodwin Goodhew, looked at each other with a calm kind of trepidation in their eyes. The three had developed a strong bond since the games had begun, and were rarely apart.

"I don't care," Tanya said. Her short red hair was still matted to her forehead with sweat. "I don't care about any of this!"

"Fine, fine," the Producer said. "That's just fine. Now, follow me, and we'll begin today's video diary."

The Producer beckoned, and then began walking around the circumference of the island, making his way to the living quarters.

"He can't follow you!" Gwen said, and Cobalt tried to sit up, but pain rocked through him and he lay back down.

"Too bad," the Producer said as he walked. "If he's not at the living quarters soon, he'll be relieved of his pain."

Gwen, Tiger, Alasdair, Kodi, and Emerson all helped to lift the boy with the broken leg and carry him as carefully as they could back to the bedrooms. Every step sent a bolt of agony through Cobalt, but they had to keep up. They had to keep going.

They made it back to the other side of the island. More bedrooms had been disassembled and removed from the beach, and the remaining bedrooms had been cleaned.

By who? Emerson wondered.

But she didn't dwell on it. They placed Cobalt carefully on his bed, where he lay sweating and trying not to move.

Emerson looked at the leaderboard; the top five positions had changed, and Imelda was no longer first.

Place	Contestant Name	Contestant #	Follower count
1.	Gwen Perez	7	714,907
2.	Imelda Fleet	33	696,315
3.	Decker Shimada	25	544,835
4.	Delilah Scattergood	21	507,351
5.	Steele Sawyer	18	484,610

Emerson looked over to Imelda, who was staring at her name in second place and clenching her jaw.

At the bottom of the leaderboard, Teller had dropped down; Kodi had stayed at fifteenth place. Emerson had climbed up two places, and now had a significant amount of followers—so many, in fact, that her brand credits would be worth more than double the value of physical cash.

Place	Contestant Name	Contestant #	Follower count
13.	Teller Sanderson	20	82,755
14.	Emerson Ness	16	82,404
15.	Kodiak Finch	1	80,100
16.	Nick Mason	4	76,628
17.	Gamble Delaney	6	75,901

For some reason, Emerson found herself staring at the fish carcass that the latecomers had caught with their plastic spears two days before. It was rotting, and seagulls were circling above it.

"By now, you all know what to do," the Producer said, gesturing toward the bedrooms. "Record your video diaries. Be lively, be eager, be dishonest! Show the people what they want to see. Take them out of their drab lives for a moment and let them live vicariously through people who are better than them! Give one hundred percent!"

This time there was no cheering or clapping from the crowd, not even from Imelda, who couldn't take her eyes off her name in second place.

"Diary recording begins in five minutes. Good luck."

The Producer walked away, and the remaining contestants made their way to their bedrooms.

Emerson sat down on her bed. Never came over and joined her.

"They've really got us trapped, don't they?" Never said.

"What do you mean?"

"I mean, they've thought of everything. We gotta do what they say: If we don't try hard in the games, we face the vote; if we're not popular enough, we face the vote; if we don't stay focused, we die. We gotta earn followers twenty-four hours a day or we lose. They've got us working nonstop, doing things we don't wanna do, changing who we are, for a goal we can never reach. We are trapped."

Emerson nodded once, slowly. "You're right."

"And Cobalt," she said, looking over to the boy who was blowing out rapid breaths. "He can't survive like that. They're gonna let him die . . . die in agony."

"They're monsters," Emerson said.

"They're the elite, you know? The people who set this up. The superrich."

"Of course," Emerson replied. "I mean, they built an entire island, took over an entire cruise ship. They're obviously rich."

"It's more than that, though. It's the show itself. I'm not saying everyone with money is bad, but there's a type of person . . . only people who think of themselves as elite could come up with something like this. They love to see disadvantaged people suffer; it lets them enjoy what they have a little bit more."

"What do you mean?" Emerson asked.

Never kicked at the sand and then looked out to the ocean. "There was this airline a few years back that decided to convert their fleet of turbojets into all luxury-class. Every seat reclined into a bed, everyone got champagne on arrival, the food was beautiful, and every passenger had their every need catered for. It went bust within six months."

"Not enough rich people to fill up the planes?" Emerson asked.

"No, there were plenty of rich people, they just all wanted to fly on the airlines that had first- *and* second-class sections."

"Why?"

"Because there's a certain type of person who can't enjoy nice things unless they know there are people beneath them."

Emerson thought about that for a long time. She didn't want it to be true. She wanted to believe that every person had the capacity for empathy and compassion, but she knew that Never was right.

"Do you think we'd become like them, if we won the games?" Emerson asked finally.

Never thought about it for a while. "I'd like to think we wouldn't, but I've seen good people change. Give a person money and they always want more. Give a person power and they always want more. Give a person influence and they always want more. All these social media companies know that there is nothing more addictive than attention, and they offer it for free to children."

Emerson couldn't help but laugh. "So, you ready to perform for the cameras? Diary starts in one minute."

Never laughed too, and then sighed. "Yep, better get into character, huh?"

She went over to her bedroom and waited.

The screen flickered, and the scoreboard disappeared. The countdown to the recording began.

As the light turned red on the drone that hovered in front of her, Emerson thought about when she had set up her first social media profile, a Content-Plus account. She had been eleven years old, and she had been obsessed with her favorite social media stars: Devon Dislikes the World, Press Paws, Magical Melody, and at least a dozen others. She had dreamed about being just like them, but when she filmed herself on her ancient camera phone, in her broken-down old bedroom, it just wasn't the same.

She had uploaded the videos anyway. Her big idea was to review reviewers. She would watch videos of people reviewing the latest products and movies and toys, and she would review their review. Okay, it wasn't the greatest idea, but she couldn't afford to buy things to review, and she couldn't afford to see movies, so it was her only option. The hate she got for the quality of the footage, the poor sound, the ugliness of her room, her lack of charisma, the fact that she was so plain-looking—it hurt. It hurt a lot. She deleted her account after uploading five videos, but nothing is ever gone from the internet forever, and a group of boys in Stone's Throw High School found her old content and shared it with everyone. She was already the girl who stole money, and now she was the thief who failed to grow an audience, the magpie without a brand.

"I've been thinking a lot recently about how cruel people can be," Emerson started, looking into the lens of the drone. "We turn on each other and hurt each other and ridicule each other. Why? I think there are two reasons: The first is to feel better about ourselves. My friend Never helped me to see that. The second reason is because we're all so scared that *we* will be the focus of the hate that we push it away from ourselves and onto other people. Bullies are the biggest cowards of all. I know that sounds like a cliché, but it's true. Bullies are so scared of being hurt that they build shields of hate and cruelty to stop it from coming back at them. Don't get me wrong, I don't pity bullies. I don't feel bad for them; they can all go to hell as far as I'm concerned. Just because you're a coward doesn't mean you get to ruin people's lives. Anyway, the biggest bullies of all are the people who set up this game show. Forcing kids to entertain you, hurting and killing kids for amusement . . . how weak and pathetic must you be to do something like that? I know this won't affect them in any way, because people who are willing to do something like this must lack any trace of empathy, but I want them all to know that the good, decent people of the world think that you're demons from hell."

Emerson smiled suddenly and brightly at the camera. "Thanks for watching."

After her sarcastic sign-off, the camera drone stopped recording and disappeared.

Emerson watched the others. A camera drone hovered over Cobalt as he squirmed and moaned in pain; Gwen continued to tease her viewers, asking them if they'd like her to take off an article of clothing; Teller did shirtless sit-ups; Imelda emoted and laughed away, but there was less energy from everyone now. The weight of all the death and destruction had finally gotten to be too much.

When the diary recording ended, the leaderboard hadn't changed much at all. Everyone had gained a few thousand more followers, but no one had overtaken anyone else.

"Congratulations on getting into first place," Imelda called over to Gwen.

"Uh, thank you," Gwen replied, pushing her pink hair behind her ears.

"Of course, I could easily get the top spot back if I bribed viewers with promises of showing my naked body too. Pathetic." Gwen lowered her head and bit her lower lip as Imelda continued. "Honestly, what you're doing is basically prostituting yourself. Are you proud?"

Gwen spoke quietly. "What am I supposed to do? The viewers stopped caring about my and Harlow's pranks after the first day. I'm not beautiful. I'm not charismatic. I'm not talented. I'm not the type of person who others gravitate toward, so I guess that means I'm worthless. How is that fair? I'm shy and I don't know how to be funny, so I don't get to have nice things? I don't have any other options, Imelda. Either I take my clothes off or I fall behind. Those are my choices."

Imelda didn't speak for a while. She appeared to steel herself against whatever emotions were trying to break free. "Yeah, well, they'll get bored of you soon."

The Producer walked onto the beach and addressed the contestants.

"Contestants, you have completed your third task, and completed your daily video diaries. The footage is being aired as we speak; soon we will take a snapshot of the leaderboard to find out which of you will be facing Tanya Moon in the viewer vote. Once again, I want to thank you for making this episode the best yet. Well done. Now let's find out who today's winner is. Ten, nine, eight, seven, six, five, four . . ."

No one joined in the Producer's countdown, and yet he was so animated and full of energy that you'd think he was standing on a stage in front of a stadium full of adoring fans.

". . . three, two, one, zero! Congratulations to today's *Kill Factor* leader, Gwen Perez!"

Emerson and a few others clapped to counteract the silence from Imelda and her crew, of which Gwen was clearly no longer a part.

The crackle and pop of the fireworks juxtaposed the look of shame on Gwen's face as the Producer put an arm around her.

"How does it feel to be at the top of the leaderboard with so many fans?" he asked.

"It feels great," Gwen said without any emotion at all.

"I bet it does. Now, Gwen, you were invited onto *The Kill Factor* because of mistakes you made in the past, is that right?"

"That's right," Gwen said, nervously pushing her pink hair behind her ears.

"What were those mistakes, if you don't mind me asking?"

Gwen looked at the Producer and then down at the sand. "I killed a girl."

There was an audible gasp from several people on the beach.

"And how do you feel about that now that you have gone through several steps of rehabilitation?"

Gwen seemed to think about it for a while. "I wish I hadn't killed her. I didn't mean to kill her. I hit her and she fell . . . She bullied me every day, made my life miserable, laughed at me, slapped me, mocked me, turned my friends against me. But she didn't deserve to die. She was a bully, but she didn't deserve to die."

"And do you think the process of *The Kill Factor* has changed you?" the Producer asked.

Gwen raised her eyes and looked at Imelda. "I still hate bullies, but I wouldn't kill anyone."

Imelda seemed to shrink back into the growing darkness.

"Congratulations once again, Gwen Perez," the Producer said, and then turned to face the remaining contestants. "Now, it falls on me to announce the contestant who ended the day with the least number of followers: The contestant who will be joining Ms. Moon in the viewer vote is . . . Gamble Delaney."

The spotlight drones shone their beams on Tanya and Gamble, and Emerson wondered what task the Producer would set up to make the contestants fight for votes. Whatever it was, she was glad she wasn't a part of it, and she was glad that Kodi was safe too.

25
CHAPTER

Emerson lay in her bed, watching the stars burning high above, and thought about how there was no happy ending to all this. She and Kodi would be dead or in prison by the time the games were over. She had come to this island with the sole objective of earning enough followers to get Kester through college, and she had gone and fallen in love. It wasn't fair.

Just an hour earlier, Tanya Moon had been escorted off to the prison. She had stood onstage for three minutes alongside Gamble Delaney as the Producer asked them each to share their most embarrassing moment, in a last-ditch effort for the viewer vote. But Tanya had refused, instead staring defiantly past the cameras that hovered around her while Gamble proceeded to share a memory of his first year of high school, a Halloween party in the woods where the popular crowd had convinced him to wear a bunny costume to match his big teeth. They then abandoned him the woods. It was clear that Gamble had won, and yet the Producer drew it out anyway, finally announcing the outcome.

Emerson felt a kind of sadness creeping over her—no, it

was more than sadness; it was hopelessness, desolation, despondency.

Never was right. They were trapped.

The night drifted by in restless slowness. The only sound other than the steady crash of the waves was the sound of Cobalt crying and moaning at the pain in his leg. The short bursts of sleep that Emerson did manage to get were filled with terrifying dreams that faded away like old photographs burning on a fire, until all she could remember was the sense of helpless dread.

When morning finally broke, Emerson stayed in bed, feeling the horrible heat of the sun baking down on her. In her mind, she listed the dead.

Wolfgang Jorgensen, Carter Boyd, Juliette Star, Zach Dobler, Levi Russo . . .

She thought about their faces as they passed through her mind: alive and vibrant and happy.

. . . Harlow Wozniak, Billie Joe Walker . . .

They had personalities, ambitions; they made mistakes; they loved and hated and . . . and now they were dead.

. . . Cameron Angus, Hugo von Hugo, Vintage Patel . . .

"Hey, Em, you staying in bed all day?" Emerson let the faces of the dead contestants float away, and she turned her eyes to Kodi. Despite the deep chasm of depression that had opened up in her mind, she felt a spark of light at the sound of his voice.

"I was considering it, yeah," she replied.

"I don't blame you," Kodi replied. "I thought about the same thing."

"Oh yeah? What got you out?"

"I don't know, really. Maybe hope got me out. Maybe I still believe there's a way out of all this."

"Hope?" Emerson said, and laughed. "What hope?"

Kodi laughed too. "Yeah, I guess you're right. Hope is like . . . I don't know, hope is like an addiction, don't you think? You'd need a nicotine patch to get off it."

Emerson nodded. The phrasing struck her as strange, though. She had heard the term *nicotine patch* only twice in her life, and both times were in the last week . . . A thought struck her in that moment, and she looked into Kodi's eyes. He replied with a subtle nod. He was trying to tell her something.

"Yeah," Emerson said, trying to maintain a natural facade. "Hope is a tough addiction to shake."

"Definitely," Kodi agreed. "We should have a group meeting of all the addicts on the island. We can meet at three p.m. and say things like, *My name's Kodi, and I'm an addict.*"

Emerson nodded again. "Yeah, count me in."

She felt adrenaline rushing in her bloodstream now. Of course, the Nicotine Patch service that the cruise ship offered. What had Tiger said? Something about how they interfered with electronic signals so people couldn't use them to send out live broadcasts. If they could get some of those Nicotine Patch drones onto the beach, they would interfere with the actual camera drones and maybe . . . maybe they could escape? Emerson didn't know what

Kodi's final plan was. The one thing she knew was that hope really *had* come back.

× ✖ ×

Time slipped by fast and slow.

Emerson watched Kodi go from contestant to contestant, trying to surreptitiously get across his message of sabotage, and she readied herself.

When the time finally came, and the light on the island was beginning to turn golden, six contestants gathered at the shore: Kodi, Emerson, Never, Tiger, Alasdair, and Nick.

"Time travel is real, you know?" Nick said, grinning madly at the group. "Oh yes. It was invented more than a hundred years ago, but the world government doesn't want you to know about it."

There was an uncomfortable ripple among the other five.

"Right, okay," Kodi said, finally, and then turned to the group. "I'm going for a swim," he said. "I miss that old cruise ship. I think I want to get close enough to get a good look."

And with that, he stripped down to his underwear and ran into the undulating waves.

Without hesitation, the others followed his lead while Never stayed behind on lookout.

The water was cold, seemingly too cold for the hot summer's day, but the temperature change was welcome on this hot afternoon.

As she swam, Emerson looked out into the water in front of her, watching for killer jellyfish or whatever else might be lurking in the blue waves.

They swam for five full minutes before catching up with Kodi, who had stopped and was treading water. The *Calypso* sat shimmering fifty yards away. All around them, camera drones buzzed and hummed.

Kodi looked around at those who had joined him. He shrugged, and then yelled out as loud as he could. "*Calypso!* Nicotine Patch!"

Emerson joined in, screaming the words as loud as she could. And then all of them were yelling out for the cruise ship's artificial intelligence to hear them and give them what they were asking for.

Finally, after thirty seconds of shouting, they all fell silent, and waited.

Nothing happened.

The buzz of the camera drones remained constant and maddening; the roar of the rolling ocean boomed quietly around them.

"Shit," Alasdair whispered.

"Wait," Tiger said. "What's that?" She lifted a shimmering finger out of the water and pointed to a speck in the sky that grew as it approached.

And then there were more of them. The Nicotine Patch drones that had been designed to appease the addiction of attention were flying toward them. And when the first one got within ten yards of Kodi, all the camera drones that surrounded him dropped away, falling into the ocean.

"It's working!" he yelled.

Emerson watched as one of the drones flew high up into the sky and a strange thing happened. A seagull that was flying above the drones disappeared for a moment and then came back as the drone went by. Emerson blinked and shook her head. Salt water must've gotten in her eyes.

The other Nicotine Patch drones arrived, and for the first time since waking up in a coffin on that godforsaken artificial island, they weren't being filmed. They whooped and celebrated and hugged one another. Kodi swam over to Emerson and kissed her, his fingers running through the wet, matted hair at the back of her head.

"We have to go," he said, looking into Emerson's eyes, and then—forcing himself to break away from Emerson—he spoke to the group. "We have to get back to the island as fast as we can. If these things are powerful enough to shut off all the other camera drones, there might be a chance."

They began to swim as fast as they could, kicking their legs and carving out paths in the water with their arms.

"What are you going to do once the cameras are out?" Emerson asked, drawing alongside Kodi.

"I'm going into that hatch beneath the heart-tree, and I'm going to kill anyone I find."

Emerson felt her heart thunder in her chest. "If you kill them, you'll be exactly what they said you are: a criminal."

"I didn't come to this island as a murderer, Emerson, but their idea of rehabilitation might have turned me into one."

"Think about this, Kodi. There's got to be another way."

"There isn't. If I take them out, the rest of you can get out of here."

And with that, he sped up, pulling out in front of the others and making it to the beach first.

Emerson watched as Kodi picked up the sharpened stick that the latecomers had made to spear fish, and stormed toward the heart-tree.

As Emerson, Alasdair, Tiger, and Nick made it to the beach, all the camera drones dropped out of the sky.

"Hey! What's going on?" Imelda asked, and then pointed to Kodi. "Where's he going? What is this?"

Emerson ran after Kodi and grabbed his hand. "Wait! Just listen."

"We're not going to get another chance, Em! This is it!"

"What are you doing?" Imelda screamed. "You can't do this! You can't ruin this for me!"

Emerson and Kodi ignored her. "Try to find another way, please," she said, and for a moment, there was a look of hesitation in Kodi's eyes.

"Stop them! You have to stop them!" Imelda cried. And before anyone could react, Teller slammed into Kodi, throwing him to the ground so violently that the spear went flying from his hand and landed in the sand twenty feet away.

"No!" Emerson cried, and Teller began to hit Kodi over and over again.

She tried to grab Teller and drag him away, but he was too big, too strong.

"Emerson, go!" Kodi yelled as a fist slammed into the side of his head. "This is our only chance!"

Emerson tried again to pull Teller away, but he didn't budge. She reared back and kicked him in the side, but he didn't flinch; he just kept on hitting Kodi, who had managed to free one arm and was trying to block the punches.

"Now!" Kodi screamed.

And Emerson ran. She tried not to think, tried not to wonder what happened next. She grabbed the spear from the sand, and ran to the hatch beneath the heart-tree.

26
CHAPTER

Emerson ran so fast that she was ahead of the Nicotine Patch drone when she made it to the hatch.

She pulled on the hidden handle. It didn't budge at all.

Locked, she thought. *It was all for nothing.*

But as the Nicotine Patch drone caught up with her, it short-circuited whatever electronic mechanism was keeping the hatch shut, and it flew open so suddenly that Emerson fell back into the plastic roots and fake fallen leaves.

She scrambled to her feet, grabbed the spear, and looked down at the steps that descended into a bright white tunnel below.

She froze in fear for a moment, wondering what fate awaited her at the foot of those stairs. "Go," she whispered to herself, and then she was running.

The entire tunnel was made of thick white plastic. The sound of her footsteps fell flat in the seemingly endless tunnel at the foot of the stairs. Round light fixtures were molded into the walls, giving off bright, lifeless light that made the tunnel look infinite.

As she ran, her mind went out to Kodi, and she hoped he

would be okay, but she reminded herself of his words: *This is our only chance.* And she ran faster.

Finally, she reached another set of stairs. This one was identical to the one she had climbed down at the start of the tunnel, only it went up to the surface instead of down.

She climbed the stairs, stumbling in her adrenaline-fueled efforts. When she got to the top, a second locked hatch clicked to open as her Nicotine Patch drone came near.

Emerson threw open the small door and stepped out into a dark room filled with blank TV monitors and a desk with sliders, buttons, and dials. There was no light in the room, just the remaining sunlight seeping through the windows.

"What is this place?" she wondered out loud, and almost at the same time the words came out of her mouth, she realized that she knew exactly what this place was: It was an editing room, the place where all the footage from the games was mixed and amended until it was ready for TV.

For a minute, all Emerson's focus was taken up by the array of screens and dials, but as she looked up and out of one of the narrow windows, she saw exactly where she was on the island: the very center. And through the windows separating the room from the world outside were thousands and thousands of white walls that looked to be made out of the same plastic that had made up the tunnel that had led her here.

"A maze," she said, staring at the parallel walls that twisted and turned in all directions, splitting into three lanes, then turning in on themselves over and over. She turned slowly around, looking at corridor after corridor of paths that turned to dead ends or junctions with multiple options.

This must be part of another game, she thought, and as her eyes traced the seemingly endless pattern of white walls, she saw something else that caused her to freeze in place.

As she looked up in the direction of where the bedrooms on the beach would be, she saw, towering up into the sky, the prison, only it wasn't a prison at all. It was a flat wooden wall held up by steel poles that had been driven into the fake ground. It was no more than a stage set, or a vintage Hollywood movie backdrop.

"What the hell?" Emerson muttered to herself.

Her attention was drawn away from the prison and the maze when the sound of the hatch lock sliding back into place filled the room.

Emerson ran to the hatch and tried pulling it toward herself. It was locked fast; the Nicotine Drone that was hovering over her left shoulder was apparently no longer doing its job.

"No!" Emerson whispered as she pulled at the hatch, willing it to open. "No! No! No!"

Suddenly, the dim room grew a little brighter, then brighter still. Emerson turned to see the blank monitors switching on, one by one, and the control panel was lighting up in reds and greens. The camera drones of the beach had come back online. She looked to one of the monitors and she could see the Producer walking along the sand with a look on his face that somehow conveyed both deep rage and joyful avarice.

The Nicotine Patch drone suddenly fell out of the air,

catching itself just before it hit the ground. It made grinding crunching noises, and then fell completely.

"Ladies and gentlemen," the Producer said, his voice coming through the speakers in the control room, sounding tiny and shrill. "Somebody is missing. That person has two minutes to get back to this beach, or their fellow contestants start to die. Your time starts now."

The lock on the hatch clicked open.

"No!" Emerson cried out. And then she was running.

She hauled open the hatch and ran down the plastic stairs as fast as she could. The dull, empty sound of her footfalls mocked her as she pushed herself onward. The corridor had grown longer since the first time she had run along it. She was certain of that. She didn't care that it was impossible, she *knew* it to be true. The staircase at the far end never seemed to get closer.

Finally, she made it to the staircase and sprinted up, her legs burning, her lungs bursting. She crawled out beneath the heart-tree and ran to the beach, where the enormous screen showed a clock at zero seconds.

"Too bad, Ms. Ness, you didn't quite make it in time," the Producer said, and there was no smile on his face now.

"I ran as fast as I could," Emerson breathed. "Please . . . please don't."

"Rules are rules," the Producer said. "A contestant will now be chosen at random to die."

The screen flashed, and photographs of all the remaining contestants appeared on the screen. Each of the photographs began lighting up one at a time in rapid succession until the screen looked almost like a strobe light, and as the time went on, the light began to slow down.

Emerson's own face was lit up for half a second, followed by Nick's, then Imelda's. The light slowed down further and Emerson knew what she was looking at: Whoever's face was illuminated when the ten seconds ended would be the contestant chosen to die.

"Please," Emerson begged. "Please. I'm sorry. I'm so sorry. It was my plan, it was all me, none of these people knew anything about it. Punish me, not them."

"Ms. Ness," the Producer replied calmly, "I *am* punishing you."

The faces were lighting up so slowly now that Emerson knew the ten seconds were very nearly over.

Alasdair's face, Teller's face, Never, Delilah . . . and finally it stopped.

Emerson felt her heart grow cold as Tiger's face remained lit up on the screen.

27
CHAPTER

That second seemed to last a lifetime, and then the light ticked over for the last time and landed on Delilah Scattergood.

"The decision is made," the Producer said.

Emerson looked over to Delilah, who stood grinning in the sand.

"I'm so sorry," Emerson said. "I'm so so sorry."

"It's been . . . fun," Delilah said, and the smile on her otherwise vacant face remained, although her eyes told a story of agony as the poison was released.

The morbid girl with the black eye makeup fell to her knees, and then rocked backward into an uncomfortable, twisted position. She let out one final breath, and seemed to deflate into the sand. She was dead.

Emerson's hand went to her mouth as her eyes filled with tears.

Your fault, she thought. *This is your fault. That girl is dead because of you.*

"No more mutinies," the Producer said. "No more schemes. The games will continue, but one more act of rebellion and you all die. You think I won't do it? If an example needs to be made for the good of season two, then I will make that example out of each and every one of you."

Emerson's internal pain grew as she chastised herself for feeling relief that it wasn't Tiger, Never, or Kodi who had died. This was not a time to feel anything other than guilt.

The Producer glared at them, seeming to lock eyes with everyone on the beach. There was no sound other than the rasping breathing of Cobalt, who lay sweating in his bed.

"I will return this evening," the Producer said. "To continue your rehabilitation."

He walked away. Emerson fell to her knees in the sand and stopped trying to hold back the emotion that had built up inside her.

"How dare you?" Imelda said, her voice filled with rage. "How dare you try to sabotage this show without even asking the rest of us?"

"Not now, Imelda," Kodi said, pushing past the Topsider and kneeling down beside Emerson.

"Yes, now!" Imelda cried. "Any one of us could have been killed! We should be counting ourselves lucky that it was just that freak Delilah!"

"Are you okay?" Kodi asked, and Emerson looked into his eyes, noticing for the first time the bruises and cuts that had been inflicted by Teller's blows.

"No," Emerson whispered in reply.

"Are you listening?" Imelda continued, stepping closer to the pair. "Your stupid actions could have ruined this opportunity for me, and it's your fault that Delilah is dead!"

"I know that!" Emerson screamed. "Do you think I don't know that? I'm sorry, all right? We were trying to save everyone and we . . . we . . . I'm sorry!"

Imelda took a step back, composed herself, and shook her head. "Whatever. You're losers anyway."

She walked away, followed by her cronies, and Kodi put an arm around Emerson.

"It's not your fault, Emerson. The whole thing was my idea."

But Emerson could do nothing but let the guilt bear down on her.

"Hey," a voice said, and Emerson looked up from the sand to see Gwen Perez, the pink-haired leader of the games, standing over them. "I just wanted to say . . . thank you for trying, you know? Someone had to do something. You saw an opportunity and you tried. Thank you."

Kodi nodded, and Gwen walked away.

Emerson found herself wondering if Gwen's gratitude was merely a facade for the cameras: She was Imelda's greatest competition; she had to take a contrary stance. Emerson shook her head; she didn't want to think like this anymore. Being surrounded by cameras all the time was driving her crazy. She got up and went back to her bed, where she lay down and thought about the second life she had played a part in snuffing out.

As time ticked by and Emerson lay in abject despair, caught

between the pain and guilt, she saw that her follower numbers were going up faster than ever.

Why are they so cruel? she wondered, thinking back to when Alasdair had asked the viewers to unfollow him. *Why do they enjoy my pain?*

× ✖ ×

At around five in the evening, a few people had gathered around Cobalt's bed. He had become disoriented and confused, but it seemed to pass after an hour or so.

Finally, the sun began to fall, and with it, the next game.

"Contestants of *The Kill Factor*, game number four is about to begin. Please make your way to the other side of the island," the Producer's voice commanded from the speakers.

Emerson got out of bed and watched as five contestants, including Kodi, Tiger, and Never, lifted a screaming Cobalt out of his bed and carried him as the island began to turn.

The red sun shone eerily on the Producer as he awaited the contestants.

Cobalt was placed carefully on the sand, where he writhed in pain, sweat drenching his clothes.

This time, there were fifteen tiny huts built on the sand, each one emblazoned with the numbers of the remaining contestants in little brass numerals.

"Contestants," the Producer said. "On this day, you learn about Discipline. The rules are very simple. The first person to fall asleep faces the viewer vote. There are fifteen of you remaining. For the person with the least amount of followers, Gamble Delaney, the game begins in thirty minutes; for the person in second-to-last place on the leaderboard, Nick Mason, the game begins in one hour; for third-to-last place, Tiger Quinn, the game begins in one and a half hours, and so on and so on until we reach the contestant in first place, Gwen Perez, who will start the game in seven and a half hours. I advise you to use your time wisely and try to rest. It's going to be a long, long time until you can sleep again. Inside each of the huts behind me is a room with a bed; the hut is completely soundproof and is available to you until the game begins. Good luck—the game starts for Mr. Delaney in half an hour."

Emerson shook her head and looked down at the sand.

"You okay?" Kodi asked.

"I haven't slept properly in days," she answered. "And to be honest, I don't feel like I deserve to stay in this competition anyway."

"Listen to me, Em," Kodi said, taking her hands. "This is not real life. This is not who you are. This whole island is designed to twist reality and change you. The fact that you still feel guilt is a good thing! It shows that you are still you. People have died, more people are going to die, and your only job is to stay alive and stay in the game. We tried to escape and it didn't work. Someone died, and it was *my* fault, not yours! The whole thing was my idea, never forget that. You can mourn the death of Delilah when you're home with your brother with more brand-credit value than you could ever spend, but until then, stay in the game. Okay?"

Emerson sniffed away the tears that threatened to infiltrate her eyes, and nodded her head. "Yeah."

"Good! Now get as much sleep as you can before this starts. It's going to be a difficult few days."

"You think it'll last that long?" Emerson asked.

Kodi nodded. "It could be three, four days before the first person goes to sleep."

Emerson nodded once again. Most of the contestants had gone into their temporary bedrooms now.

Never, Tiger, Kodi, and Emerson stayed behind to help carry Cobalt to his hut. The boy was hot with fever and pain, and he screamed incoherently as they got him into the comfortable bed inside.

After the door had slid automatically shut behind him, the four contestants looked at one another with grief in their eyes.

"He's not going to make it, is he?" Tiger asked, adjusting her thick glasses.

"I don't think so," Emerson said.

Without saying anything, Never turned and walked to her hut. The door opened, she stepped inside, and it closed behind her. Tiger went to her hut next.

"Get some rest," Kodi said.

Emerson was the last contestant on the beach.

She looked around, watched the sun become bisected by the horizon, felt the darkness begin to surround her, and then went to her hut.

As the door slid shut behind her, absolute silence replaced the whooshing of the waves, and perfect darkness replaced the graying air of twilight.

She lay down, and for the first time in days, her mind went completely blank, and she slept.

× ✱ ×

There were no dreams.

She was awoken by an alarm ringing inside her hut. For one second she was certain she was trapped inside a coffin, but she quickly remembered where she was.

She sat up, threw the blanket off her, and put her hand against the door of her hut. She hesitated. What would she find out there? The games were never fair, never honest, always lethal.

She took a breath, opened the door, and saw that there were five contestants on the beach, sitting around, talking. Nothing unusual, nothing extreme.

"Hey, Emerson," Tiger said, and smiled.

Emerson smiled back. "Hey, Tiger." She walked over to the group: Tiger, Nick, Gamble, Kodi, and Sadio.

"How was your sleep?" Gamble asked.

"Pretty good, surprisingly," Emerson said.

"Lucky for some," Gamble said, and smiled brightly, showing his big teeth.

"Yeah, sorry," Emerson said. "It's going to be pretty tough for you."

"I don't know," he replied. "I was thinking—what if I just go to sleep? What's the worst they can do, put me in the viewer vote?

249

I've already done that twice, and I'm bottom of the leaderboard anyway."

Emerson thought about it and couldn't see a flaw in the plan. "It makes sense," she agreed.

"I'm going to wait until everyone is here and tell them my plan; if they agree, I'll just go to sleep, and the game will be over."

"It won't be over," Sadio said, talking to someone other than Tanya and Goodwin for the first time since he had joined the ship late with the other two. He had become even more withdrawn and reclusive since Tanya had been voted off.

"No?" Gamble asked.

"No. People will still want to win. People will want immunity from the vote. People will want more camera time, more followers."

"Let them," Tiger said. "If they're that desperate, they'll never sleep again."

This made Gamble and Emerson laugh, but the others fell silent and went back to staring at the sea.

Half an hour later Goodwin Goodhew came out of his hut, rubbing the sleep out of his eyes. He joined Sadio and immediately they sat away from the rest of the contestants, the remaining latecomers together again.

In the next two hours, Teller, Alasdair, and Cobalt joined the woken contestants. Cobalt had to be carried out onto the sand, and it worried everyone that he didn't scream when he was placed down.

By the time Never came out of her hut, it was around four

a.m. and the darkness of the night was starting to clear away.

"I was expecting carnage when I opened that door," Never said, joining Alasdair, Tiger, and Emerson.

"Me too," Tiger agreed, already looking a bit tired after staying up a full night.

"Yeah, me too," Emerson said.

"Don't get too comfortable," Kodi added. "There's a long road ahead of us."

"Gamble has a plan," Tiger said, looking at Never and then over to Gamble, who was lying on his back looking up at the cloudy sky. "He's just going to go to sleep once everyone is up. He says that he's in last place anyway, so he might as well sleep because he's going to be facing the vote either way."

"Bad idea," Alasdair muttered.

"Why?" Tiger asked. "It means we can all just go to sleep, doesn't it?"

"I don't mean that his plan is necessarily bad; I mean saying it out loud while being recorded by camera drones was a bad idea."

"Why?" Emerson asked, but she thought she already knew.

"Because they won't like being outsmarted. They'll react. You'll see."

By the time Gwen Perez was woken up and came out of her hut, it was 6:30 a.m., and all the contestants had fallen into their usual groups—all except Teller, who was alone now that Harlow was gone. He sat near the shore, inspecting the cuts on his knuckles where he had hit Kodi, occasionally laughing bitterly to himself.

Gamble explained his idea and got some pushback from the contestants at the lower end of the leaderboard, but ultimately, everyone agreed that it was a good plan. He tried to go back into his hut to sleep, but the door was locked.

"No problem," he said. "I'll just lie down in the shade."

About an hour had passed since Gamble had gone to lie down when Alasdair's prediction came true and the Producer's voice came over the speakers.

"Contestants. There has been a slight change to the rules of the Discipline game. The first three contestants to fall asleep will have their poison capsules activated. The fourth contestant to fall asleep will face the viewer vote. Good luck."

The beach fell silent; heads dropped. Gamble came walking out of the trees shaking his head.

"This is your fault!" Steele growled at him, taking his sunglasses off for the first time. "Because of you and your stupid plan, three of us are going to die!"

"I didn't know!" Gamble said, holding up both hands.

"You should have figured it out!" Decker added, stepping beside Steele, forming a barrier between Gamble and the rest of the contestants.

"I thought I was helping!" Gamble said.

"What if I knock you out?" Steele asked, his huge arm muscles twitching in the morning sunlight. "Would that count as you sleeping?"

"That would . . . that would be murder," Gamble said, taking a step back.

"It wasn't me that put the poison in your body," Steele said, thinking out loud. "I had nothing to do with that." He took a step closer to Gamble.

"Stop it," Emerson said, getting to her feet and walking over to Gamble. "He was trying to help."

"Get out of the way, 16," Imelda called from a few yards away. "It's got nothing to do with you."

"You really want to be responsible for his death?" Emerson asked, ignoring Imelda.

Steele nodded slowly, not taking his eyes off Gamble. "I really do."

"Fine," Emerson said, taking a step away. "Go for it. But if Kodi's punishment for pushing Imelda off the diving board was a jump that almost killed him, I imagine the punishment for murdering a contestant will be a dose of your own poison."

Steele took another step toward Gamble, seemed to consider Emerson's premise, then turned away from Gamble.

"He's going to die anyway. He got no sleep before the game began."

"We'll see," Gamble said, and without warning, Steele spun around and slapped him so hard that Gamble was knocked off his feet.

"Yeah, we *will* see!" Steele said, standing over Gamble, who was raising a shaking hand to his red cheek.

The Discipline game had begun.

28
CHAPTER

During the first day, no one struggled with tiredness. Not even Gamble, Nick, or Tiger, who had been the first three contestants out. It wasn't until twilight that things started to get difficult.

The contestants had spent the day in their normal way, albeit with less energy wasted on things like workout routines and long runs on the beach. Imelda decided to talk her viewers through her daily routine, including all the products she used. Emerson noticed that Steele was now spending more time with Gwen, who was teaching him how to do handstands. Alasdair had gained an audience, and was running a class on sand, talking about how mineral particles in water with high calcium carbonate concentration create a special kind of sand grain called an oolite.

The contestants at the bottom half of the leaderboard took it in turns to tend to Cobalt Skiba, who lay in the sand with his eyes closed, muttering to himself in tongues. It was Emerson's turn now. She held his hot and sweating hand as his head turned slowly from side to side.

"Oh lordy, Emerson. I don't think I'm going to last much longer," he said in a moment of clarity.

"You're going to be fine, Cobalt," Emerson told him. "As soon as the games are over, we're going to get you to a doctor."

He smiled. "No . . . I don't think that's what's going to happen."

Emerson didn't know how to reply.

When evening came and the light began to dim, all the contestants could suddenly see the long night ahead, as though it were a tunnel stretching out in front of them in a seemingly endless conduit of darkness and exhaustion.

Never was sitting with Cobalt when he slipped into unconsciousness.

"No!" Never screamed, rocking his shoulders, trying to rouse him. "No! Wake up! Cobalt! No!"

"The first contestant to fall asleep," the Producer's voice came thundering out of the speakers, "is Cobalt Skiba."

"Wait!" Never screamed.

"It's okay," Cobalt managed to whisper. "I'm going to go hang out with Llanzo." And then his body fell limp in her arms. The poison had been released. He was the first to go, and—oh God—it was relief. The boy had been in agony since he had fallen from the podium nearly two days before. The pain and infection had led him into delirium, and if not for the poison, his death would have dragged on for days.

Emerson had liked Cobalt. He had made friends easily, had been kind and loyal.

"He's not in pain anymore," Tiger said, putting a hand on Never's hitching shoulder.

× ✖ ×

The second night of the Discipline game moved around them. The sticky heat gave way to thick air and the smell of ozone, and when the storm came, Gamble, Nick, and Tiger danced around and cheered. No one could sleep in this weather. Lightning flickered, turning the island into an overexposed photograph for half a second. Emerson watched the *Calypso* rocking on the enraged waves.

"It's not right," a voice said over Emerson's shoulder. It was Alasdair.

"What isn't right?" she asked.

He looked up at the clouds and the flickering lightning. He held a hand out and felt the rain splashing into his palm. "All of this. It's all wrong."

Emerson didn't want to burn the energy it would take to look up and observe what he might have been talking about. After three hours, the storm passed, and the contestants were left in the darkness. They were cold and wet. Morning seemed like forever away.

The next four hours would have been the longest of Emerson's life, had it not been for Tiger and Never, who sat with her beneath the heart-tree, telling each other stories from their childhoods. She had been avoiding Kodi. There was something about the way his presence made her pulse race just a bit more, made her consider her words just a little more carefully. She knew that being near him would take more energy out of her. And even though her biggest concern should have been the poison in her arm, she found herself hoping he felt the same way.

When dawn broke and the first rays of sunlight spilled across the beach, the contestants began to move, to stand up and walk around, to stretch out their limbs and come back to life. It was like watching bears come out of hibernation.

Emerson felt it too. The sun gave her life; it cast off the shroud of night and warmed her cold skin. She, Tiger, and Never walked to the beach, where breakfast had been served. Emerson didn't feel like eating, but Never told her she had to. She would need all the energy she could get to stay awake another day.

The drones cleared away the food, and the day unfolded.

Imelda ramped up her efforts to regain the top spot, spending hours doing a Q and A where she imagined what kind of questions her viewers might ask. There was no leaderboard on this side of the island, so no one knew if they were in the same spot they had been two days before.

Alasdair was using a plastic stick in the wet sand to draw pictures of the solar system and the moon's revolutions around the earth. He had no audience this time, but he was just as engrossed in his work.

Nick Mason was talking avidly about a secret world government that controlled everything and had planned out the future of humankind, and how time travel had been invented as far back as 1974.

Gwen Perez was sunbathing. Decker Shimada was swimming in the shallow water. The remaining latecomers, Sadio and Goodwin, were sitting cross-legged, facing each other and holding hands. They were talking quietly. Gamble sat near the shore. Kodi threw stones into the ocean.

The day dragged on. Emerson feared the setting of the sun. She knew that the third night would be much more difficult than the second, and for people like Tiger and Gamble and Nick, who had had no extra sleep before the game began, it would be hell.

× ✖ ×

The second person to fall asleep was Steele Sawyer.

He had been granted six additional hours of sleep before the game began, but it was a momentary lapse in concentration that led to his death.

At some point, just before full dark, he had sat down and leaned back against a tree. Emerson had been watching him, so had Gamble. His head rocked forward onto his chest and he woke suddenly, wide-eyed and scared. For a second, Emerson thought he had gotten away with it, but the Producer's voice broke the silence of the night.

"The second person to fall asleep is Steele Sawyer."

"I didn't!" Steele screamed, getting to his feet. "I didn't! I didn't fall asleep! I didn't!"

"Steele," Gamble called, and Steele turned to look at Gamble.

Emerson waited for Gamble's moment of bitter victory.

"I'm sorry, man," Gamble said finally.

It seemed like all the muscles in Steele's body tensed, and he fell stiffly onto his front, breaking his sunglasses on an outcrop of rock. He died ten seconds later. No one said a word.

29
CHAPTER

The third night was torture. There was no other word for it.

At some point, when the moon was at its highest peak, Emerson felt her eyes trying to close. She walked into the cold sea with no thoughts about jellyfish or anything else that might be lurking in the waves. She had to wake herself up.

Her black jeans and dark blue T-shirt soaked through and weighed her down, and she was too tired to swim. If she had gone deeper into the waves she may have been in real danger of drowning, but she walked out of the water five minutes later and collapsed onto the sand next to Tiger, who was sitting with her knees drawn up to her chest.

"I don't know how much longer I can do this," Tiger said. There was no panic in her voice, just a vague curiosity. "I think I'm just going to drift off to sleep."

"No," Emerson choked out from her prone position on the sand. She managed to pull herself to standing. "No, Tiger! Stay awake! Come with me."

Emerson grabbed her by the hand and made her walk circles around the beach.

All around them madness was setting in.

Nick Mason was rambling about time portals and how the government was lying to them. He told a stunned Tiger that he was setting up an experiment to expose the lies. Sadio and Goodwin were sitting face-to-face, chanting the words to some ancient nonsense poem. Never was lying on her side in the surf, slapping herself in the face every five seconds or so. Gwen had been running on the spot for so long that she had dug a two-foot-deep hole beneath her feet. Imelda had found a small, thin piece of flint rock and was shoving it beneath her fingernails to keep herself awake.

It felt like a thousand years later when the sun came up.

The game continued. Nobody was going to fall asleep. Nobody wanted to die.

The heat of the sun tried to convince them all to close their eyes and drift away. It would be so easy. So beautifully easy.

At some point in that day of irritation, paranoia, and emotional chaos, someone started to scream.

Emerson's first thought was *oh shut up!* And when she looked around she saw Imelda lying on her back, screaming up at the sky over and over again. Her face had turned red with effort, and her hands were balled into fists that slammed down against the sand.

No one paid much attention. And after a few minutes the screaming ended.

Teller spent three hours using a heavy rock to chop away at the base of a plastic tree. Why he was wasting all that energy, Emerson didn't know. She watched him for a while with a vague and unfocused interest, and then went back to staring at the waves.

The *Calypso* caught fire in the early evening. Emerson watched the flames engulf the enormous cruise ship, but when she stood up to get a better look, she realized it was a hallucination.

Emerson thought that Gwen and Imelda were both crying as the sun went down, but she wasn't sure what was real and what was in her mind anymore.

The two remaining latecomers were walking around the beach, picking up rocks and putting them in their pockets.

"What are they doing?" Alasdair asked.

"Huh?" Emerson replied.

"The, uh . . . them . . . 48 and 50. They're doing something."

"They're collecting rocks," Emerson replied.

There was a long pause before Alasdair replied. "Who are collecting rocks?"

"The people . . . the . . . I don't know," Emerson replied, forgetting what they had been talking about.

The latecomers were speaking. They were making some sort of announcement. Emerson couldn't pay attention to the words coming out of Goodwin's mouth. Something about freedom. Something about honor.

The Producer announced that the third contestant to fall asleep had been Sadio Sarr.

Emerson blinked, looked over to where the latecomers had been standing, and saw that Sadio was gone, and Goodwin was walking into the ocean.

"What . . . what's happening?" she said.

Goodwin's head submerged below the waves, and he didn't reappear.

"No!" Emerson screamed, suddenly realizing what was going on. She tried to run over to where Goodwin had gone under, but she stumbled and fell. By the time she got back to her feet, there was no sign of the latecomers.

"Is the game over?" Gamble asked, his eyes half-open as he scanned the beach.

"Next person to fall asleep faces the vote," Alasdair replied. "Last person to fall asleep gets immunity."

"Oh," Gamble said. "Good." And he lay down on the sand and fell asleep instantly.

The remaining contestants looked around at each other. Tiger shrugged and lay down.

"Who's missing?" Teller asked, looking around the beach.

Emerson instinctively looked around for Kodi. His blue-gray eyes landed on hers, and Emerson realized he'd been looking for her too.

"I'm going to prove it right now!" Nick Mason suddenly shouted. Everyone who was still awake turned to see him at the very top of the heart-tree. "Morally they cannot let me die!"

"What are you talking about?" Gwen called up to him.

"The time travelers!" Nick screamed "I know they exist! And because I know they exist, it is their moral obligation to save me."

"Get down from there," Alasdair called.

"They won't let me die," Nick said. "They won't let me die! They'll come back through time and stop me. They have to! And once I prove that the time travelers are real, you'll all know the truth! The moon is backward and the stars don't make sense! We're living under a dome! The world government is behind all of it!"

"Nick, wait," Emerson said, but it was too late. He jumped.

His neck snapped. It sounded like a wet branch breaking under the weight of snow.

Gwen became sick.

Teller went to sleep. So did Imelda and, a minute later, so did Gwen.

Five minutes later, and everyone was asleep on the sand.

Soon after, three beeps blasted out of the speakers, startling them all awake. The Producer asked them to meet him on the beach in one minute.

They all fell asleep again in the minute it took the Producer to arrive, and were all woken by a blaring alarm that screeched out into the air.

"Contestants," the Producer said, clapping his hands together. "You have completed game number four. Over the last seventy-six hours you learned about discipline and took another step toward rehabilitation."

They all stood around, swaying on their feet, barely able to keep their eyes open.

"The last person to fall asleep, and the person who will receive immunity from today's viewer vote, is Emerson Ness. Congratulations, Emerson."

Emerson turned her head slowly to face the Producer. She barely understood what he had said.

"Now," the Producer said. "The loser of today's game is the person who fell asleep first. That person was Gamble Delaney. If you could all follow me, we'll begin today's video diary."

The Producer walked, and somehow, the remaining ten contestants followed.

When the other side of the beach finally came into view, Emerson realized she had been walking while fully asleep for most of the journey. When she realized where she was, she looked at the leaderboard and saw that most of the names had been grayed out. She looked at the names of the contestants who remained.

Place	Contestant Name	Contestant #	Follower count
1.	Gwen Perez	7	1,358,215
2.	Imelda Fleet	33	1,277,198
3.	Decker Shimada	25	1,004,019
4.	Never-Again Jones	47	833,482
5.	Teller Sanderson	20	799,951
6.	Alasdair George William Tremblay-Birchall	42	744,773
7.	Emerson Ness	16	611,508
8.	Kodiak Finch	1	593,307

9.	Tiger Quinn	11	591,406
10.	Gamble Delaney	6	509,111

Emerson stopped walking and stared at the number beside her name: 611,508. The number changed and four hundred new followers were added to her total. She wondered if she was dreaming, and bit her tongue in order to wake herself up, but it was real.

The way the brand-credit system worked was simple. Each week you were given one hundred brand credits: ninety to spend and ten to save (any more than ten left over at the end of the week was removed from your account and given back to the government). Each digital credit was time-stamped and linked to your follower amount at the time, so right now, Emerson would have one hundred brand credits in her account worth the equivalent of $1,500. If her dad was smart, he'd have spent ninety of them on Kester's education.

$1,500 a week was good, but she'd need more to ensure that Kester got into college. Her popularity would drop when the show was over, so she would need to ensure that her time-stamped credits at this time were worth as much as possible. Her dad was legally allowed to spend ninety of her credits a week until she turned eighteen, but he couldn't touch her savings. The Producer had added a clause into her contract stating that all her social media accounts and credit accounts would be transferred to Kester as soon as the games were over. A feeling of warmth came over her. She was close to achieving her goal. The whole reason she had agreed to this was to help Kester.

"Oh no," Tiger said, her voice lackluster and hollow.

Emerson looked at Tiger's name in second-to-last place, and realized that—unless something changed during the video diary—it would be her facing the audience vote because Gamble was at the bottom of the list, but he had lost the game. "You're going to be fine," Emerson said, taking Tiger's hand in hers.

"I don't know if that's true," Tiger said, her voice shaking now. "I don't want to go to jail and be alone forever. I want to play Catan with my friends. I even want to spend time with my sisters . . . Emerson, I'm scared."

"You know the routine," the Producer said. "Mr. Delaney is once again in the viewer vote after losing the Discipline game. Let's find out who he will be facing. Diary recording begins in ten minutes."

"Oh no. Oh no," Tiger muttered.

"Hey," Kodi said, crouching down in front of the little Topsider. "Be brave, okay? Be yourself. You're a good person and people will follow you."

Tiger nodded and wiped the tears out of her eyes. She went to her bedroom to prepare.

"Do you think she's going to survive the vote?" Emerson asked.

"I don't know," Kodi admitted. "Gamble has survived twice already."

"She'll survive," Alasdair said, stepping alongside Kodi. "I'm going to try one more time to get my followers to stop following me, and start following her."

"It won't work," Emerson said. "The viewers are cruel; you saw it at the first video diary when they refused to unfollow you. I saw it when I was miserable and could barely get out of bed— they followed me by the hundreds."

Alasdair thought about this, then replied, "I think you're wrong. There are a lot of cruel viewers out there. They're anonymous and so they can act on their inner meanness—which, by the way, probably comes from their own pain—but we've found an audience now; people are connecting with us as individuals. I like science and nature, and people who like those things too follow me. It's not a bad thing. And when you were sad and going through the experience of guilt, people weren't following you out of cruelty. They were following you because they had felt those feelings too and they empathized with you. There are spiteful people in the world, Emerson, but they are outnumbered by the good people. And, in true scientific fashion, I think I'm about to prove it."

Emerson considered Alasdair's words. Could it be true? Could it be that the people who followed her when she was at her lowest point did so because they cared? Because they had been through similar experiences and wanted to show their support?

"You realize that if your experiment works, you'll go to jail for the rest of your life with no contact from anyone?" Emerson asked.

"I do realize that," Alasdair replied, and then smiled. "I was always kind of a loner anyway."

Emerson put a hand on his arm. "You're a good person, Alasdair George William Tremblay-Birchall."

He nodded. "Yeah, I know."

Emerson smiled.

The diaries began.

30
CHAPTER

"So, I guess I'm using this diary thing as a kind of therapy now, huh?" Emerson said, still fighting to keep her eyes open as the tiredness got worse.

In the room next to her, Alasdair was speaking candidly to his followers, telling them that he felt like they had grown to understand him and truly know him over the last few days.

The camera drone hovered in front of Emerson, waiting for her to continue.

"I've been in a pretty dark place since Kodi and I tried to escape and Delilah died. I got myself so wound up that I thought you guys were following me because you enjoyed see-ing me hurt, but I don't think that's true. Alasdair explained some things to me, and if he was right, then I suppose a lot of you have felt the way I felt. Perhaps some of you have felt this kind of guilt. A lot of you have experienced worse. Grief is a strange thing. I lost my mother when I was five. Being at her bedside in the hospital is one of my earliest memories. Watching my dad turn off all his emotions so that he didn't have to feel, watching him change into someone else, someone who wasn't allowed to love because love only led to pain. I don't want to be like my dad. I thought I hated him, but the older I get the more I understand him. He's human and he was hurt and he didn't know how to deal with it. God, my mind is all over the place. I'm so tired. I want to sleep. I want this to be over. I want to go home. I . . . I don't know."

Emerson stopped talking. The drone stopped recording.

She watched as Alasdair implored his viewers to stop following him and start following Tiger. And when Emerson looked over to the leaderboard, she saw that it was working.

The diary recording finished much quicker than usual. Everyone was tired and wanted this day to be over with.

The Producer stood before them and announced that the prize for first place would be a beauty filter on all their footage. The filter would give them more prominent cheekbones, fuller lips, and bigger eyes.

The Producer then froze the screen.

Alasdair's followers had come through. He was now in second-to-last place, and Tiger Quinn had jumped up to one place above the viewer vote zone.

"It is time, contestants, to count down to today's winners and losers." The Producer held both arms aloft and began to count. "Ten, nine, eight, seven . . ."

All around him the zombie-like contestants watched with little detectable enthusiasm.

". . . three, two, one, zero! Congratulations to today's *Kill*

Factor leader for the second time in a row, Gwen Perez!"

The fireworks exploded in the sky, startling Emerson back to being fully awake.

The Producer put his hand on Gwen's shoulder. "Twice in a row, Ms. Perez! You must be very happy."

"I am," Gwen said, and Emerson couldn't tell if it was the tiredness that was taking the energy out of her voice, or if the competition had finally broken her completely.

"Excellent, excellent," the Producer continued. "And can you tell us all exactly what you have learned during your time on the island?"

"What I've learned?" Gwen said, pushing a clump of matted pink hair out of her eyes. "I've learned to appreciate little things, like the sound the waves make, and how beautiful the moon is. When it can all be taken away at any second you . . . you sort of . . ." Gwen's voice drifted away as the exhaustion hit her once again.

"That's very profound, Ms. Perez. Keep doing what you're doing. The audience clearly loves you!"

The Producer stepped away from Gwen, and addressed the swarm of camera drones. "Now, ladies and gentlemen, this is the hardest part of my job: The contestant who will be joining Gamble Delaney in the viewer vote tonight is . . . Alasdair George William Tremblay-Birchall."

Gamble and Alasdair were illuminated in cold white light as they made their way to the stage.

The Producer ran one stubby finger under the flap of an

envelope he had produced from an inside pocket of his jacket, and read aloud.

"In tonight's task," the Producer said, "our two brave competitors must create a viral moment. Our viewers will vote for the moment they deem the best. The viewer vote opens in ten seconds. Good luck."

The screen flashed, and the countdown started. When it hit zero, Gamble's face appeared on the screen. Without hesitating, he walked over to the dead, rotting fish that the latecomers had caught six days before, shooed away the seagulls, picked it up, and bit into the stinking flesh.

He chewed the mouthful of rancid meat and swallowed it. Three seconds later he brought it back up again, but he didn't stop. He bit off the tail and gagged, spitting it out before biting into the head.

Emerson turned away and waited for his three minutes of humiliation to end.

It finally did, and it was Alasdair's turn to create a viral moment. When his face appeared on the big screen, he carefully stepped off the stage, walked to the bonfire, and picked up a flaming stick.

"Fire," he said, looking up at the glow, "is a fascinating event. If you think about it, this burning branch is now running in reverse. Once upon a time this branch used photosynthesis to convert heat and light from the sun into chemical bonds, and fire converts that chemical energy into heat and light. It's amazing. Nature is cyclical in all sorts of ways. The more you look at nature, the more mathematics you see: A snowflake has perfect six-fold radial symmetry; the Fibonacci sequence recurs over and over in the spirals of a pine cone, the form of a hurricane, the helix shape of shells; fractals and repeating patterns in leaves, trees, even mountains. Leonardo da Vinci encouraged everyone to learn how to see that everything connects to everything else."

Alasdair put the burning branch back into the fire, brushed the bark off his hands, and stood back.

"Be curious. That's all I'm saying. If you find yourself asking why the sky is blue, or why the mountains change color halfway up, then maybe you have a scientific mind, and maybe you can find real happiness in trying to solve problems. You might even change the world. And for my friends here on this island, I want you to remember one thing: The moon is backward and the stars don't make sense."

Alasdair still had a minute left of his time. He walked slowly back to the stage and stood beside Gamble until his time was up.

Those words: *The moon is backward and the stars don't make sense.* She had heard those words before . . . recently. It had been Nick. He said the exact same thing before he threw himself to his death.

"What does he mean?" Emerson whispered to Kodi. "About the moon and the stars?"

"I don't know," Kodi replied, looking up at the moon as it hung brightly in the sky.

Emerson was surprised to see that Alasdair's and Gamble's

scores were pretty close when the screen went blank, but when the minute time delay was over, the Producer announced that once again, Gamble had survived the viewer vote.

Alasdair was given five minutes to say his goodbyes. He was stoic as a tearful Tiger hugged him for almost the entire five minutes.

"What did you mean?" Emerson whispered as she held Alasdair close. "About the moon?"

"I can't say anything out loud," he whispered back. He pointed toward one of the many hovering drones. "But Nick was right."

Emerson pulled away from the embrace and looked into Alasdair's eyes. He nodded, imploring her to seek answers, and then the drones escorted him into the forest, and to the prison, where a fate awaited him. A fake prison, a maze, and so many unanswered questions.

31
CHAPTER

The nine remaining contestants slept all through the night and into the next afternoon.

Emerson woke first. The burning sun had caused her to sweat through her T-shirt.

She walked into the sea to cool off, and found herself staring at the *Calypso*.

The moon is backward and the stars don't make sense. What did it mean? What had Nick been right about?

She made her way back to the beach, where Kodi, Tiger, and Never were awake and picking at the breakfast that had been left by the drones.

Emerson sat with them and ate. She had to tell them about what she had seen in the center of the island, but there was no way to without being recorded.

How do I tell them without the Producer finding out? she thought.

Swarms of camera drones hovered over them, the low buzz a constant reminder of their presence. They couldn't pull the Nicotine Patch trick again. They would be killed if they tried, and besides, the Producer would have closed that loophole days ago.

Gwen got out of bed and sat down at the table with them. "Hey," she said, smiling awkwardly.

"Hi, Gwen," Tiger replied, and silence returned for a while before Tiger spoke again. "I collect board games. Mostly vintage board games."

"Oh, really?" Gwen replied, sounding genuinely interested. "I love board games."

"No way!" Tiger said, her blue eyes almost comically wide behind the lenses of her glasses.

"Yeah! I love Monopoly, Scrabble, Boggle, Pictionary . . ."

"Catan?" Tiger asked.

"I love Catan!"

"Oh my days!" Tiger said, standing up and dancing from foot to foot. "We should make a board game! It would give us something to do."

"Sure," Gwen said, smiling as she bit into a hunk of bread.

"I'm going to get started right now!"

Tiger ran away and began collecting pebbles from the sand.

"I wish I had that sort of enthusiasm," Never said, smiling as she watched her friend.

Emerson looked toward the prison in the center of the island and felt a tugging at her heart. Alasdair had been taken there. If there was no prison behind the facade, where had they taken him? And was he even still alive?

× ✳ ×

Emerson lay in her bed for most of the day, thinking through endless plans to escape the island, to free Kodi and the others, to overthrow the Producer without the poison being released into their veins, but every plan she came up with was flawed and easily thwarted.

As the sun began to go down, Tiger sat on the end of her bed.

"It isn't going to work," she muttered, dumping about thirty little stones onto the floor.

"What isn't going to work?" Emerson asked.

"The stupid board game. I was trying to make Scrabble—I found all these stones and started scratching letters into them. I drew a big grid in the sand, but it just won't work. The grid gets all messed up when you step on it, and it's going to take too long to find a hundred stones that are the right size."

"I'm sorry, Tiger," Emerson said, looking down at the stones with the letters scratched into them. "Maybe if we all helped?"

"There's no point. The next game is going to start soon. Who knows, maybe I'll die or get voted off."

"Don't talk like that," Emerson replied.

"Why not? It's the truth. This is happening, Emerson; this is real. There are nine of us left. We started with fifty!"

"But you have to stay positive. You've got a chance of winning and getting out of here."

"Not really," Tiger said, shaking her head so that her blond braids whipped around. "Not really."

The little Topsider got up and walked away while Emerson stared at the stones on the floor.

× ✖ ×

Three loud, high-pitched beeps sounded from the speakers, followed by the Producer's voice. "Contestants of *The Kill Factor*, the penultimate game is about to begin. Please make your way to the other side of the island."

Emerson stood up and waited for the island to rotate. She didn't feel scared or nervous. She felt ready and defiant. She would not lose. She would not die. She had work to do.

The island spun slowly, and the contestants joined the Producer, who stood before nine clear plastic tubes that were protruding from the sand. The tubes were fifteen to twenty feet tall, by Emerson's estimation, and big enough to fit a human inside them. Suspended above each tube was a cylindrical block of concrete that looked to weigh several tons.

"Remaining contestants of *The Kill Factor*," the Producer said, that sly and hateful smile engraved into his face. "Welcome to the Respect game. Behind me you see nine chambers, one for each of you. Suspended above each chamber is a pressing stone. During trials in a more primitive time, if a defendant refused to speak, they were crushed beneath a pressing stone until they either confessed or died. This game is not about confession, though; it is about respect. You have reached the stage of your rehabilitation where you must learn that all lives are valuable, that everyone has the right to life, and that all people deserve respect."

"That's rich, coming from you," Gamble Delaney muttered.

The Producer looked at Gamble with such demonic fury that the boy took a few steps back.

"It seems we have a contestant who is not ready to learn respect," the Producer said, pointing a finger at Gamble. "Such a shame. I thought we had made such progress with you."

"I'm sorry," Gamble said, his fingers automatically going to the number burned into his wrist, and the poisoned capsule beneath. "I didn't mean it . . . I'm sorry!"

"Too late," the Producer said. "Goodbye."

"No, please," Gamble said. "It can't end like this. I can't go through all of that just to . . . just to . . ."

He burst into tears, falling to his knees and begging the Producer not to kill him.

"Final chance, Mr. Delaney," the Producer said, looking at Gamble with disgust in his eyes. "You may enter your chambers now."

Gamble got to his feet, shaking with fear and relief.

The contestants walked over to the great plastic tubes.

Emerson saw that there was a door built into the back of each tube, and she stepped inside the one on the far left. Kodi entered the one beside her. The doors shut and locked behind them. There was nothing inside the tube except a blank screen built into the curvature of the wall.

"The game is simple," the Producer said. "You must rank each remaining contestant in order of how much you respect them. There are nine of you left in *The Kill Factor*, and you cannot vote for yourself, so if every person chooses you as the person they respect the most, you will get a score of sixty-four. This is a very unlikely scenario. However, for every point below sixty-four, the pressing stone will begin to lower. Those of you with less than half of the overall votes will be crushed to death."

"This game isn't teaching us respect," Decker Shimada said, and then covered his mouth quickly.

The Producer looked at Decker for a long time before replying. "You're quite right, Mr. Shimada. This game is merely highlighting what you should have already known: Act in a respectful manner and treat people with dignity, and they will look upon you favorably."

"So, it's just a popularity contest where the least popular dies," Emerson muttered. The Producer turned his wicked eyes on her this time.

"Voting begins in ten seconds," the Producer announced.

The screens inside the tubes flickered to life. Emerson looked down at the names of all the other contestants on one side of the screen, and a table numbered 1 to 8 on the other side.

I have to rank them? she thought, and felt physical disgust at the prospect. *I have to help choose who lives and who dies.*

A countdown appeared at the top corner of the screen, indicating that she had one minute to make her decision.

"Hey, this isn't fair," a voice called out from three tubes down the line from Emerson. It was Teller. "I can't read; I don't know who I'm voting for."

Imelda laughed. "You can't read?" she said. "I guess I know who's going bottom of my respect list."

Decker laughed hysterically.

Without thinking, Emerson slid Imelda's name over to number 8, and Decker into 7.

What have I done? she asked herself, looking at the names she had chosen as the least worthy to live.

Already the timer was down to thirty seconds.

"A quick note," the Producer called out. "Those who abstain from voting will come last and face the wrath of the pressing stones."

Emerson felt a rush of adrenaline. She began dragging names over. Kodi into first, Tiger into second, Never into third. Was that the right order? She didn't know; she had only known them for a matter of days. There was no correct answer to this death puzzle. She moved Gwen's name into fourth, then Teller, then Gamble.

It was done. Her list of who deserved to live more than others. She felt sick.

The timer told her she had three seconds left, and she thought about changing Teller and Gamble around, but a buzzer sounded.

"Voting is closed," the Producer announced. "It's time to see the results. We will begin with the current leader, Gwen Perez."

All eyes turned to Gwen's tube as the stone above her head began to slowly descend.

Everyone was silent as the enormous stone slowly made its way farther and farther down the translucent pipe.

Emerson looked around at the contestants and thought that Imelda would most likely have put her in last place, maybe Decker would have too due to his strange loyalty to Imelda, but where would everyone else have put her? Emerson looked down at her screen. She had put Gwen in fourth place. Had that decision been enough to condemn the pink-haired Topsider to death?

The stone dropped at its steady pace, lowered by some hidden mechanics buried beneath the island, perhaps even controlled from that strange plastic room behind the fake prison.

The stone was so low now that Gwen had to sit down in her tube. She crossed her legs, closed her eyes, and waited.

The stone came lower still, until the smooth gray base of it touched Gwen's bright hair. And then it stopped.

Gwen breathed a sigh of relief, opened her eyes, and began to cry. She was alive.

"Next, Imelda Fleet," the Producer announced.

Imelda's stone began to lower, and the girl inside smiled a confident, bright smile. She crossed her arms and leaned against the inside of the tube.

After fifteen seconds or so, Imelda began to look as though this whole thing was a waste of her time. It wasn't until the stone came so low, forcing her to crouch, that she began to look indignant.

"What the hell?" she asked, looking around at her traitorous peers who had dared not put her at the top of their respect lists.

Emerson watched as the stone pressed down on Imelda.

I feel nothing, she realized as Imelda began to scream. *This place is supposed to fix me, but it has broken me beyond repair.*

Imelda's screams became muffled as the stone pushed her into the sand.

All of Imelda's popularity among her group had indeed been built on fear. They had pandered to her in order to stay in her good graces, but no one had respected her, and now . . .

The stone stopped. Imelda was curled at the bottom of the tube. The stone pressed down on her, constricting her lungs. Another few centimeters and there would not be enough space to breathe, but as it was, she had just enough room to survive. Her wild and wide eyes rolled around in supreme terror.

"A close call for Ms. Fleet," the Producer said. "Next it is the turn of Mr. Shimada."

"Oh God, no," Decker said, letting out all his fear in a high and breathless exclamation.

The stone came down, and down, and down.

Decker paced the short circumference of his transparent cylindrical cell until it was time to sit down.

And still the stone kept on coming.

Decker sat on the sand, a look of resignation on his face as the stone flattened his tall Mohawk, then bent his neck, forcing him to the ground.

"Mom, I'm sorry," he said. Everyone's eyes closed tightly shut as the stone pushed him farther and farther into the sand, crushing his bones.

Emerson felt tears in her eyes, and for one second she experienced relief that she still had the ability to feel anything at all.

"A sad end," the Producer said. "But the show goes on. Next up is Ms. Jones."

Never took a deep breath and waited for her fate.

The stone came down. Never had her eyes closed for the entire ordeal but needn't have worried; it stopped before she had to move.

"Yes, Never!" Tiger shouted, clapping her hands.

Tiger was next. Her stone came down about a foot lower than Never's, but because she was so short, Tiger didn't have to move either.

"Mr. Sanderson," the Producer said, turning slowly to face Teller.

"Wait!" Teller called out from his tube as he thumped on the thick plastic. "I didn't finish voting! I couldn't read the names!"

"I'm sorry, Mr. Sanderson, the rules were made perfectly clear to you."

"No, you can't kill me for not being able to read! You need to give me more time!"

Those were Teller's last words. The stone above his head did not come down slowly. In an odd act of mercy, Teller was not made to suffer. Instead, he was crushed to death in an instant, his life snuffed out without warning or ceremony.

Gone, Emerson thought. *Teller is gone.*

There was no sign of the boy who had been standing there a few seconds earlier. Emerson couldn't even see any blood. That was how perfectly the stone fit inside the tube.

"You must listen to instructions, contestants," the Producer said, a lighthearted note of scolding in his voice. "You must pay attention and do what you are told. Let's move on, shall we? I believe the next in line is Ms. Ness."

As the Producer's eyes turned to meet Emerson's, the stone began to lower.

There was no fear inside Emerson. No thoughts of the pain that would come with being crushed to death. No sadness. Nothing. Emerson was empty of emotion, and again she thought of how this island had killed a vital part of her.

Is it killed? she wondered. *Really? Or is it just in a coma? Can it be revived? Will I ever be normal again?*

This was a question she felt she could not know the answer to until she knew whether or not she would live for more than twenty-four hours.

The descending stone pressed against her head, and she sat down. She looked out of the plastic tube and over to the rolling waves of the ocean. Her eyes turned to the moon. *The moon is backward and the stars don't make sense.* She looked for constellations that she might recognize and saw none.

The stone stopped a foot above her. There was no relief or elation.

"Mr. Finch," the Producer said, and there was some trepidation in the voice of the Producer as he turned to Kodiak. "You're next."

Kodi's stone began to lower, and Emerson watched. She felt certain that he would be okay, but still there were sparks of fear flickering inside her.

Kodi's stone halted a little lower than Emerson's. He was alive.

"Finally, Mr. Delaney," the Producer said, turning to stare into Gamble's fearful eyes.

Gamble nodded. He ran his tongue over his big teeth, and looked up at the stone as it began to fall slowly toward him.

When, after a minute or so, the stone began to crush Gamble, he screamed "Stop! Stop! Stop!" as though the people behind this game had any kind of mercy.

He died screaming.

Emerson looked at the stars once again. She desperately wanted to see one of the constellations that Kester had taught her: Orion, Cassiopeia, Draco, or Leo, but there was nothing familiar about these points of brilliant light in the perfectly black sky . . . except . . . except there *was* something familiar. Orion's Belt, a series of three stars in an almost straight line that tilted upward at a slight angle . . . only Orion's belt was facing the wrong way.

The stars don't make sense.

Once Emerson had seen Orion's belt, she could make out the entire shape of Orion the Hunter. The great constellation's bow, which normally aimed up into the night sky, was aimed down, as though he were firing arrows at Earth.

Impossible, Emerson thought. *The stars can't just flip around.*

Whatever it was that Nick had noticed before he had killed himself, or that Alasdair had figured out before he had gone to jail, she was seeing it now too. But what did it mean?

33

CHAPTER

The stones lifted and Imelda screamed with relief once she could finally breathe easy again.

"Contestants," the Producer intoned, almost singing, "you have completed game number five and taken yet another step toward becoming valued members of society." No one clapped or cheered, but the Producer stood triumphantly, as though he was about to deliver incredible news, and Emerson could imagine the editors of this hellish show adding sound effects of rapturous applause.

"Six of you remain, and only one game to go before a winner is crowned. All of you have come so far and learned so much. You are so close to being fully rehabilitated. But let's not get ahead of ourselves. There will be only one winner. Five more of you will bow out before the games are complete. And—to that end—I shall announce the winner and loser of today's game. The person who has earned the most respect from their peers, and the winner of the Respect game, is . . . Ms. Never Jones!"

Emerson clenched her fist in celebration. Tiger hugged Never.

"Ms. Jones," the Producer said, walking over to the winner.

"How are you feeling right now having won the respect of your fellow contestants?"

"I feel awful," Never replied. "Dozens of people had to die for me to still be in this game. It's all a lie. There's no rehabilitation here, just desensitization and hell!"

"Very good, Ms. Jones," the Producer replied, grinning widely. "Now, you were chosen to come to this island because you committed a very serious crime, isn't that right?"

"No," Never replied. "I stole off rich people like you because the system is rigged! I had to feed my family. I had to pay rent. How was I supposed to do any of that when your kind are hoarding all the wealth?"

"I understand," the Producer replied, a look of sympathy on his face. "And do you think the process you have been through on the island has helped you in any way?"

"No!" Never replied. "Aren't you listening to me?"

"That's so good to hear," the Producer said.

Never's shoulders slumped. "You're going to change my words, aren't you? When this goes out to all the people watching, you're going to change what I'm saying."

"That's right," the Producer replied, a look of hateful victory in his eyes. "Ladies and gentlemen, your winner, Never-Again Jones!"

Without warning, Never grabbed the Producer by the throat and squeezed as hard as she could.

"No!" Emerson screamed, knowing that her friend was signing her own death warrant.

The Producer's face began to turn purple as he fell to the ground. Never landed on top of him, not losing her grip on his neck. Emerson ran toward them, hoping that if she could get Never away from the Producer in time, then maybe they wouldn't release the poison, but as her hands grabbed Never's shoulders, she knew she was already too late.

Emerson pulled the weakened girl off the Producer. Never stared up at the backward stars.

"Never!" Emerson cried, holding her friend's head in her arms.

"I messed up," Never replied, her voice shaking.

"No, you didn't."

"I could've won this stupid thing."

Emerson pushed a strand of Never's hair out of her sweat-soaked face. "You once promised to look after my brother. Well, now I'm promising you that I'll get out of here and look after your family."

Never nodded; her hand rested on Emerson's.

Tiger screamed and fell to her knees as the life left Never's eyes.

Emerson felt Kodi's hand on her shoulder, but she didn't need comfort or support in this moment. Instead of anger, instead of pain, instead of anguish, Emerson felt a resolve growing in her. There would be time for rage and hate and sorrow later, but for now, she knew only one thing: She would get off this island, she would find all the people responsible for this hell, and she would kill them.

"Never-Again Jones will receive immunity from the viewer vote," the Producer said. Emerson turned to look at him. He was standing steadily on both feet, no sign of a bruise on his neck, no indication that Never had even shaken him at all. "Not that immunity is any good to her now."

The slight smile on the Producer's face set Emerson's resolve in stone. "I'm going to kill you first," she whispered.

"The loser of the Respect game is Imelda Fleet. Sorry, Ms. Fleet. It seems you do not command enough respect among your peers; perhaps some reflection is required."

Imelda was still shaking and sobbing from her latest near-death experience.

"Follow me," the Producer said. Again, the island began to turn.

× ✖ ×

For the first time since the first diary, Emerson refused to speak. She spent the entire time staring at the Producer, her mind turning over and over with thoughts of backward stars, fake prisons, mazes, and the giant cruise ship waiting on the waves.

"Contestants!" the Producer said. And by now, Emerson could almost speak along with what he was saying. "You have made it through the fifth game, and completed your video diaries. The footage is being aired as we speak, and in exactly one minute we will take a snapshot of your follower count and see which contestant will be facing Ms. Fleet in the viewer vote. I am proud of each and every one of you. Good luck."

The Producer counted down from ten, the screen flashed, and

Emerson looked to see which of them would be competing against Imelda.

Fireworks flashed in the sky as the Producer announced that Gwen Perez had retained her lead by a narrow margin, and would be receiving five new outfits as a prize.

It was all somewhere way in the background, though.

Emerson stared at the scoreboard.

Forty-five names were grayed out. Only five remained.

The name sitting at the bottom of the list was her own.

34

CHAPTER

Emerson felt Kodi's arms around her.

"You have to stay in the game," he whispered. "No matter what."

She looked into his gray-blue eyes and allowed that feeling of determined focus to reignite inside her. She nodded.

The drones shone their spotlights onto Emerson and Imelda as the Producer commanded them to step onto the stage. He was taking an envelope from the pocket of his suit jacket and opening it.

Emerson's body felt numb. It was all happening too fast.

She stared at her name on the scoreboard.

Place	Contestant Name	Contestant #	Follower count
1.	Gwen Perez	7	2,290,236
2.	Imelda Fleet	33	2,276,797
3.	Tiger Quinn	11	1,721,600
4.	Kodiak Finch	1	1,577,203
5.	Emerson Ness	16	1,382,509

Focus, Emerson told herself.

"Tonight's task," the Producer proclaimed, "is to confess your deepest, darkest secret. Each of you will get a chance to speak for three minutes. Good luck."

The screen flashed, and huge numbers appeared and disappeared, counting down from ten to zero.

Imelda's face appeared first. She began to speak, but Emerson could hardly hear her words through the buzzing in her ears. Whatever she was saying was surely a lie. Emerson looked around at her friends. Tiger, who had her arms wrapped around herself; Kodi, who was nodding in encouragement. Emerson felt tears running down her cheeks.

Imelda was the best actress Emerson had ever witnessed. Her inflections, her calculated pauses, the moisture she was able to push to the brink of her eyes. A single tear fell just as the countdown hit five seconds.

"It was the lowest point in my life," Imelda said.

Imelda's follower count was skyrocketing.

When zero hit, Emerson's face appeared on the screen. For ten seconds she didn't speak. Her mind was blank. And then she felt the weight of everything she had been through pressing down on her.

Kester's words flashed into her mind: *Remember that people fall in love with honesty. Be honest and you'll win them over.*

Emerson inhaled a deep breath into her lungs. It was time to stop lying to herself.

"I'm here, on this island, because I was arrested for murder," she said. "A man died because of a fire that started in a school that I was robbing. I have spent every day since I found out about the death of Marvin Tzu telling myself that it wasn't my fault, that I didn't start the fire, but the truth is: I did. I started the fire, and I did it on purpose. I wanted that school to burn." Emerson didn't hear her own words. Instead, she stood inside that dark and empty physics room in her mind's eye, and smelled the gas as it billowed out of the tap in the middle of the desk.

"That is my biggest secret," Emerson continued. "I stood in that school, in the science classroom where Mr. Abernethy would call me stupid, where Claire Tavernier and Travis Chalk would hit me with their physics books if I fell asleep, where I fell behind, where I felt like I didn't belong . . . I stood there and I hated every person who had laughed at me, called me names, made fun of me behind my back. I hated that they had families that looked out for them. That they had credits that had value, and fathers who weren't obsessed with fame, and opportunities to get out of the Burrows and make something of themselves."

She had wanted the school to burn, and all her bad experiences with it, as though a baptism of fire would purge the trauma away. It had been a silly act of childish destruction that had led to tragedy. "I turned the gas taps on and I walked away. I didn't ignite the gas, and I kept telling myself that it wasn't my fault because I didn't ignite the gas, but it *was* my fault. I killed Marvin Tzu because I was angry and I was jealous and I was weak. I'll never forgive myself for that. I don't deserve your vote. I don't deserve to stay in this game, but I want to. I want to be a better person, and I want to try to make amends for what I did somehow."

Emerson stopped talking. For the first time since Agent Dern had told her that a man had died in the fire, she replayed the events in her mind exactly as they had occurred: There were no blank spots or omitted facts. She was to blame for a man's death. She had accepted that.

Emerson's three minutes ended. She looked to Kodi, who had hatred etched onto his face. She didn't blame him.

Everyone stood in perfect silence as the one-minute time delay passed, and then the Producer spoke.

"Ladies and gentlemen, the results are in. I can now reveal that the contestant in second place got 906,192 votes when the lines closed, but the person in first place got 1,285,205 votes. Ladies and gentlemen, the person leaving the games tonight is . . ."

The Producer left the required dramatic pause, and the audience held their breath.

". . . Imelda Fleet."

For perhaps the first time since Emerson had met Imelda Fleet, she observed genuine emotion as it took hold of the girl. It was a look of complete devastation. But to Emerson's shock, she felt nothing in return. Not sympathy, not even triumph.

Okay, Emerson thought. *Let's get the hell out of here.*

35
CHAPTER

Dawn broke on the day of the sixth game.

There were five bedrooms left. Imelda's bedroom would be dismantled while the remaining contestants were competing in game six, so time was running out. She had to act fast. It was the only remaining room with a mirror.

Everything was in place. Emerson had spent the night slowly and carefully collecting Tiger's game stones and arranging them under her pillow to spell out her plan. There were only enough letters to write three simple words: GLASS. CUT. POISON. But if Tiger and Kodi understood, and she could keep the information away from the drones somehow, then it was all they would need.

Once they had cut the poison capsules out of their wrists, they would have to take their chances and swim to the *Calypso*. Then it was all about luck. They'd have to find their way to the ship's control room, start up the engines, and pilot the enormous thing out of there. All of this relied on there being no remote kill switch that would shut off the ship entirely, or armed guards hidden somewhere on the beach who would kill them before they got near the boat, or *Kill Factor* employees aboard the ship who would apprehend them as soon as they boarded.

It was impossible. Emerson knew that, but impossible seemed so much more beautiful than the inevitable.

The sun was still crawling up into the sky as morning came to life on the island. Emerson watched the few remaining contestants as they roamed around the beach aimlessly. She glanced at the leaderboard.

Place	Contestant Name	Contestant #	Follower count
1.	Gwen Perez	7	2,478,811
2.	Tiger Quinn	11	1,919,944
3.	Kodiak Finch	1	1,687,441
4.	Emerson Ness	16	1,523,016

Four left. Four people fighting for freedom and for their lives. Emerson wondered if she was being selfish, if her plan was taking away an opportunity from Tiger and Gwen, who actually stood a chance of winning, but she dismissed the thought. There was no winning in this game.

It was time. No point in putting it off any longer.

"Kodi, Tiger," Emerson called out.

She watched Tiger, her red eyes meandering over the beach and finding Emerson. She had aged ten years in the short time she had been on this island. Her sense of humor had been killed, her enthusiasm euthanized, her personality sedated and subdued until it was a ghost of what it had been.

They came over and sat next to Emerson. Kodi did not make eye contact with her. Thirty or more camera drones hovered around them, revolving and canting to find interesting angles.

She had to show them the stones without the drones seeing. Emerson's only thought was to pull the blanket over all their heads and show them the words beneath her pillow before the drones could react, but she didn't get a chance. Before Emerson could even open her mouth to speak, the island began to revolve.

Emerson's heart stopped.

The Producer knows, she thought.

"What's going on?" Tiger asked, getting off the bed and out of the room so she could walk along with the revolving ground.

"I . . . I think this is my fault," Emerson said.

"What do you mean?" Kodi asked. "What did you do?"

"I tried to . . ."

But the Producer's voice echoed out over the beach from the hidden speakers.

"Contestants," he said. "The final game is about to begin."

36

CHAPTER

Every step along the rotating sand was a step closer to death. Emerson was certain of that.

Emerson reached for Kodi's hand, but he pulled it away and walked faster. Her heart hurt, but she understood that she was not the girl he had thought she was. She was a killer.

The competition side of the island came into view. Four chairs sat on the beach in a horseshoe shape, all made of thick and solid-looking planks of wood, all with heavy-duty leather straps on the armrests and legs of the chair.

The Producer arrived, walking toward them through a heat haze, like a bleak vision of evil.

Emerson waited for his eyes to meet hers. She waited for his look of disappointment, his words of judgment, and then the feeling of the poison being released into her body, the pain, and then the nothingness of death.

Instead, the elderly and youthful man stood before them, beaming his Hollywood smile. Finally, he spoke.

"Welcome, contestants, to the sixth and final game. In this competition, you have the opportunity to learn Restraint. The game is simple. Kill one of your fellow competitors, and the games are over."

Waves rolled against the shore. A cloud rolled over the sun.

"I don't understand," Gwen said cautiously.

The Producer turned his hellion eyes on Gwen, and smiled with such ferocious delight that Emerson felt cold just watching him.

"Take the life of one of your peers," the Producer clarified, "and the project comes to an end."

The silence seemed to come up from the ground, surrounding the remaining contestants.

"What if we just choose not to kill each other?" Kodi asked.

"Then you will have shown great restraint, and proven that you have truly been rehabilitated," the Producer said.

"Then that's what we'll do," Gwen said, her voice filled with cautious hope. "We'll just wait it out until the game is over and we'll all be in the final, right?"

"Excellent," the Producer said, clapping his hands together. "Nothing would make me happier. This is a marvelous opportunity to prove that you have truly changed. Show restraint, and prove that you could be a worthy winner. Take a life, and the game ends with one less person competing for the coveted top spot on the leaderboard! It is up to you. There will be no more diaries, no more viewer votes. This is it. Play this final game, survive, and you will be in the final group. If you could all take a seat in one of the chairs, we will begin."

"Wait," Emerson said, and the Producer's dark eyes rolled over to hers.

"What is it, Ms. Ness?"

Emerson swallowed. "Why now? The games always happen at night. Why is this one starting in the morning?"

The Producer smiled. "Ah yes, there is one final thing I forgot to mention. There is no time limit on this game except the time limit enforced by your own will to live. You will not receive food or water until one of you kills another. As to why the game is beginning right now . . . well, some decisions are proactive, others are reactive, Ms. Ness."

"So either one of us dies or all of us die," Kodi said.

The Producer nodded.

And with that, Emerson knew two things: Someone would have to die in this game, and the Producer had seen her hidden message. Why he didn't just have her killed, she didn't know, but she suspected that the more people involved in his final game, the more interesting it would be for the viewers.

"Ms. Perez, this seat is reserved for you." The Producer gestured toward the seat nearest to him. Gwen swallowed hard and sat down. The Producer tightened and secured each of the four straps one by one until Gwen was fastened to her wooden chair, no way of escaping at all. "Ms. Quinn, this one is for you."

As Tiger sat down on her chair, Emerson saw in the young Topsider's eyes that she felt very much as Emerson did: broken, lobotomized, gone.

Emerson was next to be restrained in her seat, and finally, Kodi. Emerson watched as the Producer tightened the straps around his arms, and then patted him on the hand.

The chairs were angled in an arc that allowed all the contestants to see one another. Emerson looked into the fearful eyes of Gwen, the lost eyes of Tiger, and the determined eyes of Kodi, and she wondered what the others saw when they looked at her: Terror? Disenchantment? Confusion?

"And now," the Producer said, sounding eerily like an old-timey circus ringleader, "the means by which to win this game."

A mechanical whirring emanated from behind each chair. The sand beneath their feet began to shudder and displace. Emerson watched as a metal arm rose up from behind each chair. Attached to each was an ancient-looking wooden crossbow with a fearsomely barbed arrow loaded into each. The one above Gwen's head was pointing right at Kodi's chest. The crossbow above Kodi's was pointing at Gwen, the one above Tiger's chair was aimed right at Emerson's own heart, and she could only assume that there was a fourth weapon above her own chair pointed right at Tiger.

"From now on, you should all watch your words," the Producer said, barely able to hold back his glee. "Say the name of one of your peers, and the corresponding bolt will fire from the crossbow, killing the named contestant and ending both their life and the competition. The game has begun, and it will not end until one of you has killed another. Good luck."

The Producer turned, leaving them to stare at one another,

allowing the reality to sink in. The cloud finally moved on, and the sun beat down upon them once more.

No one spoke for a long time.

Gwen bit at her lower lip. Tiger's half-lidded eyes gazed at the sand. Kodi shook his head solemnly.

"I know what you're all thinking," Gwen said finally, looking at the bolt that was aimed at her and then back to the other players of the game. "I'm at the top of the leaderboard, right? So it makes the most sense to kill me."

"No one's thinking that," Kodi replied.

"Why not?" Gwen asked. "I'd be thinking that if I was in your shoes. Kill the leader and maybe you'll win the games."

"No one is going to kill anyone else," Tiger muttered.

"We have to," Emerson said quietly.

"What?" Tiger asked.

"We have to. You heard what the Producer said; no food or water until one of us kills another. You can only live without water for about three days, and we'll be losing our minds long before that. Someone has to kill someone else."

The waves rocked against the beach. The sun sat stoically in the sky. The contestants waited.

"You want to know something?" Kodi asked, offering a smile that was filled with sadness. "I've known since before the show began what it was going to be. I knew it was going to be pain and suffering and torture. I decided before we boarded the ship that I wasn't going to make friends with anyone. In fact, I was going to make enemies. I was going to be the worst version of myself. That way I would be able to let everyone around me suffer and die and I wouldn't have any emotional attachment. That was the only way to make sure that *you* got out of here alive."

Emerson's eyes rose to meet Kodi's. He was looking right at her. There was something wrong.

"What do you mean?" Emerson asked.

"I've been lying to you from the start."

Emerson felt the skin tightening around her body.

"I knew who you were before we met at the docks. I came here to make sure you lived," Kodi continued, staring into Emerson's eyes.

"What are you talking about? You didn't know me before all this."

"Yes, I did. I was there the night you robbed the school," Kodi continued. He held his eye contact. "I followed you. I knew what you were planning to do, and I was going to steal the money off you when you left. It's how I make money. How I *made* money, at least. Followed thieves, and mugged them for their take."

Emerson was crying now. The words seemed to circle around her consciousness, refusing to sink in, refusing to be real.

"I was the one who lit the gas in the school. It was taking too long, so I decided to smoke you out. The cops showed up so quickly, though, and I left. When I found out what had happened to Marvin Tzu, I felt . . . I hated myself. I *still* hate myself. I never wanted anyone to die. I don't want to be my dad."

"It's not true, it can't be," Emerson whispered. She still didn't understand.

"It is true. My father and I, we're from the Burrows, but I hadn't seen him since I was six years old. He went to jail for murder. I never knew the details of his case, but I hated him . . . I *hate* him so much. When the real producers of this show made him the presenter, I convinced him to get me onto the island with you. Nepotism at its most pitiful."

"I don't understand," Emerson said. "What are you talking about?"

"The Producer," Kodi said, a film of tears in his eyes now. "His name is Lester Finch. He was a serial killer on death row. He's my father."

Emerson's mind spun. She shook her head. "No. No, that doesn't make sense."

"It's true," Kodi replied. "And I need you to know, before . . . before the end, that I really do love you."

"Don't," Emerson choked out, suddenly knowing what he was about to do. "Don't."

More tears rolled down Kodi's cheeks, and he smiled once again. "I grew up terrified that I would be just like my dad: something missing inside me, but I knew when I met you that I was all right. I love you, okay? Always remember that."

"Listen to me," Emerson said, but words stuck in her throat.

"I always hated my name," Kodi continued, looking up at the clouds as they strolled calmly over the blue sky. "My psycho father named me after a type of bear because he wanted me to be fierce and strong and brave. I suppose I tried to be those things at times, but I never liked the name . . . Kodiak Finch."

"No!" Emerson screamed as the crossbow above Gwen's head let out a hollow *thunk* sound as the wire that held back the arrow let go.

The bolt hit Kodi in the heart.

There was a moment, as Emerson stared at the growing patch of blood on Kodi's white shirt, when her fractured soul told her it wasn't real, that she could undo it, that she could make it so that nothing had happened, but it passed like the second hand on some infinite clock ticking away moments of hope in a world full of bad things.

"I'm so, so sorry," Kodi whispered, the words coming with great effort. Please make it off this godforsaken island.

His beautiful eyes closed. His head fell forward. His hair spilled over his face, and he was gone.

"I love you," Emerson managed to say through the earthquake of pain that was ripping her apart inside. "I love you, Kodi. I love you."

For some time after that, the world seemed to fade away from Emerson Ness.

37

CHAPTER

Emerson was seven years old and Kester was dying.

The old-fashioned phone had to remain plugged into its charging cord or it would die instantly. It was slippery in Emerson's sweating hands.

"I'm sorry, madam," the emergency services operator was saying in curt tones, "but the ambulance will not go any farther than New Third Avenue. You'll have to meet them there."

She wanted to scream at the bad woman on the other end of the phone. She wanted to say, *I'm little! I don't know what to do! My brother is just a baby. Why won't you help me?* But Emerson was seven, and you have to be polite to adults, so she just said, "Okay, I'll go there now."

The walk through the Burrows at night with a rasping and horribly warm little baby was like walking through a vivid nightmare.

There were users plugged into old electric car charging ports with ancient VR headsets on. A burning delivery vehicle sent flickering shadows into the darkest corners, where milky and hopeless eyes watched the roads. All around her were the worthless: people whose brand credits were just meaningless numbers in their virtual accounts. Nobody followed these people. A group of young boys, most of them with no shoes or shirts, came running out of a house with boarded-up windows. One of them had blood on his hands; all of them were laughing.

When the patched and uneven road finally began to rise up to meet New Third Avenue, Emerson dared to let herself feel a moment of relief, but when she made her way to the Topside, there was no ambulance.

She stood there, a little girl with a dying infant in her arms, and wondered if she was too late. Had the ambulance waited around, assumed it was a prank, and then left?

Kester had fallen silent, and Emerson began to cry.

More than anything or anyone else, she hated her father. This was his fault.

When the blue and red lights finally turned the black street into a disorienting strobe of color, Emerson closed her eyes and prayed that her little brother was still alive.

The paramedic stepped out of the cab and wandered casually over to Emerson. "This is the boy?" he asked, scratching his nose.

"How could you not come down to get him?" Emerson asked. For the first time in her life, she could not hold back the anger inside her. "You're a bad person. You're bad people. He's a baby! He's sick and he's in trouble and you wouldn't come for him!"

"Hey, little girl," the man with the short, curly hair replied. "It's company policy. It's not personal. Now, do you want us to help the kid or not?"

Emerson handed over her feverish brother and got into the ambulance.

Hatred and disbelief filled her. The world wasn't fair. It was clear and obvious and no one was going to do anything about it. The people who had the power to change it didn't care, and those who did care didn't have the power to change it.

But all of that had been years ago. Now she was somewhere else. On a beach. On an island.

No, Emerson thought.

She did not want to come back to reality. She didn't know what awaited her there; she only knew that it was a chasm of unfathomable pain.

Please, no.

But things were coming into focus now. Senseless stars in a wrong sky, a moon that was backward, an island where the wind never blew and the rain fell straight down. An island where she had fallen in love with a boy name Kodi, and then watched him die.

No.

It hit her like an avalanche of misery. All the things her brain had been keeping from her were released at once and it was like a swarm of locusts in her soul.

Emerson lay on her bed, wishing she could return to the bliss of ignorance, but that refuge was gone forever and she knew it.

Kodi had lit the fire that killed Marvin Tzu. He had been there that night to rob her. He was the reason she had been caught by the police. He was the reason she was on this hellish island . . . and yet she loved him still. She didn't care about all the things he had done wrong—he had given up his freedom to come here and protect her, he had tried so hard to get them off this island, and he had given his life so that she could remain in the game.

Lying asleep beside her was Tiger, one arm draped across Emerson's shoulder.

Emerson stirred and felt Tiger's arm pulling her close, comforting her, and she felt the faintest moment of light. That light went away as quickly as it had arrived, though. Yes, there were good people in this world, but good people rarely were allowed to shine. Never had been poisoned. Alasdair had been taken away. Kodi had been killed. Tiger would go soon too, and so would she, and maybe that was okay.

There was no way out of this. No way off this island. Kodi's plan to use the Nicotine Patch drones had failed. Her own plan to write out a warning had failed. They could not outsmart the Producer (or whoever was really in control of the games). They could not escape the island. They would all die here, she knew that. There was no prize; there was no freedom even if you won the whole thing.

Emerson felt an acceptance growing inside her. Why fight when you can't win? Why bother?

She watched the stars and planets and galaxies moving slowly clockwise across the sky, and she tried with every fiber of her being to think of absolutely nothing at all.

It would be over soon regardless; why suffer? Just think of nothing and wait for the end.

No more anger.

No more rage.

No more pain.

No more . . .

No more.

38

CHAPTER

Dawn broke.

Emerson watched the sun throw orange rays across the water, and saw the grayness of sunrise give way to the stinging brightness of morning, and none of it mattered.

Somewhere in the far corners of her mind she wondered if Kester really would get the benefit of her now over two and a half million followers, or if that was a lie too. She hoped—with whatever ability she had left to hope—that he would.

Tiger stirred, clambered higher up so that she could kiss Emerson on the cheek, and then rested her head on Emerson's shoulder.

"Are you okay?" the little girl whispered.

Emerson closed her eyes, opened them slowly, then replied, "No. I'm not okay."

"I know," Tiger said. "I'm so sorry."

Again, Emerson felt that flickering light inside her, and again she let it die. She loved Tiger, but love wasn't enough anymore.

"Hey, Emerson," the lost voice of Gwen Perez called out.

Emerson turned her head and saw that Gwen too was lying in her bed, unmoving.

"Yeah," Emerson called back.

"I can't do this anymore."

"I know," Emerson replied.

"The Producer said it's over," Gwen said, her voice flat and hollow. "But it's not over. I know it's not over. Do you know how I know?"

"No."

"It's not over because we're still alive. It'll only end when everyone is dead, won't it?"

"I think so," Emerson replied.

And they were silent again after that. The whoosh and roar of the calm water breaking gently on the beach was the only sound.

Drones flew in with breakfast that no one ate, and sometime later they took it all away.

At some point, Emerson looked at the scoreboard. She could barely take in the information.

Place	Contestant Name	Contestant #	Follower count
1.	Gwen Perez	7	3,878,811
2.	Tiger Quinn	11	2,919,944
3.	Emerson Ness	16	2,523,016

It meant something, or perhaps it meant nothing. Emerson didn't know and couldn't make herself care.

She got out of bed when the sun was directly above the island and walked to the water's edge. There was something distantly comforting about how the afternoon light turned silver and gold against the ripples of the waves.

She stood there for some time, allowing herself to get lost in the mesmeric dance of colors, but then came crashing down when the Producer's voice blared out over the island.

"Finalists of *Kill Factor*. All of you should be very proud of yourselves. You have learned valuable lessons during your time on the island. You have transformed from criminals into valuable members of society, and for that I applaud you. But there can only be one winner. Please make your way to the far side of the island."

"I thought he said there were no more games," Tiger said, but her voice carried no anger or fear or any emotion at all, for that matter.

The island revolved and the three girls walked the familiar path to the other side.

As the staged area for the finale came into view, Emerson saw that each piece of apparatus for all the games they had played since the beginning were there: holes in the beach with coffins inside, the enormous diving board platforms, the fifty-foot-high running track, the huts for the sleeping game, the tubes for the Respect game, and the chairs they had sat in the day before. Emerson looked at the wooden seat where Kodi had died and felt the wound reopen.

The Producer walked on the spot among all the equipment and smiled as his finalists approached.

The island stopped spinning, and the four of them stood in silence for a while.

"Welcome," the Producer said. "Here you are, the finalists of the first-ever *Kill Factor*. I told you a long time ago that we were going to make history here, and we have, by God we have! You don't know this, but the world has gone crazy for *The Kill Factor*: Protests in every major city in America! Online frenzy begging governments to intervene, boycott threats, people promising to hack into our systems and find out where the island is, anger and furor! But most of all, the highest viewing figures of any show in the history of broadcasting."

"But the people hate it," Gwen said. "You just said there have been protests and threats and boycotts!"

"There is no better advertising than outrage, Ms. Perez. And the numbers don't lie. We're a hit. Yesterday's game was watched by over two hundred million people worldwide, and when the figures come in for today's broadcast, I think we'll hit a new high."

"How can they stand for this?" Tiger asked, her voice still vacant. "How can people . . . stand for this?"

"Oh, there is outrage, of course. There always is when something new comes along. It has been the same way throughout history. People like to think that they will fight for what's right, and they will . . . for a while, but then something new comes along and takes their focus away, and that thing that so enraged them becomes commonplace. In ten years *Kill Factor* will be an accepted part of life, and no doubt there will be other presentations that come along and push the boundaries even further. Who knows? But for now, we are the only show in town, so let's sparkle!"

"No," Emerson said, sounding almost bored.

"No?" the Producer repeated, his voice full of good humor.

"I can't. I won't. I'm not going to do this anymore. You'll just have to kill me. That's what you're good at, isn't it? Killing people?"

The Producer smiled. "Oh yes, I had forgotten that my darling son made many dying confessions. Needless to say, it only adds to the drama of the show! That being said, Ms. Ness, you *will* take part."

"And what if I don't? What's the worst you can do?"

"The worst? The worst? That's a good question. I suppose I'll kill Tiger if you refuse to participate. And if Tiger refuses to participate, I'll kill Gwen, and if Gwen refuses to participate, I'll kill you."

Emerson sighed. Once again she had been checkmated by a mind of pure evil. "Okay," she said. "I'll do it."

"Wonderful," the Producer said. "When the cameras come on, all you have to do is beg for your lives. When the ten minutes are over, the person with the most followers will win the inaugural games. On this one occasion, the footage will not be edited, it will not be delayed; it will be going out live. You can say what you want, do what you want, but remember, you're begging for your lives. Make the most of your time. Good luck."

The Producer walked away. Emerson watched him go. She looked down at the sand and for some reason she expected to see that he had left no footprints, but instead she saw the half-moon shapes left by the heels of his shoes, and she saw something else too—the drawing that Alasdair had left in the sand during the sleep game.

Emerson walked over to the image, which was faded now. She could make out the circular shape of the moon, the points in the sand that represented the stars, and a crude image of the island beneath the celestial bodies. And surrounding all this was a half-circle, enclosing all of it like a snow globe.

. . . my friends here on this island, I want you to remember one thing: The moon is backward and the stars don't make sense.

Alasdair had said that. Nick had said it too. And she herself had noticed that Orion was indeed facing the wrong way, but what did it mean?

Large camera drones, the same ones that filmed the video diaries, appeared from within the plastic forest, and the red lights came on.

Kodi's last words echoed in her mind.

Please make it off this godforsaken island.

Emerson no longer believed that anyone was going to make it out of here alive.

Ten minutes of unedited time with her audience. Ten minutes to say whatever she wanted.

The moon is backward and the stars don't make sense.

Ten minutes to speak the truth. Ten minutes to inform.

The moon is backward. Nick was right.

Ten minutes to talk to her brother one last time.

The stars don't make sense . . .

Something clicked in her mind. Finally, she saw what Alasdair had seen, and what Nick had seen before him.

CHAPTER 39

Emerson looked at the camera drone with its red light, and then back down at Alasdair's drawing in the sand.

It was obvious to her now. The way the rain had fallen straight down, the way no wind ever blew across this island even though it was in the middle of the ocean.

They were living under a dome. Nick had said those words right to her, only she hadn't listened because it had come in the middle of a string of conspiracy theories and crazed ramblings.

She had seen it when the Nicotine Patch drones flew too high and the seagull had disappeared. They had short-circuited the panels of the dome for a moment. The dome, which projected clouds and the sun and the moon—the moon, which traveled clockwise across the sky. And the stars, which were flipped the wrong way around. Someone, somewhere in the production team, had messed up and no one had noticed except a few kids who had been forced to live on this island. If she could somehow get this information to Kester, maybe—just maybe—he could use the massive electronic signal to figure out where they were and get them out of here.

Emerson looked directly down the barrel of the camera, and something else occurred to her. The Producer had told them that more than two hundred million people were tuning in, and yet only around ten million people were following the three remaining contestants. That surely meant that the other viewers were . . . what? Watching to see if something would be done? If law enforcement would intervene? If someone would escape? Maybe. It was her only hope.

And it hit her as clear as day. It would be difficult, but she would have to have two conversations at the same time: one with her hands, using sign language, and the other with her mouth, using her spoken words. She would sign all the vital information to Kester and at the same time speak directly to the people who were watching in hopes that this horrible show would come to a burning end.

The moon moves across the sky in the wrong direction, Emerson's hands said.

"I had never been in love until I came to this island," her mouth said. "I never had time for things like that. But here, in this terrible, terrible place, I fell in love with Kodi, but there can be nothing good here, so they took him away from me. I have never felt pain like it, and it will never go away."

And the stars are backward, like I'm looking at them through a mirror.

"I know there are people out there who have felt this kind of pain before, and I wish I could speak to you right now. I want you to tell me it gets better, because right now, I don't believe it ever will."

The water is freezing cold. Too cold for the warm climate of the island.

"They tell you that they sent us here because we're criminals who need to be rehabilitated, but there has been no rehabilitation, just trauma and pain and loss."

We were injected with something on the cruise ship and were unconscious for a long time.

"I wasn't born a criminal. I never needed to be rehabilitated. I was born into an unfair world. It's the system that needs to change, not me . . . not us!"

The entire show is filmed beneath a dome. The sky isn't real.

"Follow me. Get me off this island and I'll show you what a criminal looks like. I'll show you what vengeance looks like. I will spend the rest of my life tearing this show to the ground and holding every single person involved accountable for their part in the murder of dozens of kids. If the authorities have been paid off, and if the government won't help me, I'll take the law into my own hands, and they will suffer. I promise you they will suffer for what they have done. I know it goes against what you believe in, but follow me and together we'll crush them! Join me and no one will have to suffer for entertainment ever again."

Emerson had played her final game, and all there was left to do now was wait and see if she had done enough to win.

Tiger was talking quietly to her drone. Gwen had tears rolling down her cheeks as she spoke.

Time ran out, and the large camera drones disappeared.

Emerson made eye contact with Tiger, and smiled. Tiger smiled back. Emerson tried not to think about how hard she had worked to gain more followers than Tiger, how hard she had tried to condemn the little girl to whatever fate lay beyond the fake walls of the prison, inside the maze with its white walls.

I'll get you out of here, Tiger, she told herself.

The sound of one pair of hands clapping interrupted the silence, and the three remaining contestants of *Kill Factor* turned around to see that the Producer had reappeared.

"The results are in," he said. "We have our winner."

CHAPTER 40

The Producer did not announce the winner right away. No, there would be no theater in that. Instead, the island revolved back to the bedroom side. The bonfire was still burning; the bedrooms had been cleaned. The scoreboard was blank, however, so that the surprise of the winner would not be revealed.

The Producer ordered each of them to go to their bedrooms and change into their final outfits for the live show.

Emerson walked slowly toward her room, and saw that the green dress from the Infinity Suite was hanging on the frame of one of the fake walls. Emerson looked at it for a long time. She ran her hand along the material, felt it between her fingers. A pair of beige shoes with a short heel at the back had been placed beneath the dress.

She put the dress on and for a moment she wished she could see what she looked like. She sat on the edge of her bed and looked at the beige heels. She didn't know why, but she decided to put her black boots on instead.

"Five minutes until the live show begins," the Producer's voice thundered out of the speakers.

Emerson sat down on her bed, and Tiger joined her.

"I hope you win," Tiger said, putting an arm around Emerson's waist.

Emerson rested her head on top of Tiger's. "If I win, I'll get you out of here, Tiger."

"I know you will. That's why I hope you win."

A shadow fell over the two girls, and Gwen stood before them. "Do you . . . do you guys mind if I sit with you? I'm scared."

"Of course," Tiger said, and patted the bed beside her.

Gwen sat down and the three of them sat together, arms around one another.

Not long after, lighting drones began to appear, zipping out of the plastic forest and illuminating the early evening with reds and greens and blues, twirling and dipping and swooping around until the beach was bathed in light.

The scoreboard came to life, but instead of the usual list of names, there was an enormous face watching with eager eyes. The face split into two, and then four and then eight. More and more faces of viewers all around the world with fanatical smiles and greedy eyes. Sixteen faces, then thirty-two, sixty-four, and on and on exponentially until it seemed that every pixel of the screen was filled with eager expressions.

"Ladies and gentlemen!" the Producer screamed as if he were trying to be heard over a roaring crowd. "I want to thank each and every one of the nearly two hundred and fifty million people watching around the world right now! From the bottom of my heart, this means the world to us here at *The Kill Factor*. We've seen the protests, we've heard your calls for boycotts, we've felt your outrage, and we can sincerely say that we hear you and we see you and we'll do our best to make the necessary adjustments so that future installments of the show will be more palatable for all. And now, for your viewing pleasure, here's a quick recap of all the events that have led to this moment."

The faces on the screen began to disappear one by one, getting faster and faster until only a black screen remained. And then Emerson saw herself on the screen: She was in the cabin on the cruise ship; Imelda was standing in the doorway calling her a rat. When she stormed out of the room, Emerson watched herself upend Imelda's suitcase out the window and then throw it out into the harbor.

Next the screen switched to Tiger singing a ballad in her room as the Nicotine Patch drone hovered around her. The scene changed to Gwen trying on different outfits in the Infinity Suite.

Suddenly, the footage was on the beach, and Emerson saw herself break out of the coffin. She had to look away as Kodi ran up to her and asked her if she knew CPR. She could hear her rasping breaths coming from the speakers as she failed to resuscitate Jorgensen. And then Kodi's voice again: "He's gone. Help with the others."

The scene switched to Gwen gasping for air inside her coffin, and then Tiger being hauled out of the sand by Kodi.

The horrible montage continued for what felt like a lifetime. Emerson tried not to look when she heard Never's voice, and Alasdair's, and Kodi's, but she couldn't help it. She relived the moment that she had first kissed Kodi on the diving board, the moment that Teller had tried to make her promise that she wouldn't fall in love with Kodi, the moment Never had told her the story of the first-class airline, and—worst of all—the moment Kodi had died. During that short segment she had fought hard not to cry, and lost.

Finally, the screen faded out on a shot of the three remaining contestants sitting where they were now, on Emerson's bed, arms around one another.

"It has been an emotional and educational time," the Producer said, "but all good things must come to an end. And the end is now. Ladies and gentlemen, it is time to reveal the results of *The Kill Factor*. Remember, the contestant with the most followers wins their freedom."

Emerson felt Tiger's arm tighten around her, and she kissed the young girl on top of her head.

"It's going to be okay," Emerson whispered.

"In third place, with 4.1 million followers . . ." Emerson held her breath, waiting for the Producer to say her name. "Is Tiger Quinn!"

Emerson turned to Tiger, held the young girl's face gently in her hands and told her once again that she *would* save her, then she kissed her on the forehead.

Tiger joined the beckoning Producer—her eyes were no longer filled with that terrible emptiness; there was something new there, perhaps the same determination that Emerson herself felt.

The Producer spoke to Tiger; he put his arm around her

shoulder, an action that caused Tiger to shudder with disgust. She answered his questions with monotone syllables, but Emerson wasn't listening. She was looking at the rising moon as it illuminated the evening. It looked so real, so perfectly genuine, that she questioned whether she had been right about the dome at all. Most of all, Emerson was waiting for something to happen. Waiting for Kester to get her out of here somehow.

Drones came out of the plastic forest and began to guide Tiger away.

"Tiger," Emerson shouted. "I'll see you soon, okay?"

Tiger nodded, and then she was gone.

The Producer turned to the two girls, who sat side by side. Emerson hoped it would be the last time she had to look at that awful smile.

"Emerson Ness and Gwen Perez, the final two. Words cannot express the pride I feel at how far you have both come. From criminality to reformation. You are my greatest accomplishments, but—as you know—there is only one prize in this game. So, without further ado, it is time to find out which of you will be going home, and which of you will be imprisoned for life."

Gwen took Emerson's hand and held it tightly. Emerson steeled herself.

The Producer took an envelope from the inside pocket of his jacket and opened it.

"The winner of the first-ever *Kill Factor* is . . ."

The pause that the Producer left stretched out into infinity, and for some reason, Emerson thought of something that Kester had once told her: Zeno's dichotomy paradox, in which some ancient Greek philosopher said something like *if a person tries to walk to a destination, they can never truly arrive, as they first must walk half the distance, and then half the remaining distance, and then half the remaining distance again, and so on forever as there will always be distance remaining.*

It hadn't made sense to Emerson at the time, and it didn't make sense now, but she saw that infinity was possible, that the Producer would be halving the distance until he announced the winner forever and ever.

His eyes flicked up from the piece of paper in his hand and looked first at Emerson, then at Gwen. And, finally, he spoke.

"Emerson Ness."

41

CHAPTER

There had been an explosion of fireworks, hundreds of camera drones swarming around her, music had played from somewhere, the audience faces had reappeared on the screen all screaming and whooping with delight, but Emerson had not reacted at all. There was still work to do.

"Congratulations to Emerson Ness, the first-ever winner of *The Kill Factor*!" the Producer was yelling, his face distorted through the glittering scraps of red confetti.

Gwen began to sob at Emerson's side. Emerson leaned in close and whispered to the distraught girl, "It's not over."

But the Producer was pulling Gwen to her feet and commiserating with her.

The Producer told Gwen how proud he was of her, and how far she had come, and Gwen told him that none of it mattered if she was going to be locked up for the rest of her life.

Emerson watched the skies, hoping against all hope that the dome would begin to glitch and malfunction, or that the whole thing would come crashing down, or a swarm of military boats would arrive with soldiers and guns.

"Please, please, please," Emerson whispered.

"Emerson Ness!" the Producer was announcing, and when Emerson looked over, she saw that Gwen was being led away, and it was her turn to face the Producer. She got to her feet and walked over to him, her eyes still scanning the darkening sky.

"Emerson, I think part of me knew you were going to win the first time I met you," the Producer said.

Emerson did not reply; instead she looked to the screen, which once again showed the scoreboard, only this time there were forty-nine names that were grayed out, and only hers left.

Place	Contestant Name	Contestant #	Follower count
1.	**Emerson Ness**	16	11,728,411

It had worked. She had spoken directly to the people who were watching in the hopes that something good would happen.

"There was a grit about you, a determination!" the Producer continued. "How does it feel to have won your freedom?"

Emerson looked from the scoreboard to the Producer. "It doesn't matter what I say, you'll just change my words, but at least I can tell you the truth. It feels like hell. It feels like you've put me through torture and killed people who I loved. You have not made me a better person. You have snuffed out parts of me that made me who I am. You traumatized me for your precious viewing figures. You never cared about helping anyone. You're a monster."

The Producer smiled widely and laughed. He held Emerson's

hand aloft in triumph. "One last time, congratulations to our winner, Emerson Ness!"

More fireworks. More confetti. More music.

The Producer and Emerson stood in their false victorious pose for a full minute. The music stopped, the last firework exploded above them, and all the camera drones fell out of the sky.

"And that's a wrap," the Producer said.

"What do you mean?" Emerson said, looking around at the suddenly desolate-looking island.

"The show is over, Ms. Ness."

The sand was littered with glimmering scraps of confetti; the place was empty apart from the Producer and her, and suddenly it all appeared even more pointless than it had seemed before.

"What now?" Emerson asked.

"Now," the Producer said, sighing. "One last game."

42

CHAPTER

"What do you mean?" Emerson asked. "How can there be one last game? There's no one left to compete against."

The Producer sat down on the sand and looked out toward the cruise ship. "Do you know why they named the ship the *Calypso*?" he asked, his voice wistful and somehow sad.

"No," Emerson replied, her mind still spinning.

"Calypso was the name of a Greek deity, a type of fantastical being who lived on an island. According to legend, she imprisoned a king on her island for seven years."

"But there is no prison here," Emerson said. "I've seen it with my own eyes."

"No, there's no prison," the Producer agreed.

"Then where have you taken them? What did you mean when you said there was one last game?" Emerson asked, bracing herself for the answer.

"How many contestants started the games?" the Producer asked.

"Fifty," Emerson replied.

"Wrong," the Producer told her, removing his suit jacket

and placing it on the sand beside him. "There were fifty-one."

Emerson, doubting herself for a moment, looked at the scoreboard. There were still forty-nine names grayed out and hers alone at the top. "There were fifty contestants."

"I was the first to be recruited," the Producer said. "You know my secret; my son told you the truth. My role on the show was to be different from everyone else's. Don't get me wrong, Emerson. This is not a moment of redemption or a cause for pity. No, my crimes were far worse than any of yours, and I don't feel any remorse about what I have put you through or the lives I have been complicit in taking. There are much higher powers than me on this island, and we are both beholden to them now."

"He hated you, you know. Kodi hated you."

The Producer grinned and then shrugged. "I was on death row when they came to me. They told me there would be no more appeals, no more delays, and certainly no hope of a pardon. I had a choice: die by lethal injection tomorrow, or take part in a new game show. If I live through the show, I can go free and come back to host the following year. If I die, the winner of the game show will become the new host."

Emerson's eyes met the Producer's. "What are you saying?"

"You were right all along," the Producer said, all grandiosity gone now; he was just an old man on the beach. "There is no freedom. There is no prize. The best you can hope for is to live and take over my role as host of the games next year."

"No," Emerson said, her voice shaking. "No, it can't be . . . no."

"Yes," the Producer replied, nodding.

"I won't do it."

"Good. In that case I'll get to live another year. All you have to do is lose the final game."

"What is the final game?" Emerson asked.

"The final game is our last chance to learn a lesson. The lesson is Loyalty."

And as though by speaking the word the Producer had summoned some ancient evil from within the island, the sand began to shake beneath their feet, and the entire man-made landmass began to rise out of the ocean.

Emerson stumbled and fell back. Sand poured off the perfectly rounded edge of the island and down into the water below. Up and up the island rose, until it was higher than the diving boards had been.

The Producer sighed, put on his jacket, and stood up.

"It's time," he said, and began walking toward the center of the island.

Emerson hesitated, looked to the top of the dome, where dark clouds drifted across a purple sky, and hoped one last time for her brother to save her. Then she followed the Producer.

The plastic branches ripped at her skin as she pushed her way through the fake foliage, keeping the Producer in her sights as she moved deeper into the island, the prison's fake wall looming ever larger in front of them.

After seven or eight minutes of walking, they came to a large circular river filled with fast-flowing water, and a drawbridge lowered down to let them across.

Now they stood before the prison wall, and though it was not real, it was still imposing as it rose up before them.

"Two doors," the Producer said, pointing to the black door and the white door that were built into the wall. "One for you, one for me. Any preference?"

Emerson looked at the two doors. They were identical apart from the colors they were painted in. She pointed to the one closest to her, the white door.

"Very well," the Producer said. "See you on the inside."

"Wait," Emerson said, and the Producer turned to face her. "Where are the camera drones? Are they not filming this game?"

"The show's over, Emerson. This one is just for the management."

"I don't understand."

"You never will, Emerson. You never will."

And with that, the Producer stepped through the black door, and was gone.

Emerson stood outside the white door and took a deep breath. She thought back to a moment on the beach, standing with Kodi as he told her that the perfect ending she had imagined, where her genius brother saved the day, would never happen, and she hoped that he had been wrong. "Come on, Kester," she whispered. "Please."

And then she too stepped through the door.

43

CHAPTER

Emerson was in complete darkness.

It was cold here, beyond the white door, and the blackness that surrounded her was so thick that it seemed impossible. It was quiet too, the kind of quiet that was so all-consuming that Emerson could hear her own pulse thundering through her body.

And then she was surrounded by a light so blinding that she had to screw her eyes shut in pain.

Finally, the light dimmed, and Emerson saw that she was in a small room with gray walls.

She turned around slowly. There was the white door through which she had entered, and another door opposite. The only other item in the room was a stand that held a crossbow and a belt with ten arrows. Emerson's heart stopped when she saw the crossbow. She begged her mind not to replay the moment the arrow had struck Kodi in the heart, but she couldn't stop it. She saw his eyes grow wide, his mouth grimace against the pain, and she saw the life drain from him once again.

A voice came through hidden speakers in the room. A voice disguised by distortion and pitch shifts until it was unrecognizable as human.

"Emerson Ness, the final game has begun. Six contestants remain alive in addition to yourself and the producer: Their names are Andrew Matthews, Tanya Moon, Alasdair George William Tremblay-Birchall, Imelda Fleet, Tiger Quinn, and Gwen Perez. Here you have an opportunity to display your loyalty to us. Take the weapon from the stand and the ammunition provided, enter the maze, and kill them. Only you and the Producer will be armed. The game ends when only one person remains alive. Good luck."

The door in front of Emerson swung slowly open, revealing the white walls of the maze beyond.

"Wait," Emerson said, trying to process the instructions of the final game.

I have to kill the people who were voted off, and kill the Producer before he kills me.

"I can't," Emerson said. "I can't kill my friends."

There was no reply from the horrible and distorted voice that had spoken to her before.

Emerson's mind raced. She had to act quickly because the Producer would already be in the maze, hunting those who remained alive.

She grabbed the ten extra bolts that were clipped onto the belt. Emerson quickly fastened the belt around her waist, and pulled one of the short but gruesome-looking bolts free. She held the arrow in her hand and felt the sharp, barbed tip with her finger. It would work.

Without allowing herself time to think, she gouged the tip of the arrow into the number 16 that had been branded into her wrist, and ripped open the skin. Blood poured out, dripping down to her elbow and onto the floor of the gray room.

She dropped the arrow and pressed a finger and the thumb of her left hand into the wound she had just made. She tried not to think of the pain. She tried not to imagine the game organizers watching her and releasing the poison before she got to the capsule. She tried not to picture herself lying dead in this room that was gray not only in color but in character too.

She gripped the capsule. It was no bigger than a headache pill. She pulled it free, and as she held it up to her eyes, she heard a pop, and the capsule burst open, spilling its poisonous contents.

She dropped the capsule, picked up the crossbow, and stepped into the maze.

It was cold inside the network of white plastic walls that rose up around her, at least forty feet high and perfectly smooth. No way of climbing them.

She had one objective: kill the Producer before he could kill anyone else. After that, all she had was hope; hope that her brother could find her and bring this whole thing down.

The crossbow felt heavy in her hands, and yet it was comforting—she would not be helpless if the Producer was waiting around the next corner. Would she have the mettle to pull the trigger and take a life if that moment of kill or be killed should arrive? She thought she would. She was driven not only by her animalistic instinct to survive but also a snarling hatred of the man who had pulled the strings that made them all dance like marionettes and die like forgotten soldiers. She didn't care that he too had been forced into his role; she didn't care that he was just another contestant in the games. He had *enjoyed* it; she had seen it in his gleeful eyes over and over again.

The white plastic floor beneath her feet sloped down, and she walked through a tunnel that emerged on the other side with three options: left, right, or straight ahead. Emerson turned right, then right again. The ground sloped upward to a bridge over yet another white path below. The entire structure was so plain and repetitive that it was hard to tell where you had been or where you were going. If it hadn't been for the blood dripping down from Emerson's wrist, she might have gotten turned around a dozen times.

This new section of the maze sloped down into a covered corridor, and Emerson began to slow as she heard sobbing from somewhere up ahead. Alone in this lifeless place, the sound was eerie, like something out of a horror movie.

Emerson crept forward as quietly as she could. She inched around a long, curving corner, and finally, she was close enough. She saw Andrew Matthews lying on the cobblestones, his head resting awkwardly against the wall. He had lost a lot of weight in the six days he had been in here, and Emerson wondered if he'd been fed anything at all.

"Andrew," Emerson said, running to him and skidding to a stop beside him. "You have to come with me," she said, taking Andrew's hands and trying to pull him to his feet, but he was too weak. "Listen to me, I can get you somewhere safe, we just need to follow the blood back to the gray room."

Emerson was aware that she was rambling, but she needed to get Andrew out of the maze and away from the Producer. The emaciated boy looked at her with a dazed kind of understanding. He forced himself to stand, and as he did, a loud clicking sound echoed around the white walls, and a crossbow bolt entered through one side of Andrew's neck, exited out the other side, and stuck in the plastic wall behind him.

"No!" Emerson screamed, and turned to see the Producer reaching for a second arrow.

Andrew looked around as though he were seeing the world for the first time. He coughed violently, blood spraying out onto the floor below. He swayed on his feet, and then he fell down dead.

The disembodied and distorted voice echoed around the maze: *Seven contestants remaining.*

Emerson saw that the Producer had reloaded his crossbow.

In a split second she weighed up the distance between them, the time it would take to raise her own weapon and fire back, and the odds that she would fire a terminal shot, and she decided that her best bet was to run.

Emerson sprinted down the corridors and tunnels, along the bridges and walkways.

The Producer's voice boomed after her. "We should team up,

Emerson! The quicker we kill them, the quicker you and I can settle this once and for all."

She turned left, right, right, left. There was no way of finding her way back now; she had doubled back on herself several times, her shoes smearing blood drops that she had left behind five minutes earlier.

Six contestants remaining, the ethereal voice announced, and Emerson wondered who else the Producer had killed.

She kept running, certain that at any second she would come face-to-face with the Producer. She imagined them pulling their triggers at the same time, two arrows finding their marks, both of them dying, and there being no winner to this terrible competition.

Five contestants remaining, the voice rang out again.

Four contestants remaining.

"No!" Emerson screamed. The Producer had killed two more contestants.

Please not Tiger, please not Tiger, she thought, and then realized that she was indirectly hoping for the death of Alasdair, or Gwen, or Imelda.

As she ran, Emerson heard a shuffling noise to her right. She spun and aimed the crossbow at the sound. She could feel her heart thumping, her wide eyes taking in every part of her surroundings. It was Imelda Fleet. She had tucked herself deep into an indent in one of the plastic walls and was cowering there.

"Imelda," Emerson said.

"Please," Imelda begged. "Please don't kill me."

"I'm not going to kill you," Emerson replied. "I'm going to get you out . . ."

A bright bolt of pain sprang in her right thigh. Emerson screamed and fell down.

"It's almost over," the Producer said as he loaded another arrow into his crossbow.

Emerson looked at the bolt that had gone almost right through her leg, just above the knee. The green dress rippled against the steel of the arrow, and Emerson felt the world swirling away from her. She had dropped the crossbow in her agony, and now she reached for it. The Producer kicked it away, and almost simultaneously fired again. Emerson waited for a fresh burst of pain, but it didn't come. The Producer had fired at Imelda instead, hitting her just below the left cheek.

"What a game," the Producer said. "The adrenaline alone almost makes it worth it. You could get hooked on a thing like this."

As he spoke, he loaded another arrow into the bow.

"Just you, me, and Tiger left," he said, pulling on the crossbow wire until it clicked into the mechanism. "Once you're out of the way, the game is as good as over. I might make it last, though. I might savor it."

Emerson felt a moment of sorrow flow through her. The Producer had killed Gwen and Alasdair. They had been good people, good friends. Now they were gone.

"You said you were like us," Emerson pleaded, sliding back to lean against the hard plastic wall. "You said that they took you out of prison on the promise that you might get to live. Why do you fight so hard for them?"

The Producer lowered the crossbow and fired. This time the pain exploded in her left shoulder. Emerson screamed so loud and so long that her throat ached. She looked down at her shoulder and saw the bolt there. It had gone right through and stuck into the wall behind her, pinning her there.

The Producer seemed pleased by this outcome. He smiled and then began to speak as he loaded the crossbow one more time. "I've always been different, Emerson. Always been a little theatrical, a little heartless, a little bit emotionally distant. By the time the police caught me, I had killed eleven people. They called me prolific. I didn't see it that way; I was only just getting started. You see, Emerson, I'm what they call a psychopath. A very high-functioning psychopath, but a psychopath nonetheless. When they came to me with their offer, I didn't hesitate. It wasn't so much the chance to carry on living that appealed to me, it was the chance to continue my quest. So, in answer to your question, *why do I fight so hard for them?* Because I *enjoy* it."

Emerson felt her heart sink. She wondered just how close she had come to escaping this place. The pain that throbbed all the way through her almost made her wish the end would come quickly.

"This has been fun," the Producer said, and aimed the crossbow at her head. "Goodbye."

The nearly instant click of the mechanism and slap of the wire filled the world, and Emerson waited for the end of everything. Instead she heard the Producer choking and growling.

The shot that the Producer had fired was sticking out of the wall a few centimeters from the side of her head. Imelda Fleet—with an arrow sticking out of her head—had grabbed a bolt from the Producer's belt and shoved it deep into the side of his neck. She was pushing it in as hard as she could as the ageless man tried desperately to thrash her off his back.

Emerson gritted her teeth and began to lean forward. The feeling of the arrow in her shoulder scraping along her clavicle almost made her pass out with the impossible agony of it, but she kept going, feeling the wide end of the arrow, with its plastic flight, enter the hole in the shoulder, widening the wound as she roared through the pain until she was free from the wall.

The Producer was still flailing around, and Imelda was losing her grip on him.

Emerson's left arm was nearly useless, and she wondered if the arrow that had gone through her shoulder might have severed some tendons, but she managed to hold a bolt in place as she loaded her crossbow.

The Producer threw Imelda to the ground and pulled the arrow from his neck. He screamed in fury as his blood flowed out of him. And then he turned his livid eyes to Emerson.

"You don't have what it takes to pull that trig—"

But that was all he had time to say. Emerson had fired her

shot, and the arrow dug deep into the left side of his chest, piercing his heart.

All the anger seemed to leave him then. He seemed confused for a moment, and then a look of clarity overcame him.

"It's all going to get so much worse now," he said, and then dropped to the ground, dead.

Three contestants remaining.

Emerson dropped the crossbow and then fell down, no longer able to hold her own weight. Blood dripped steadily from her wrist, and flowed constantly from the wounds in her thigh and shoulder.

She sat there, in the white maze, and looked at the Producer's dead eyes, and she was glad that he was gone.

"Emerson?" a voice to her left said. It was Imelda. "Emerson, are you there?"

"Yeah," Emerson replied, no energy left at all.

"I can't see," Imelda said.

"You saved my life."

"Yeah . . . I'm sorry I called you a rat."

"I'm sorry I threw your stuff overboard."

"It's just stuff," Imelda said, and then she died too.

Two contestants remaining.

Emerson watched her own blood pooling around her, and wondered how long it would take to die.

Tiger is going to win, she thought, and smiled, until she remembered what the Producer had told her: There was no freedom; there was no real prize—all the winner got was the opportunity to become the host of the games the following year, and she knew that Tiger would never do that.

She began to feel cold and wondered if this was the first stage of her life slipping away. It would probably take hours to die from the wounds she had, hours and hours.

From here she could see the stars, and wished they were real and not just a projection on a dome, but they were beautiful nonetheless. She looked at the backward Orion's Belt and laughed. How had she not seen it before?

The center star of Orion's Belt went out, and Emerson stopped laughing. She stared at the place where the star was supposed to be, and waited for it to come back. It did not.

More stars started to go out all across the sky. Hundreds of them, flickering and disappearing. The moon seemed to shimmer for a moment, and then it was gone too.

"What's going on?" Emerson asked aloud.

The entire sky turned a hallucinatory shade of green, and an error message blinked across it in enormous letters.

And the island was plunged into darkness.

44
CHAPTER

Emerson sat in the white maze, surrounded by blackness, waiting for something to happen.

Nothing did.

The fake sky was gone. Every hidden light inside the maze was gone. Not a single sound broke through the deafening silence of the island.

And then there was something. A buzzing sound that was all too familiar to Emerson. It was a single camera drone roaming through the corridors of the maze. Was it looking for her?

For a while the buzzing grew louder, then quieter again, and then it came back, this time louder. Emerson could see the glow of its light approaching her, and she didn't have the energy to run from it.

The drone came around the corner, spotted her, and zoomed toward her at high speed. It stopped, seemed to look at all the blood, and then hovered in front of her face.

It stayed there, presumably waiting for her to do something, and as she stared back at the little drone, she became more and more certain of what it was.

"Kester?" she asked, and the drone remained there, unmoving. Emerson held up her hands and signed his name instead.

The drone moved excitedly up and down, up and down.

It is you? Emerson signed, and again the drone moved up and down, up and down before gesturing down toward one of the corridors over and over again.

Follow you? Emerson signed.

Up and down, up and down.

Emerson gritted her teeth and let out a guttural sound as she pushed herself to standing. The effort alone made her nearly pass out, but she limped after the drone as it led the way into the maze.

The drone looked back, and Emerson signed for it to wait. She couldn't leave without Tiger. The drone nodded, and continued to lead her through the winding paths. Emerson staggered and swayed on her feet, but the more she moved, the more she found she *could* move.

Finally, the drone stopped at a junction where six paths merged, and there was Tiger standing in the center of all the roads, like a ghost in the darkness.

Emerson hugged her and felt the girl's arms tighten around her.

"Is it really you?" Tiger asked.

"It's me," Emerson said, and when she pulled away, she saw that she had left blood all over Tiger's clothes.

"You're bleeding," Tiger said.

"I'm going to be okay. We're getting out of here, okay?"

Tiger nodded, and Kester continued to lead them out of the maze.

It seemed to take forever, but soon they were walking past bloodstains that Emerson had made when she had first entered the maze, and then they were at the gray room.

They stepped inside. Emerson limped over to the white door and tried the handle. It was locked. The drone hovered over to the door, and after a few seconds, they heard a click. Emerson tried the door again and it was open.

When they stepped out, Emerson and Tiger both took one last look back at the enormous fake wall that made up the nonexistent prison in the center of the island, and then they moved as quickly as they could through the plastic trees and the artificial plants.

They had been making their way through the forest for about a minute when they began to hear a new sound. Footsteps.

"Go!" Tiger said, and Emerson ignored the electric pain in her leg every time she took a step.

Panic drew them onward. The sound of more than a dozen footsteps running through the forest was eerie, and was made doubly eerie by the fact that the pursuers did not say a word; they just ran after Emerson and Tiger with terrifying speed.

And then Emerson did hear a sound, a sound that she wished she had not heard. One of the chasers laughed, as though this were a child's game. And the laugh was terrible, almost demonic.

"Run!" Emerson screamed.

They had made it to the beach, and Emerson's heart broke at what she saw.

She had forgotten that the island itself had risen up out of the waves until it was so high that no one would survive the jump off the edge.

"No!" Tiger screamed.

More of the hunters were laughing now. To them, this was a joyous thing. It was a thrilling hunt, and when they appeared from the trees, Emerson was certain they would be hideous creatures from the depths of nightmares, all pointed teeth and black eyes.

Emerson and Tiger continued to follow the drone as it made its way to the edge of the towering island. But it froze, hanging in the air.

Emerson got there first and saw what the drone was showing them: The enormous mechanism that had ratcheted the island up and up into the air could act as a kind of ladder all the way down to the water.

"You go first," Emerson told Tiger, knowing that there was no guarantee that her pierced leg and shoulder would hold out long enough for her to make it all the way down.

Tiger's pale face turned even whiter as she looked down to the water, but there was nothing else to do. Tiger lowered one shaking leg onto the cog-like strip of steel that ran all the way down, and began to lower herself, one step at a time, to the water.

Emerson went next, placing a weak foot onto the greased-up metal and praying it would hold her.

The last thing Emerson saw as she too lowered herself down

was a hundred indistinct figures bursting out of the forest. They may have been human. They probably were human, but in that moment, they could have been monsters.

The climb down to the water lasted a hundred lifetimes, and by the time Emerson was close enough to just let go and fall into the freezing waves, her arms were burning, and the muscles in her legs were ready to give up completely.

As she lay on her back in the water, she looked up one more time. A dozen faces stared down at them. Human faces, of course. They didn't seem to be panicking about the contestants who were escaping; they only watched, curiously, to see what would happen next.

45

CHAPTER

There were a few moments, during the swim to the cruise ship, that Emerson came very close to losing consciousness, and by the time she had gripped the cold rail that led all the way up to the top deck, her vision was graying out at the edges.

Tiger got to the top first, and lay on her back in a puddle of cold seawater, watching her breath make clouds over and over again in rapid succession. When Emerson got to the top, she lay beside Tiger, and the two of them stayed there for a full minute until they could no longer ignore the frantic buzzing of the drone as it zipped around them.

Emerson rolled over, and the pain erupted inside her all over again as if the arrows had been fired into her once more. Her muscles were stiff and cold, her joints were aching, but it wasn't over yet.

She lurched after Kester as he led the way to the front of the ship, and to a small metal door with BRIDGE written on it. Emerson tried the handle, and it opened.

The drone went in first, followed by Tiger and Emerson.

Inside was a room of such futuristic qualities that Emerson

wondered for a moment if she had set foot on a spaceship. Narrow windows encircled the entire room. Several different stations were dotted around with various screens and navigation tools—all the screens were blank, but they looked complex nonetheless. Two comfortable-looking leather chairs sat front and center, with dozens of dials and touchscreen pads and readouts.

"What do we do?" Tiger asked.

And to Emerson, the little Topsider's voice sounded miles away.

The drone moved to the big leather chair on the left and bobbed up and down above a small metal key that was already slotted into a housing on the arm of the chair. Tiger ran to the key and turned it. Nothing happened. The drone moved to the second chair, where an identical key sat. Tiger turned that one too.

Lights came on around the ship; screens came to life; 3D maps appeared, hovering in midair.

"Is that it?" Emerson asked, her voice hoarse and quiet.

The drone moved up and down. Emerson collapsed into one of the chairs with a view through the enormous window. There was nothing to see except the inky ocean moving perpetually.

The ship began to rumble and shake as the engines came to life. Kester had control now. Emerson slumped in the seat and smiled as the ship began to move slowly, slowly.

Tiger sat down beside Emerson.

"We're going to make it out of here, aren't we?"

Emerson nodded. Her green dress was now almost completely

red from the blood that had poured out of her, and her skin had grown pale, almost transparent.

They picked up speed with agonizing sluggishness, and Emerson wished she could see the island disappearing into the distance. As if Kester had read her mind, a new 3D display rose up in front of her with a perfect high-definition video feed of the island. It was lowering slowly down until it was in line with the water's edge once more, and Emerson could see the people standing there, watching them go, unmoving.

A siren sounded inside the bridge, and Emerson—with great effort—turned her head to the window. There was a vast nothingness before them, a place where the waves stopped and a void began. It could only be the edge of the dome.

"This is it," Tiger said, her voice filled with panic.

Emerson could no longer feel the pain in her shoulder, or her thigh, or her wrist, and somewhere in the back of her mind, she thought that was a bad sign.

Warning, an electronic voice said. *Impact imminent. Adjust course immediately.*

Tiger gripped Emerson's hand. Emerson looked back to the image of the island. Why were they just standing there, not moving, not trying to bring their lost contestants back? Emerson didn't know, and she didn't have the energy to care.

Warning. Impact imminent. Adjust course immediately.

The whir of the engines grew in pitch and volume as Kester told the ship to go faster, faster! He must have been overriding fail-safe features constantly, but it was working: The ship went faster and faster, and the enormous nothingness got closer and closer.

Warning. Impact imminent. Adjust course immediately.

And then the ship hit the dome.

The sound was enormous. Tiger and Emerson were thrown from their seats, and for a brief moment, all the pain in Emerson's body returned in lightning-bolt brightness.

The screech of metal, the crash of glass, the grinding sound of the engines fighting against the obstacle.

Emerson got back to her feet. She had almost no breath now, and sweat was pouring from her, but when she collapsed back into the seat and looked out the cracked window, she had to blink several times to believe what her eyes told her.

No more than three hundred yards away was the same dock they had left from all those weeks ago. Her own city took up the horizon: the unique skyscrapers, the famous advertising boards, the weaving, winding roads with a thousand auto-taxis moving serenely through the crowded streets.

Emerson laughed; she couldn't help it. It was, somehow, all so funny.

The effort of that laughter, though, was the last of her energy. Her vision blurred, she felt her life slipping from beneath her, and then the world went blank.

46
CHAPTER

Death was not how Emerson had imagined it. There was no bright light, no sense of floating up to the afterlife, no feelings of bliss or awe. There was only darkness.

The darkness was complete and all-encompassing. There was no sound, there was no feeling, there was no thought.

And then, a million lifetimes later, there was something. It was merely an awareness of existence, but it was something other than the darkness.

Slowly, over an impossible timeline, that sense of awareness grew into the ability to think.

Where am I? Who am I? What happened?

And with those thoughts came a feeling deep within her, an instinct to put up walls, to not allow the answers to come just yet. No, instead just exist as no one, nowhere, with no past or future. Be ignorant to all of it, because none of it could bring happiness.

The self is persistent, though. It wants to be known, and a few hundred years later, she told herself her name.

Emerson Ness.

Emerson Ness became aware of a persistent beep. That beep came over and over again in a steady, maddening rhythm. It had been there this whole time, she knew that, but once she had become aware of it, she could not let it fade away into the background again.

Beep... Beep... Beep.

Emerson Ness, she thought, and more of herself came back to life.

When, finally, she opened her eyes, a new thought entered her mind.

What kind of game is this?

Her brain felt disconnected from her body. She couldn't make her arms lift up from the strange white bed she was in.

They've drugged me again, she thought. *The Producer, the people in charge. They've drugged me, and now they want me to escape before the walls close in and I'm crushed to death, or the room fills with water and I drown, or fire engulfs the bed and burns me alive.*

But her eyes began to adjust to the darkness, and she saw that she was not on the island anymore. She was in the hospital.

The last thing she remembered before falling unconscious was Tiger begging her to stay awake. They had been on the cruise ship, the *Calypso.* They had escaped ... they had escaped.

It came back to her in fragments: the maze; the blood as she cut the capsule from her wrist; the arrows hitting her leg and her shoulder; watching the Producer die; swimming to the cruise ship as the figures on the island watched on, motionless; breaking through the dome to find out that they were back where they had started.

Relief flowed through her. They were safe now, her and Tiger. They had escaped.

She rested her drowsy head back on the comfortable pillow and whispered into the dark room, "I made it, Kodi. I made it."

And for the first time in a very long time, she felt safe.

CHAPTER

The news sites were filled with nothing but *Kill Factor* headlines.

A thousand reporters were camped outside the hospital, desperate to get a quote or a photograph of the two girls who had survived and escaped the island.

Emerson watched the TV in the hospital with Tiger lying beside her.

The authorities had found nothing on the island, and they had found nothing on the cruise ship either. All electronic files had been wiped; there were no fingerprints anywhere; there was no trace of any person who had been involved in the competition other than the corpses of some of the contestants.

There were a thousand conspiracy theories, and almost every person who commented on the articles and videos spoke of how impossible it would be to keep something of this scale secret. Hundreds of people must have been involved: engineers, mechanics, programmers, producers, directors, editors, and more, and yet no one was found, and no one was speaking out.

Companies were offering hundreds of brand credits linked

to a million followers for anyone who could prove that they were involved to speak to them completely anonymously, but no one had taken up the offer so far. And Emerson was certain that no one would. Kodi had been right: This was something so big, and so clandestine, that it had to be government run.

"What do you think's going to happen now?" Tiger asked.

"I really don't know," Emerson admitted.

"Well, you're now the most popular influencer in the world, so at least there's that."

"I really don't want to be the most popular influencer in the world," Emerson replied.

"Yeah, but it gives you a kind of protection, don't you think?" Tiger asked.

"How do you mean?"

"Well, like, you're going to be watched twenty-four hours a day for the rest of your life, so it's not like they can ever get you back onto another *Kill Factor*."

Emerson thought of the calm faces that had watched them escape from the island, and a shudder ran through her.

"Not for the rest of my life," Emerson said finally. "I've got a year in juvenile detention to get through first."

Emerson had been told earlier that day that when she was healthy enough to be discharged, she would be serving a sentence for the crime of arson. The authority of *Kill Factor* was apparently never going to be recognized by the courts, and yet they were showing great leniency in reducing her sentence, citing time served and the suffering of cruel and unusual punishment. Tiger would be imprisoned too, but only for three months.

"Juvie will be nothing compared to the island," Tiger said. "We'll both sail through it."

Emerson nodded. The truth was, she was glad that she would serve time for the death of Marvin Tzu. Yes, it had been Kodi who had lit the fire, but when she had turned the gas on, she had *wanted* the school to burn. She felt like she deserved the punishment. She would not argue or appeal; she would do her time, donate a hundred brand credits to Marvin's family, set up a scholarship for his grandkids, and of course make sure that Never's family were financially supported, and then ... and then what?

She had made a promise to all those who followed her on that final day on the island, a promise to spend the rest of her life bringing the organizers to justice.

Now was not the time to think about it, though. She had a few more days in here with Tiger, alone, avoiding the reporters, the cameras, the questions. After that, a year of prison, where she would be safe from secretive agencies and powerful organizations that could disappear without a trace.

She would use the time to become a better person: a much easier endeavor when you had the money to back your plans.

Emerson had spoken once to her friend Never, and had asked if she thought that money would change them. Never had said, *I've seen good people change. Give a person money and they always want more. Give a person power and they always want more. Give a person influence and they always want more.*

Emerson was determined that this would not be her. She would do good things with her newfound wealth; she would invest it in the people who needed it. She would give opportunities to the forgotten, give hope to the invisible.

In an hour, visiting time would start, and she would see Kester for the first time since he had saved her from the island. That was what she was looking forward to the most, seeing her brother, and saying thank you.

Tiger had fallen asleep with her head on Emerson's chest, and Emerson kissed the young girl's head. She looked out the window and watched a blackbird sailing across the afternoon sky, and she smiled. Soon she too would be free, just like . . .

Emerson's blood suddenly ran cold as she watched the bird. For a second it disappeared. Emerson sat up. Tiger stirred but didn't wake. The bird had reappeared now, and was once again sailing across the blue sky without a care in the world.

I imagined it, Emerson told herself. *I just imagined it.*

But then the bird flickered like a glitching image.

It was a sign. A message.

The games were not over yet.

Acknowledgments

I loved writing this book. It was the type of story that just flows from start to finish. There's so much action and adventure, and the characters seemed to come alive and make decisions for themselves. That so rarely happens for me, so I tried to enjoy every second of it.

I want to thank my wife, Sarah, for continuing to believe in my writing, and for lying around on the couch and watching nonsense on TV with me.

I also want to thank Sam Palazzi, Kesia Lupo, and Chloe Seager for once again helping one of my novels make it from my mind to reality. All of your ideas, enthusiasm, and belief make the final book so much better than I could ever manage on my own.

Everyone at Scholastic and Chicken House—it means so much to me that you champion my writing and help me make these pipe dreams a reality.